BOOK 1

‖‖‖ ‖‖‖‖‖‖‖‖‖‖‖‖‖‖‖‖‖‖
P9-CDV-945

DISCARD

SISTERS OF MERCY FLATS

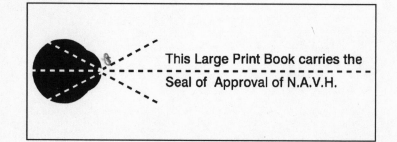

This Large Print Book carries the
Seal of Approval of N.A.V.H.

SISTERS OF
MERCY FLATS

LORI COPELAND

THORNDIKE PRESS
A part of Gale, Cengage Learning

Detroit • New York • San Francisco • New Haven, Conn • Waterville, Maine • London

GALE
CENGAGE Learning®

LIBRARY OF CONGRESS CATALOGING-IN-PUBLICATION DATA

Copeland, Lori.
  Sisters of Mercy Flats / by Lori Copeland.
    pages ; cm. — (Thorndike Press large print Christian fiction)
  ISBN-13: 978-1-4104-5882-7 (hardcover)
  ISBN-10: 1-4104-5882-2 (hardcover)
  1. Large type books. I. Title.
PS3553.O6336S58 2013b
813'.54—dc23   2013009383

Published in 2013 by arrangement with Copeland Incorporated

Printed in the United States of America
2 3 4 5 6 7 17 16 15 14 13

To Kathleen Kerr

ONE

July 1863
Houston, Texas

"Best lookin' herd of beef I've seen this side of the Colorado!" A.J. Donavan knocked the dust from his hat and then pitched it onto the bar. "Texas Longhorns are a scroungy-looking lot, but this herd is prime hoof."

A three-bladed overhead fan in The Silver Slipper labored to stir the midday heat as Donavan signaled to the bartender for another shot. Turning to the cowboy standing next to him, he asked, "Got any idea who owns the herd?"

Ealy Moore turned his eyes to the ceiling pensively. "Nope."

The bartender eyed the cattleman as he set a shot glass of whiskey in front of him. "You in the market for beef, stranger?"

"I'd be interested in buying that particular herd," A.J. admitted. Tossing the drink down, he motioned for another one. "I've been on the trail for over a month now and I'm dry as a tick feather."

"Don't guess it would be too hard to find out who owns the cows." The bartender lifted the bottle to refill the glass. "My guess is they belong to one of those drovers who were in here round about noon. They were bragging about bringing in a big herd."

"Know where the men went?"

"Said they were going over to the hotel for a bath and a shave and then they were gonna get skunk drunk —" The man's voice faded when a shadow fell across the doorway of the bar.

The room's occupants glanced up to see three nuns standing in the entryway, their hands resting lightly on the heavy gold crosses that hung around their necks.

The men gaped at the sight. A reverent hush had suddenly enveloped the room. The sisters were young and exceptionally comely. Not remarkable, but it was noteworthy to find such rare, wholesome beauty hidden beneath dark habits.

The women remained in the doorway, their gazes moving slowly about the room, pausing momentarily on the table where four men with cigarettes dangling from the corners of their mouths were engaged in a game of jacks high. When they spotted the women they quickly folded their hands and crushed their smokes. Overhead a fly droned.

Moving with somber dignity the women glided across the room, their black habits brushing quietly along the wooden floor. The watering hole was near empty this afternoon. The earlier drinkers had gone about their business, and the evening crowd wouldn't be in for a while.

The air in the room was close; silence stretched. Others around the bar stood, glasses posed in midair, watching as the women approached.

Pausing in front of A.J., the middle sister spoke. "I understand you are interested in purchasing our cattle." Her soft voice was peaceful, befitting her calling.

A.J. straightened. "Er . . . those your longhorns, ma'am?"

The sister smiled. "Are you an interested buyer?"

"Well . . . yes ma'am. I'd be real interested, Sister . . ."

Sister's eyes lowered submissively. "Sister Anne-Marie."

"Pleased to meet you, ma'am . . . er, Sister." He hurriedly wiped the dust from his hand and then extended it to her. "A.J.

9

Donavan's the name, cattle's my game."

Sister's head lowered. "Mr. Donavan."

"Pleased to make your acquaintance, Sister. You say you want to sell your herd? That's mighty fine beef."

Sister Anne-Marie lifted mournful eyes — a most uncommon shade of jade green. One man murmured. Exquisite. The term fit; still, it fell short of the breathtaking beauty that lay in the emerald pools.

"The cattle are a gift to our mission," Sister Anne-Marie explained, her hand waving graciously to include the other two women.

"A gift, you say?" Surprise lit his craggy features, apparently astounded that women would be in charge of the sizable herd.

The sisters bowed their heads, murmuring softly in unison, "Praise be to God," Sister Anne-Marie continued. "If it were not for the kindness shown by others, our mission could not survive."

The bartender leaned closer. "What mission is that, Sisters?"

"Our Lady of Perpetual Grace."

He frowned, shaking his head. "Don't believe I've ever heard of it."

"It is but a small, modest mission," the nun conceded.

A.J. frowned. "I don't understand, Sister.

10

If the cattle are a gift —"

"A gift we cannot keep," Sister Anne-Marie acknowledged. "We have no means to care for such a large herd. Our order is small, and our funds are meager. With the help of some very kind hombres, Sister Amelia, Sister Abigail, and I have managed to bring the herd here to sell. The money we receive from the cattle sale will help see us through the coming winter."

A.J. shifted to face the other two sisters. They nodded gravely.

"They're mighty fine-looking animals," he admitted. "How many head you got there? Twenty-five, twenty-six hundred?"

"No sir. Only twenty-four hundred thirty-three head," Sister Anne-Marie said. "We began the journey with twenty-five hundred, but we suffered losses along the way."

Sister Abigail reached to lay her hand upon Anne-Marie's arm. "Still, we have been most fortunate. The Lord has smiled upon us, for we only lost sixty-seven head in all."

Sister Anne-Marie nodded, clearly repentant. "Of course, Sister. We have been most blessed."

"You must have had good grass and water along the way. The cattle appear to be well fed," A.J. noted.

"The Lord smiled on us, Mr. Donavan."

"Well, ladies," the cattle baron nodded, "if you're willing to sell the longhorns at market price —"

"Oh no, sir." Sister Anne-Marie held up a hand to stop him. "We couldn't do that."

"Now ma'am, as fine as those cattle are I'd have to think about paying above market price." His expression said that he wasn't about to be fleeced, even by a nun. "You got a mighty fine herd, but I couldn't pay above three dollars a head."

"Kind sir, it would only be fair if we sold the cattle for a dollar a head below market price," the nun insisted.

"A dollar *below* market price?"

"Below market price," she stated firmly, and Sister Abigail and Sister Amelia nodded in solemn agreement. "It is imperative that we sell the cattle and return to the mission as quickly as possible. The vaqueros who have so kindly helped us drive the cattle here have families who need tending, and the return trip is long and arduous. Even if we leave before sunset, we shall travel for days before we reach home again. Since it is we who find ourselves on the horns of this dilemma, it is hardly fair to ask you to pay market price." Sister Anne-Marie glanced at Sister Abigail and Sister

Amelia, who were again nodding in full agreement. "If you want the cattle, the herd is yours for a dollar a head below market price."

A.J. turned to face the room. "You're sure? A dollar a head below market? You all are witness to the offer?"

Men's heads nodded in unison.

"We are quite certain," Sister Anne-Marie said. "If we are able to begin our return journey back to the mission within the hour, the sacrifice will be warranted."

"Sister," A.J. said, extending his hand, "you just got yourself a deal."

Sister Anne-Marie smiled. "May God richly bless you, Mr. Donavan, as He has so richly blessed us."

"If you'll wait right here, it'll only take me a minute to go to the bank and get your draft."

"Cash," the sister corrected. "Cash would be most suitable."

"Cash it'll be." Reaching for his hat, A.J. motioned to the bartender. "Get the sisters a glass of sarsaparilla while they're waiting."

The women exchanged a glance, their eyes silently condoning the slight stimulation.

The clock on the wall slowly ticked away the minutes as the sisters sat at a table near

13

the doorway, sipping their sarsaparilla. The men had drifted to one corner of the bar, obviously trying to look inconspicuous until Donavan returned with the money.

Exactly fifteen minutes from the time he left, A.J. reentered the bar. The sisters quietly rose when he hurried toward their table.

"Here you are." He pressed a large brown envelope into Sister Anne-Marie's hand. "You'll find the full amount, plus an extra hundred." He offered a benevolent smile. "A little something for the mission from me."

"Bless you, Mr. Donavan. Bless you." Sister Anne-Marie squeezed his hand and then carefully tucked the envelope beneath her robe. "If you will be so kind as to provide a piece of paper and pencil, I will write you a bill of sale."

The bartender rummaged around and eventually came up with a label torn from a whiskey bottle.

"And something to write with?"

A piece of charcoal was located, and Sister Anne-Marie quickly wrote out the bill of sale on the back of the label, signing her name in bold letters.

"And now, gentlemen, if you will excuse

us we must gather our men and be on our way."

"Of course, Sister. Mighty good doin' business with you."

A.J. and the men stepped back as the three sisters floated across the room, the whispering hems of black habits disappearing out the door.

Breathing a sigh of relief, the men returned to the card game as A.J. stepped up to the bar.

"Well, Mr. Donavan, looks like you got yourself a real fine deal," the barkeep congratulated as he filled A.J.'s glass.

"Yes, sir," A.J. tucked the bill of sale away in his pocket. "It ain't often a man falls into a herd of prime longhorns and comes out smelling like a rose. Hate to take advantage of the little women that way, but you saw what happened. It was all their idea."

The two men chortled.

"Yea, it was their idea, all right. Two dollars a head. Mister, you just stole those cattle."

"Yes, sir." A.J. leaned back, grinning. "I surely did."

Abigail McDougal stepped out of the bar, turning in unison with her sisters down the planked walkway, quickening her pace.

15

"Shoot! I thought we'd see some loose women," Amelia complained.

"Really Amelia," Anne-Marie chided. "You can think of the silliest things."

"What's silly about wanting to see a soiled dove? I've never been in a real saloon before, and from everything I've heard, that's where they —"

"Will you pipe down? They can still hear us," Abigail whispered, casting an uneasy glance over her shoulder.

"Will you stop being so bossy?"

"Will you both stop bickering!" Anne-Marie snapped. "Abby's right. We're not in the clear yet."

Amelia lowered her voice. "All that money — how much did we make, Abigail?"

"I don't know — the envelope looks pretty heavy. How much do you think, Anne-Marie?" She'd never been good with figures — especially in her head.

"Two thousand four hundred and thirty-three dollars times two."

The sisters hurried along, their expressions studious as they multiplied beneath their breath.

"Four thousand eight hundred sixty-six dollars!" Amelia squealed and Abigail elbowed her into silence.

"*Nine* hundred sixty-six," Anne-Marie

corrected. "You forgot to add Mr. Donavan's generous donation."

The sisters solemnly returned the sign of the cross to two passing men when they cut across the street. Disappearing around the corner of the mercantile, they emerged a moment later on horseback.

Amelia gloated. "How lucky can we get? We happen to walk by a bar, overhear Donavan talking about that herd, and suddenly we're rich!"

"How many times do I have to tell you, Amelia? Nothing just *happens* with us," Anne-Marie corrected. "Because we work for a worthy cause, we are given certain opportunities we wouldn't otherwise encounter."

The sisters turned to look back at the bar, then at one another. Their eyes met and they snickered.

"Men. How gullible can they get?" Abigail sighed. She didn't have much respect for the male gender and A.J. Donavan had once again proven what a dimwitted lot they were. Swayed by a pretty face and religious garb, most men would sell their grandmothers.

Amelia sobered. "Wonder who does own those cows?"

Shrugging, Anne-Marie visibly tightened

the reins around her gloved hand. "Who cares? What I can tell you for certain is who doesn't own the cattle."

The sisters exchanged looks and grinning, they crowed in unison, "A.J. Donavan!"

Kicking their horses into a swift trot, the McDougal sisters rode out of town, considerably happier — and richer — than they'd been when they rode in an hour earlier.

TWO

March 1864
Five miles from Nacogdoches, Texas
Some folk said they had it coming; others said it was a shame the McDougal sisters hadn't gotten their due justice sooner.

A March wind savagely whipped the jail wagon along the dusty road as three young women dressed in nuns' habits clung desperately to the bars, eyes clamped shut, praying out loud for deliverance.

The driver, slumped over the front of the wagon, could do little to console the screaming women, considering he had a Comanche arrow sticking through his back. The shotgun rider fired back, but he was clearly outnumbered.

War whoops filled the air. Four young braves chased behind, their black hair whipping wildly about their bronzed faces as they rode hard to overtake their prey.

"What do they want?" Abigail shouted,

her voice nearly drowned out by the sound of thundering hooves.

Anne-Marie, eyes closed, gripped the side of the wagon until her knuckles were white. "Lord God, send us help," she murmured. "We need You now —"

Amelia answered. "They want the horses!"

Abigail's heart pounded like the heathens' war drums as the savages continued to gain on them. "Tell them they can have them!"

"I hardly think they're listening!"

Anne-Marie's pleas increased. "Oh, Father! Save us!"

"Oh, this is so typical." Abigail gritted her teeth and gripped the jail wagon bars. Anne-Marie prayed and Amelia fell apart at the slightest sign of adversity. Of course, this could turn out to be more than a slight turn of misfortune. Her eyes darted back to the braves, but she wasn't worried. God had always seen the McDougal sisters through the worst of times, and He wasn't likely to fail them now.

"If you'd listened to me and let Abigail handle it," Anne-Marie shouted, "we wouldn't be in this pickle! I told you we shouldn't have tried to trick Ramsey Mc-Quade!"

"How was I to know he'd catch on to the ploy?" Amelia frowned. "He was ripe for the kill. Posing as a wealthy Negress was brilliant — Abigail could never have pulled it off!"

Abigail lifted a brow. "And you did? Ramsey knew exactly what you were doing. A beautiful black woman with our eye color? Are you mad? Just because most men are naïve doesn't mean they all are. If you ask me . . ."

"No one did, Abby!"

". . . Ramsey McQuade didn't look naïve standing beside the sheriff on the outskirts of town when we rode out with his money. He looked pretty smart to me." She shot a scathing look at her sister as the wagon lurched over a rut, pitching it into the air and Amelia to the bottom of the floor. Clasping her hands over her face, she began crying and wouldn't stop, even when Anne-Marie shot her a warning look. When the visual reprimand had no effect, Anne-Marie diverted her litany long enough to give Amelia a swift kick with the toe of her boot.

"For heaven's sakes, control yourself!" Abigail snapped when the young lady bawled harder. "You'd think you're the only one about to be scalped. Besides, nobody is going to be scalped." As far as Abigail was concerned, the braves could have the horses and the wagon but if they laid one hand on her or her sisters, she'd personally see that they'd rue the day they were born.

Farther to the west, a dapper man riding a dark sorrel sawed back on the bridle reins as he caught sight of the spectacle. Absently removing his spectacles, Hershall E. Digman wiped away the thick layer of dust coating the lenses. The sight of four young braves in hot pursuit of a wagon was of little concern to him. He didn't borrow trouble, thank you; he had quite enough of his own. And it wasn't unusual for the Comanche to be stirring up trouble. With the attraction of Mexican horses drawing them south, they were raiding deeper and deeper into Texas. The wagon was of no value, so the young bucks were obviously in pursuit of the horses and there was little he could do, or planned to do, about it.

Flexing his sore shoulder muscles, he lifted his face to the sun, momentarily dawdling as he soaked up the warm rays.

To the east, Morgan Kane slowed his horse to a walk. When he spotted the trouble he was inclined to ride to the women's aid. Even from this distance, he could see the wagon driver was dead or gravely injured and the fellow riding shotgun wasn't going to hold out much longer. The parties were at the Indians' mercy, and Morgan knew that with the Comanche, there would be none.

As much as he would like to help, he felt his sense of duty outweigh his instinct. Weather had already delayed him by several days; he didn't need another interruption. But as the women's cries shattered the peaceful countryside, he shifted uneasily in his saddle. A gentleman by nature, he wasn't happy about the situation. The wagon whipped down the road, the horses out of control now.

Soiled doves on their way to jail, an inner voice nagged him.

No one deserves a death like those women are about to face, common sense argued back. Between the Comanche and the war, a man wasn't safe traveling the main roads.

Lifting his arm to wipe the sweat off his face, Morgan fixed his eyes on the braves as they drew closer to the wagon.

To the north, an Indian riding a large chestnut stallion topped the rise. Tall and notably handsome, his piercing black eyes, straight brows, high cheekbones, and prominent nose bespoke his Crow heritage.

The wind whipped his jet black hair as his

dark eyes studied the scene below him.

Comanche.

Kneeing his horse forward, he rode closer, his eyes focused on the scene below.

The jail wagon bounced along, tossing the McDougal sisters around like rag dolls. The savages were so close now that Abigail could see their dark eyes and youthful grins through the dust boiling up through the wagon floor. The boys couldn't be more than fifteen or sixteen — youths looking for adventure.

Averting her gaze, she tried to block out the sound of thundering hooves. She had heard stories of women being captured by Indians and taken to live as their wives. Never in her wildest dreams could she, Abigail Margaret McDougal, imagine being a sixteen-year-old boy's squaw. She couldn't imagine being any man's squaw, and she'd fight until there wasn't a breath left in her if one of those heathens tried to make her one! Her face puckered with resentment. If they caught her, she would fight and fight dirty. She would pinch and spit and hit and bite and if that didn't work, she'd kick.

Her eyes darted back to the young brave drawing even with the wagon. Jumping astride the lead horse, the boy tried to slow the team. The animals, wild-eyed from the harried chase, ran harder.

Hershall Digman sat up straighter, watching more closely as the ruckus neared a rowdy climax. By Jove! Those weren't women; those were nuns in that jail wagon!

Amelia's throat was hoarse from screaming, but she couldn't stop. The sounds of war whoops and hollering as victory drew closer would terrify a saint!

Glancing frantically over her shoulder, she groaned when she saw a bend coming up in the road. That was all they needed. They would be killed for certain now!

The team galloped around the turn, and the wagon tilted sideways. Clutching the bars, she bit her lip until she tasted blood when she felt the wagon tip — then roll precariously on two wheels.

"Pray!" Anne-Marie demanded. "Pray!"

Morgan Kane edged his horse closer to the edge of the knoll. Either his eyes were playing tricks on him, or those were *nuns* in that wagon.

Nuns.

The wheels hit another pothole, and the

wagon went airborne as the horses thundered around a second bend in the road. Female screams filled the air as the right front wheel snapped. Lurching to its side, the wagon skidded across the road toward a briar-infested ravine.

A victory shout went up as Hershall Digman spurred his horse into action. Holding his bowler hat in place with his hand, he plunged his horse down the ravine.

Morgan Kane was already thundering down the hillside when the Crow kneed his horse and sprang forward. The wagon tumbled end over end down the incline, violently tossing the McDougal sisters inside the small cage.

When the conveyance came to rest on its side at the bottom of the ravine, two braves were already working to free the horses. Blades glinted in the sunlight as leather harness was slashed. Then, with another victorious shout, the youths mounted the two horses and rode them up the steep incline.

Kane was riding hard as he approached, but the Indians whipped their animals into a hasty retreat. Yelping with triumph, the braves galloped off to rejoin the remainder of their raiding party that could be spotted waiting a safe distance down the road.

The braves cut their ponies across the

open plains, their jubilant cries ringing over the hillsides.

Dropping off his horse, Morgan ran to peer down the steep slope where a trail of dust marked the vehicle's lightning descent, but the wagon was nowhere in sight.

Whirling, he reached for his gun at the sound of approaching hoofbeats. A Crow riding a large chestnut stallion was moving in fast.

Morgan took aim but stopped short when the man lifted his hand in a peaceful gesture. As the horse came to a halt, the Crow slid off the animal's back and hurried to peer over the side into the gulch.

A moment later, both men spun at the sound of a horse thundering toward them.

When Morgan saw that the approaching rider was having difficulty controlling his animal, he shouted and both men jumped free of his path. Hershall shot into the clearing. Sawing back on the reins, the red-faced shoe salesman managed to stop his horse inches short of plunging headlong over the ravine.

When the dust settled, he calmly settled his bowler back on his head and then climbed awkwardly off his mount.

Shrugging his shoulders uncomfortably in

the too-small jacket of his striped seersucker suit, he tipped his hat at the two men cordially. "Afternoon, gents."

Morgan nodded, slowly holstering his gun.

"My, my, my, my!" The newcomer, round-eyed now, scurried to gape over the rim of the gulch. Fishing a large handkerchief from his pocket, he mopped anxiously at his perspiring forehead. "A most frightful turn of events," he fretted. "Are the women . . . ?"

The three men edged closer to the ravine, their eyes searching to locate the wagon.

"Guess there's only one way to find out." Morgan glanced over his shoulder. "We'd better make it quick. Those young bucks are spoiling for a fight."

"Oh, my, my, my, my! The thought of those savages simply makes me ill! Why ever do you suppose nuns would be riding in a jail wagon?"

Morgan shook his head. "I couldn't say."

The Crow was already making his way down the ravine. His moccasin-covered feet slid in the rocks and loose dirt as he worked his way down the incline.

Hershall cupped his hand to the side of his mouth and whispered, "Does the savage speak English?"

"I haven't heard him speak a word." Morgan started down the ravine, following behind the other man.

Glancing anxiously at his carpetbag full of shoe samples, Hershall joined the two men. The Crow was already halfway down the slope.

By the time they reached the bottom they could see the jail wagon tipped on its side with the back door broken open. The three nuns lay inside in a broken heap.

Morgan solemnly made the sign of the cross and then strode to the broken wreckage. "We'd best get them buried."

"Oh, my, my, my, my." Hershall touched his temples. "I'm developing a simply pounding headache from it all."

Shoving the broken wreckage aside, the Indian ran his dark eyes over the crumpled heap of women. His fingers touched the side of Anne-Marie's wrist. Stirring, she opened her eyelids. Bolting upright, she screamed and the Crow, Morgan, and Hershall jumped as if they'd been shot.

Hershall attempted to calm her. "It's all right, Sister. You're safe now."

Bewildered, Anne-Marie shook her head, clearly disoriented.

Amelia and Abigail slowly came around. Groaning, Abigail tried to untangle her limbs from Amelia's. "Sweet Mother of Mercy, every bone in my body's broken!"

"Sister Abigail." Abigail winced at the sound of Anne-Marie's admonishment.

"Your habit, Sister. It's askew."

Pushing herself upright, the nun shook the woman lying beside her, her gaze fixed on the three men staring through the bars at her. Her gaze traveled the length of a tall man with broad shoulders and then shifted to the dapper dandy in a puckered seersucker suit, whose main concern at the moment seemed to be preventing his hat from blowing off. And then she was looking at the splendid-looking savage.

"Oh, dear goodness," Amelia muttered, glassy-eyed and rolling to her back. "Did a train hit us?"

Sister Abigail punched her warningly. "Is anything broken?"

"Are you crazy? Yes! My . . ."

Abigail swiftly elbowed her again, quelling Amelia's unsavory retort. Amelia's eyes switched to the three men gaping at her. She pasted a serene smile on her lips and hastily made the sign of the cross. "Why, no, Sister. I believe I've survived the fall quite nicely."

"God has smiled on us again," Anne-Marie said. "We must thank Him for His graciousness."

"We need to get you out of the wreckage."

Morgan's gaze focused on the mangled spokes. "You must have broken bones — or bruises?"

Abigail grunted, trying to sort her arms and legs from Amelia's. "Sister, would you kindly get *off* me?"

"Certainly, Sister, if you will kindly remove your foot from my pocket."

"Well, nothing seems to be amiss," Anne-Marie assured the men brightly. She straightened her veil.

Hershall bolted forward to assist Abigail from the wagon. Removing his bowler, he placed the hat over his heart, bowing from the waist down. "Hershall E. Digman at your service, ma'am."

Eyeing him sourly, Abigail slid out of the wagon before he could help her, but Hershall insisted on leading her to the nearest rock. Seating her, he wrung his hands with despair when he noted the beginnings of a dark bruise forming on her temple.

"You are most fortunate," he fussed, "most fortunate, my dear lady, that you weren't killed."

Pushing back the sleeve of her habit, Abigail examined her skinned elbow. "I don't feel fortunate. I've just eaten ten pounds of dust and nearly been scalped. If I get much luckier, I won't live to tell about it."

31

Anne-Marie swayed and the Indian quietly stepped forward to assist her.

"I'm a little lightheaded," she confessed. He helped ease her out of the wagon, her hand resting lightly on his bronzed forearm. The Crow stilled, lifting his hand to command silence. Nodding toward the road, his eyes mutely warned of impending trouble.

Panic seized Amelia. She might die yet. The group strained to listen to the sound of approaching horses.

"The remainder of the raiding party," Morgan guessed.

"Oh, my, my, my!"

"We'd best be on our way, gentlemen."

"Oh, yes, I think that would be most prudent of us," Hershall agreed. "Most prudent." Pushing his glasses up on the bridge of his nose, he extended the crook of his arm to Abigail.

Morgan reached for Amelia and urged her toward the incline. "The name's Kane — Morgan Kane. We don't have much time. If you can't make it up the hill, I'll carry you."

"I can make it," she said.

"Wait," Anne-Marie murmured, closing her eyes. The Indian paused, supporting her weight until the light-headedness passed.

Morgan and Amelia were already scrambling up the hillside. Amelia's boot slid in the loose dirt, but Morgan's hands boosted her onward. She turned, offering him an affronted glare. "Sorry, Sister — we have to keep moving."

The Indian and Anne-Marie systematically made their way up the incline. When she occasionally lost her footing, the Crow's hand was there to steady her.

Hershall attempted to assist Abigail but she repeatedly pushed his efforts aside. Scrambling up the incline, she glanced over her shoulder, concerned about Anne-Marie, who was disoriented.

Abigail felt her feet slipping in the loose dirt, but Hershall's hand chivalrously shot out to support her. She irritably swatted it aside and muttered, "Stop it!"

"Only trying to help!" Jerking his waistcoat back into place, he stepped back. She'd offended him, but this was neither the time nor place to make amends. The six scrambled over the gully and spotted the dust of the returning Comanche raiding party.

"They're moving in fast," Morgan noted.

"We'll have to make a run for it," Hershall concurred.

Morgan caught Amelia around the waist and lifted her into the saddle. Springing up behind her, he turned to the others. "We need to split up!"

Whirling, Hershall fled to his horse, dragging Abigail with him.

The Indian bolted onto the stallion, pulling Anne-Marie on behind.

Hershall's horse sidestepped nervously when he attempted to mount. Abigail glanced anxiously at the approaching cloud of dust, then back to Hershall's bumbling attempts.

When it became clear that they were going to be scalped if he didn't get his foot in the stirrup soon, she smothered a sigh and irritably hoisted him into the saddle with her shoulder.

"Why, thank you, my dear —"

"Just be quiet."

Planting her foot atop his, she gathered her habit, grasped the tail of his coat, and hefted herself up behind him, forcing him to grab frantically for the saddle horn to keep them both from being hurtled to the ground.

Giving the horse a sound whack across the rump, Abigail sent it bolting into a full gallop as Hershall held tightly to his hat.

"Abigail! Anne-Marie! Remember Church Rock!" Amelia shouted as the Indian turned his chestnut stallion and rode off in a northerly direction.

Amelia waved in mute acknowledgment.

Gripping tightly to Hershall's flying coat-tails, Abigail noted the message and gritted her teeth as the horse loped off to the south in a bone-jarring gait.

Why? She lifted her face to appeal to a higher source. *Why, with three choices, do I have to get stuck with Hershall E. Digman?*

THREE

Once Hershall had the horse going in a straight line, he kicked it into a full gallop. Clinging tightly to his coattails, Abigail prayed he was a better horseman than he looked.

"Can't you go faster?" she shouted.

"I'm going as fast as I can, Sister."

"Do you want me to take the reins?"

"I do not."

He batted the black veil away from his face as he raced the horse across an open field, heading for a stand of timber. Once they reached the woods, he wove the horse in and out of the trees at a heart-stopping pace in an obvious attempt to lose the zealous young braves riding close on their heels.

"I don't know what all the fuss is about!" Abigail could barely make herself heard above the crashing of thicket and flying hooves. "They're only young boys! You can take them."

"Young boys who know how to use a knife as well as their fathers!" He blustered now, spurring the horse faster.

It was close to an hour before he allowed the horse to slacken its pace. By now Abigail was thinking that her spine was driven straight through the top of her head, but the young braves had grown tired of the chase and turned away. "Do you think we've lost them?"

"I certainly hope so." He reached for his handkerchief to mop his forehead. In her first sane moment of the past hour, she noticed he wasn't as old as she'd first thought. Or as homely.

"Can we stop for a moment?" She viewed the particles of twigs and leaves stuck to the lenses of his glasses with open contempt.

"It isn't safe."

It was the same response he'd repeatedly given. "Where are we going? And what about the others — will we try to catch up with them? They're my sisters, you know." *Careful, Abigail. You don't know this man.* "My convent sisters," she amended. Who knew if he'd heard of the McDougal sisters? It seemed their reputation in these parts was growing.

"Catching up would be impossible. We'll ride until I feel it's safe to stop, and then we'll discuss what we're going to do about your situation."

She noticed that although he'd modified the horse's pace, he continued to ride at a brisk gait. He occasionally glanced over his shoulder to make certain they weren't being followed. When there was no sign of the Indians, he seemed to breathe easier.

As the day progressed, the sun slid in and out of innocent-looking clouds. In the late afternoon, the mild breeze they'd enjoyed all day took on a sudden chill.

She pressed closer to his back, trying to protect herself from the rising wind. It was a strong back — strapping and not frail as she'd suspected. Taut ridges and sinewy muscles. It was finally sinking into her that the McDougal sisters were at the mercy of three strangers, and the realization was frightening. She had never been apart from Amelia and Anne-Marie — not ever. And this odd assortment of men who'd rescued them from certain death — who were they? Where had they come from?

More importantly, what did they plan to do with them?

For the moment she felt reasonably safe. Hershall Digman didn't appear to present a threat to her, but what about Amelia? Amelia was with — what did he say his name was? Martin Lane? Morgan Spain? Everything had happened so swiftly, she couldn't recall.

And poor Anne-Marie. Her fate lay in the hands of an uncivilized heathen! Abigail shuddered when she pictured the savage's dark, foreboding eyes. Black as the devil himself.

"Are you cold?"

Startled, she realized that she had forgotten where she was for a moment. "Yes, a little."

He reached into the saddlebag, removed a heavy coat, and handed it to her. "Wear this."

"Don't you need it?" The thin suit jacket he was wearing furnished little protection from the sudden temperature drop.

"I'll put on an extra shirt when we make camp."

He was only being benevolent. He had to be as cold as she was, but if he was silly enough to offer her the coat, she'd gladly wear it. "I hope that's soon," she said.

"I think it prudent we ride until nightfall."

"Wonderful," she murmured, determined to maintain her disguise. If Hershall were to discover that she wasn't a nun, he might not be so eager to help. And as much as she hated to admit it, she knew she'd need his help to see her safely back to Church Rock Cemetery. The meeting place had long been their agreed-upon destination should the sisters ever be temporarily parted. That day had come.

They rode for over another hour before he finally thought it safe to make camp. Studying the darkening sky, the lines around his eyes deepened. The low-hanging clouds nearly obscured the sun now.

"Looks like weather is moving in."

Pushing aside the end of her veil, Abigail studied the churning sky. She couldn't argue: It looked ominous.

"What should we do?"

"We'll make camp soon." They started off again as the sun disappeared behind another dark cloud.

"Where were you and the sisters going when the Indians attacked the wagon?" He made his first attempt at conversation as the horse trotted down the road.

"To jai — Sister Jane's," she amended.

"Sister Jane's?"

"Yes, she teaches a small — yes, a small school," Abigail decided. Anne-Marie warned that although they took from the wealthy for a good cause, they shouldn't lie. The Good Book said lying was a sin, but she, for one, had a hard time getting around the truth without stretching it. "Sister Jane is ill. She sent word that she needed help, so that's where we were going." She smiled, more confident with her tale. "To help Sister Jane."

He turned to look over his shoulder, meeting her gaze evenly. "Sister Jane is gravely ill?"

"She has smallpox."

He visibly recoiled. "Nasty affliction."

"Oh, you needn't worry. We haven't been around Sister yet, but they say she looks wretched." Leaning closer, she lowered her voice, sensing that Hershall was a bit squeamish about the subject. "Big, ugly, runny sores, oozing with goop —"

He paled, turning the collar of his suit up closer.

"Are you cold?"

"A sudden chill, nothing serious."

"Smallpox. A terrible death, they say. Simply terrible. Have you ever met anyone with smallpox, Mr. Digman?"

His jaw firmed and he shook his head.

"Perhaps you'd like to meet Sister Jane? She's a pure delight — and she makes the most delightful herbal tea."

He shook his head again, kicking the horse to pick up the pace. The stallion had the worst gait Abigail had ever endured. It was like riding on a wagon full of rocks, and Hershall didn't help matters. He was a terrible horseman.

"Please," she finally muttered through clenched teeth, "could you either slow down or speed up? This gait is jarring."

Hershall temporarily allowed the horse to drop back into a smoother gait. Shifting her weight more evenly in the saddle, she adjusted her habit to a more dignified angle.

Actually, he'd said little since the small pox conversation but now he asked. "Why were you traveling in a jail wagon?"

"It was the only conveyance available — is there a town coming up?" she asked, hoping to change the subject. She should keep this encounter as impersonal as possible. He didn't appear to be the sort to take a disguise — especially the holy cloth — lightly.

"I'm not certain."

"I hope there is." A frown creased her forehead. "I must send word to the mission."

"What mission might that be, Sister?"

"It is but a small, insignificant mission near the Mexican border." He wouldn't recognize the name, nor did she plan to offer it. Surely the brief encounter would end soon.

"The Mexican border?" He frowned. "That's a considerable distance from here."

"Yes, our work takes us on many long journeys. The sisters and I have vowed that if we are ever parted, we will return quickly to a cemetery near there to be reunited."

"Why the cemetery?"

"It's a place of special significance." She didn't elaborate further; he knew too much now. The ground held no significance other than that they'd played among the stones as children.

"Well, as soon as I find a stage road, you'll be on your way," he promised.

Her heart seized. She had never been alone — never without Amelia and Anne-Marie — and she wasn't exactly the best with direction. Anne-Marie took care of that detail. As badly as she hated to admit it, she was at this man's mercy. "Mr. Digman, I was rather expecting you to escort me there."

He shifted, meeting her gaze. "To the border?"

"I know it would be a small bother, but —"

"No, ma'am. I can't take you to the border, but I will see you safely on the stage coach," he promised.

"What are you doing that's so important

that you can't take me there?" Surely he could spare a few days' delay in order to do a good deed.

He turned to peer over his shoulder at her.

"I mean," she amended her tone, "can you not spare a bit of time to help a woman in need? Are you married? What do you do for a living, Mr. Digman?"

"I'm not married, and I sell shoes."

She smiled. "Oh, how nice." She might have known. Shoes. Now that was some excuse. Like everyone was running around barefoot?

Glancing at the sky, he frowned. "Weather's moving in."

She looked up. If the clouds held as much snow as she suspected, travel would be unpleasant.

Another twenty minutes passed before he found a small clearing that looked promising. "This seems like an acceptable place to camp for the night," he announced.

Abigail slid stiffly off the horse the moment he stopped. If she'd had to stay in that saddle another five minutes, she would have screamed. The wind was steadily picking up, whipping the trees and bushes nearly to the ground. Hershall held on to his hat with one hand while he secured the horse to a nearby tree.

"Well," he said, rubbing his hands together as he scurried back, "some hot coffee should help chase the chill. I'll get a fire started, rig some sort of shelter, and then see what I can scare up for supper."

"May I help?" she asked, more from grudging obligation than real interest.

"Oh, no, no, no. You just make yourself comfortable." She stepped aside and watched as he bustled away to put on an extra shirt before he began setting up camp.

Folding her arms about herself for warmth, she paced, pausing occasionally to try to stamp some feeling back into her feet.

When he returned, he was carrying a bedroll and a few cooking utensils. "Just have a seat, Sister," he yelled above the howling wind. "This will only take a minute."

"I'll stand, if you don't mind." *If the simpleton doesn't hurry, we're both going to freeze to death!*

Clasping her wrists beneath the sleeves of her habit, she paced faster.

Although she tried not to, her eyes kept returning to his suit. The thin fabric was totally inadequate for blizzard attire. The linen seer-sucker was a most unattractive brown stripe that puckered at the seams. The trousers — way too short, but it didn't matter, because they matched the sleeves, which were too short too.

And that ridiculous bowler he was so afraid the wind was going to snatch away. The silly-looking hat hid most of his hair, but that was all right too, because he had it slicked down with some sort of greasy pomade.

She had to admit his square jaw made him seem a tad more attractive than she'd first thought, but the spectacles ruined the one concession. They kept sliding down his nose, and he kept shoving them back up with his forefinger until she wanted to rap him across the knuckles and tell him to stop it.

"Are you comfortable, Sister?"

"Just dandy, Mr. Digman!"

"It won't be long now," he promised, and her smile encouraged him to take all the time he needed.

Unrolling a piece of heavy canvas, he shook out the wrinkles. A sudden gust of wind caught it and snatched it out of his hands. The material winged off, landing a few feet away in the clearing.

When he ran to get it, the wind caught his hat and sent it skipping across the ground.

Forgetting his purpose, he scrambled after the bowler, chasing the hat around the small clearing, darting to and fro, to and fro, as the wind repeatedly caught it and sent it soaring out of his reach.

She sat on a rock, watching him dart in and out, chasing the canvas, then his hat, then the canvas, then his hat.

Absolutely pathetic.

The tent soared in her direction, and her left leg snaked out, trapping the canvas securely beneath her foot.

Hershall, still in pursuit of the bowler, scrambled down a slight ravine and disappeared momentarily. She assumed that he thought they could sleep in the hat tonight, since he had lost interest in the tent.

When he emerged from the gully, he looked ready to burst into tears. "Oh my goodness! I've lost the tent!"

"I have the tent, Mr. Digman."

"Oh, you do?" His face brightened. "Wonderful!"

She kept her foot firmly planted on her one means of survival as Hershall scrambled up the ravine and ran to her.

Lifting her foot, he smiled as he dutifully removed the piece of canvas. "Oh dear me, dear me! We would have been in a fine pickle if we had lost our tent."

If we *had lost our tent*? "Indeed we would have, Mr. Digman."

47

Scurrying over to a sturdy-looking bush, he draped the canvas over a low-hanging limb. "I'll have us set up in no time at all," he called brightly.

"Take your time, Mr. Digman." Which he undoubtedly would. She was hard-pressed to remember ever meeting a man like Digman.

Twenty minutes later, Digman managed to get all four canvas corners staked to the ground. She could have helped — the gusty wind made the task near impossible for one person — but he insisted that she sit and watch. So she had.

"There now." He stepped back to admire his work. "You sit inside where it's warmer. I'll build a fire."

"I could help —" she began, blinded by visions of a wayfaring stranger finding them frozen stiff as wash on a January clothesline by the time he had a fire started.

"No, no, I wouldn't hear of it. I'll have a roaring fire going in no time at all. Then we'll both feel better." He edged her toward the opening of the small lean-to. "Go on now; it's cold out here."

She reluctantly crawled into the shelter, wishing to high heaven he would let her help. She had a hunch that she was more adept at starting fires than he was.

Dropping the flap back into place, he scurried off again.

Twenty minutes later she lifted the canvas, watching Hershall scurry about the campsite, still gathering fallen limbs and bits of twigs for the fire.

"Better lay some rocks in a small circle to contain the fire, Mr. Digman," she called out.

"Thank you, Sister!"

Seconds later she called again. "I'm really quite efficient at starting fires — I could help, Mr. Digman!"

"You're much too kind, Sister. Remain where you are."

Huddling deeper into the fleece lining of Hershall's coat, she tried to think of something warm. The image of Amelia and Anne-Marie surfaced to mind and she felt better. They'd only been apart for a few hours, but she missed them fiercely. Anne-Marie's cool head; Amelia's amazing perception.

Easing the flap aside, she peeked out again. She knew it. Hershall was kneeling beside a circle of rocks, wasting matches. Time after time the wind blew out the match but he patiently removed another from the box and struck it.

After repeated failures to produce even a tiny spark, she was ready to scream. Glancing down at her lap, she found her fists balled tightly together. Her fingers itched to burst out of the tent and snatch the match out of his hands. She'd have had the fire lit thirty minutes ago!

By the time he managed to coax a tiny spark, she had nearly bitten her tongue in two trying to keep quiet.

She watched through the tent flap as he bent over the thin thread of smoke, blowing, and then carefully feeding leaves into the flame, blowing, adding a few shavings more, blowing —

Puff . . . puff.

The flame struggled to ignite as he hurriedly fed it more small twigs, then larger branches. Just when it appeared to ignite, a sudden gust of wind snuffed the feeble attempt and he resignedly reached for the box of matches again.

She couldn't stand it any longer. She didn't know how many matches remained, but it wasn't enough.

Bolting out of the tent, she marched toward him, set on taking the matches away from him. The man was doubled over the flame, carefully fanning the smoldering embers.

"Mr. Digman!"

Whipping upright, his spectacles plunged

to the bridge of his nose. "Yes?" He squinted to meet her gaze.

"Please . . ." she blurted. "I'm really quite good at starting fires —"

"Nonsense." He smiled, pointing to the thin wisp of smoke starting to curl from the pile of sticks. "As you see, I already have one started."

A blazing inferno!

Motioning her back to the tent, he returned to the business at hand.

Rolling her eyes with disgust, she checked her foot short of booting him face-first into the fire. There he was, hunkered over a pile of twigs and leaves, his too-short pants exposing his hairy ankles above the tops of his shoes, while she sat inside that miserable excuse for a tent, freezing.

When the flame caught, he slowly got to his feet. The branches popped and crackled noisily now, sending a plume of white smoke into the air. He arched his back and lazily stretched.

Striding past him, she threw her foot against his back, hard.

Before he could catch himself, he pitched forward. "Mother of Mercy!" he burst out, managing to catch himself before plunging headlong into the fire, she noted.

"Oh, my goodness!" Her hands shot to

51

her mouth in horror. "Did I bump you?"

He began jumping up and down, slapping wildly at his smoldering pant leg.

"I'm so sorry," she cried, trying to look properly repentant.

"Just *look* at my spats!"

She looked. They were all sooty.

"Oh, how could I be so clumsy? In my zest to warm myself by this nice, toasty fire I was reckless." She dropped her head remorsefully as Hershall Digman muttered and wiped at his spats. Then, as if to add insult to injury, the wind snatched his bowler again and sent it skipping across the small clearing into a nearby briar patch.

"Oh, dear, there goes your hat, Mr. Digman. Let me fetch it this time."

His jaw firmed, and his expression hardened. "Just tell me where it is," he ground out.

Turning, she pointed to the hat, ensnared in the thickest part of the barren blackberry patch. "Right over there."

Jerking his waistcoat into place, he spun on his heel and stalked into the weeds.

"Hurry back," she called.

Or don't. By now she was ready to be rid of this man.

FOUR

A cold rain started to fall, and the temperature dropped at an alarming rate. The smell of coffee bubbling on the fire was the only thing warding off abject misery as darkness encompassed the campsite.

"I apologize for the meager fare." Hershall crawled inside the tent, half frozen. He lit a candle and stuck it into the ground. "We'll have something hot to drink soon. I'm afraid chicory is all I can offer, but the coffee will help wash the jerky down."

"I'm sure the fare will be adequate," Abigail returned staunchly.

"Perhaps in the morning I'll shoot a rabbit, and then you can have a hot meal."

She had to admit a hot meal would be welcome, but at the moment she wouldn't turn down anything. She tried to remember the last time she'd eaten. Sometime yesterday? The jailers had set three bowls of something that resembled gruel inside the dank cell. The meal was as cold and merciless as the jailers, and Abigail hadn't been able to make herself eat. Anne-Marie warned that she must eat enough to keep her strength up, but Abigail flung her bowl across the cell, vowing to starve first. And her chickens were coming to roost.

Since death now appeared an imminent possibility, she gratefully accepted the cup of coffee that Digman handed her. Sipping the scalding brew, she allowed the comforting heat to penetrate her fingertips.

"Careful, Sister, you'll burn yourself."

"I would consider it a blessing, Mr. Digman."

He laid the jerky on a cloth and handed it to her. Then he scooted to the opposite side and began to eat his meal.

Before he had finished one strip, she had polished off both of hers and was eyeing his hungrily. The meal was tough and dry and she felt like she had swallowed a ball of cotton, but she was grateful to be eating.

Biting off a piece of jerky, he chewed thoughtfully. She felt his eyes on her. A smile quirked the corners of his mouth. "I have to admit, Sister, you're younger and prettier than the nuns I've met," he said. "My teachers were old, pudding-faced disciplinarians with hair growing on their upper lips, and all of them were handy with a ruler across my knuckles." He glanced at her. "And all insisted on prayer before meals."

Sister absently shrugged. "Forgive my oversight. I haven't eaten in a while."

"Yes," Hershall mused. "I can see that."

Later he came to his knees and began to neatly rearrange the blanket he was sitting on.

Abigail watched the motherly manner, shaking her head in amazement. He was so persnickety she wondered how he'd made his way in this rough country, especially with a war going on.

The rain fell harder, driven by a howling wind that threatened to collapse the small lean-to.

"I'm sorry I can't offer better facilities, but I didn't expect to spend the night on the trail," he apologized. When the blanket was free of any sign of wrinkle, he sat down again.

Removing his specs, he polished them with a white cloth he'd extracted from his saddlebag. "This part of Texas usually enjoys moderate weather this time of year," he remarked. "But I suppose in March you can expect most anything."

"Yes I suppose that's true," Abigail agreed.

She wondered exactly how old her companion was. Late twenties? Early thirties? It was hard for her to judge — but older than her. Much older, she decided.

"Have you served in the war, Mr. Digman?" Selling shoes seemed hardly a goal any man fancied after the war. Not that folks didn't need shoes, but most chose to farm or rebuild their homes. This man appeared to drift, going from here to there.

His gaze avoided hers. "For a short interlude, but I was wounded." He fell quiet, and she could see he found the subject most distressing. "They thought it best that I sell shoes."

"I'm so sorry."

"Oh, don't fret. The wound healed quite adequately."

She sipped her coffee, nodding. "Where did you say you were going, Mr. Digman?"

"Louisiana," Hershall said.

"To visit family?"

"Oh, no. My work takes me there."

"And I suppose you're married? Children?"

His features turned crimson. "Oh my, no. I am a lone spirit."

"What a pity. A fine-looking gentleman such as yourself?"

His face turned hotter. "I know, I know,

but to be frank, Sister, I've never had much luck with females," he confessed.

"No," she scoffed.

"Oh, I know what you're thinking. Many a woman would consider herself blessed to have a man such as myself, but" — his sigh turned wistful — "my work keeps me busy." He hooked the rims of his glasses over his ears and peered at her. "Of course, having taken a vow of chastity, you don't have to worry about such things."

"What 'things' are those, Mr. Digman?"

"Taking a husband."

She smiled. "No."

"Having taken the vow of obedience and poverty, your needs are simple."

She nodded subserviently, aware that a woman's needs would have to be simple with a man like Hershall.

"Who do you sell your shoes to, Mr. Digman?"

"The army," he stated. "An army marches on its feet, does it not?"

"Yes, but times are hard. I've heard that some Confederate units are in such bad shape they barely have shoes at all." Abigail knew little about the war. She'd heard talk, but since she didn't know anyone involved in the fighting, current affairs were of little concern to her.

"There are some who are able to afford my wares," he assured.

Setting her cup beside the candle, she noted how he dug into the saddlebag for his map. Lowering it closer to the flame, he studied it.

She made her tone casual — so far the ruse was working. He didn't suspect her ploy and she planned to keep it that way. "What direction are we traveling?"

"Northeast."

"And we will come to a town soon?"

"We should."

"It is imperative that I leave as soon as possible," she reminded him. "Sister Amelia and Sister Anne-Marie will be sick with worry if I fail to meet them at the cemetery within a few days. They'll worry themselves sick."

"Now, now, Sister, you needn't be concerned." He folded the map and put it back in the saddlebag. "It will also take a few days for the sisters to reach the cemetery."

"Mr. Digman." She bent to lay her hand on his arm. "Isn't there some way I can persuade you to escort me to Mercy Flats?"

"Mercy Flats?"

"That's where the cemetery is located — the cemetery where I'm to meet the other sisters."

His features closed. "I'm sorry. That would be impossible. I must be in Shreveport by the end of the month."

"But this is a mission of the Lord. Surely you can spare time to serve the Lord," she coaxed.

"Ordinarily I could, Sister, but it's important that I conduct this sale. We can't have the South marching barefoot, can we?"

"From what I hear, the South has been marching barefoot for some time."

His brows lifted. "Are you a Northern sympathizer?"

Turning away, she jerked the blanket tighter around her neck. "As a servant of the Lord, I take no sides. It was merely a comment. God loves everyone."

"Yes, ma'am, He sure does." He tipped his hat graciously. "And now I'd best say good evenin' to you."

"Are you going somewhere?"

"Well, it's late, and we have a long ride ahead of us tomorrow. It's time to blow out the candle."

She leaned closer, her eyes meeting his pleadingly. "Please, Mr. Digman, won't you reconsider your plans? It would only take a few days to escort me back to Mercy Flats. I'm . . . very eager to be reunited with my sisters."

"I noticed the strong resemblance between you and the nuns you're traveling with." He glanced up, assessing her. "Your eyes are a most remarkable green. Is it fair to assume that the three of you are blood sisters?"

Tears welled in Abigail's eyes, and her resolve weakened. She didn't see that it would hurt if he knew that Amelia and Anne-Marie were her real sisters, and it might even make her feel less lonely to confess it. "Yes. This is the first time we've ever been apart."

"I know it isn't proper to ask a woman's age."

"I'm eighteen. We're close in years."

His gaze skimmed her lightly. "You're not ancient. You got a lot of life waiting for you out there. I'm sorry. It must be difficult for you to be separated from your sisters."

She gazed up into his eyes, finding a spark of hope at last. "Does that mean you'll take me?"

He turned a deaf ear, preparing to retire for the night. "It's late, Sister. It's time we turned in."

Well fine! Let him be that way. She didn't need his help. She'd get back to the cemetery on her own. Scooting to her side, she rearranged the blanket. She should have known better than to ask a man for help in the first place.

"You may have the extra blanket," he offered.

She glanced around the tightly confined area. "Where are you going to sleep?"

"Due to the nasty weather, we'll have to share quarters." When her lip curled, he added, "The Lord will understand."

"Of course Mr. Digman. If you would be so kind as to allow me a moment of privacy . . . my devotions, you understand."

"Of course." He obediently crawled to the tent opening. "I'll wait outside."

"Thank you. You are ever so kind."

Hershall consulted his watch. A chill rattled his frame. Twenty minutes. She'd been at her devotions more than *twenty minutes.* How long did it take to thank the Lord? He stood in the blowing rain, turning his collar up, and then made a mad dash to a large oak for shelter. Sleet was falling in a peppery sheet now.

Yawning, Abigail stretched lazily and then pulled the blanket closer. *Simpleton.* She closed her eyes, wondering about the funny Mr. Digman. *Why couldn't I have been rescued by someone with half a brain?*

■ ■ ■ ■

Thirty minutes passed. Sleet lay heavy on the ground. Hershall's boot crunched under the icy pellets as he paced back and forth beneath the tree, stamping his feet and rubbing his hands together as he studied the worsening weather. His eyes darted periodically to the tent for any sign that Sister's devotions were complete, but he found none.

What was taking so long? His suit was soaked, and his feet felt like two blocks of ice.

When an hour passed and the sister still hadn't called, he was fit to be tied. How long could one woman pray? If he didn't know better he would swear the woman was a fraud — a complete counterfeit. But that would make the other two bogus . . .

Blowing on his hands he tried to restore feeling. He struck off in the direction of the tent when Sister Abigail finally sang out, "You can come in now, Mr. Digman!"

Gritting his teeth, he muffled a curse against the fates that had set him on the rise that day. It would be a cold day in August the next time a jail wagon full of nuns got his help.

Throwing back the tent flap, he entered the shelter like a bull moose. His seersucker suit was soaked through. Snow piled in the brim of his bowler hat and ice formed a ring around the perimeter of his spectacles, rendering him practically blind.

Rolling to her back, Abigail yawned, primly adjusting her blanket. "Is it getting worse out there, Mr. Digman?" Her gaze slid his way.

Apparently he could not bring himself to answer with a civil tongue. His knees knocked together so hard that he was barely able to wrap himself in the one blanket he hadn't given her.

"My, my. You look half frozen," she chided.

Refusing an answer, he pinched the candle flame. The tent turned black.

"Goodnight, Mr. Digman." Abigail's words rambled in the void. "I'm ever so grateful you gave me the extra blanket. I'm so warm and cozy and I'm sure I'll have a wonderful rest. In my prayers, I told the Good Lord how grateful I am."

She heard him clamp his teeth shut. Poor man. Hitching the blanket closer, she smiled. He'd regret the day he refused to help her.

Before the hour passed, she heard soft snores coming from his side of the tent. Easing out from the covers, she pushed aside the canvas flap and peered outside.

Snow fell in fat cotton flakes, slow and steady now. Worsening conditions would make traveling difficult, if not impossible. *Rooster spit!* she thought. *I can't find my way in a snowstorm!* The horse would leave a trail a blind man could follow.

Resigned that she'd have to wait until better weather to make her escape, she crawled back to the blanket, determined to make the best of a disturbing turn of luck.

FIVE

"Sister Abigail! Come and get your meat before it burns," Hershall called out as he rustled around the fire the next morning. Dumping a fistful of chicory into the pot of boiling water, he tested fresh game roasting on the fire for tenderness. "Yoo-hoo, are you awake?"

Lifting her head, Abigail squinted into the darkness. Egad. It was barely light enough to see her hand in front of her face. What fool was yapping this early in the morning?

Digman. And he sounded cheerful as a goat in mash. Apparently his anger had cooled and he was in a more tolerant mood this morning.

Wonder how long he can stay that way?

"Hurry, hurry, hurry," a male voice sang out brightly.

Rolling onto her back, she winced when she realized she must leave the pallet's warmth.

"Come, come, come now." He clapped both hands briskly. " 'Tis a new day!"

" 'Tis a new day," she mimicked.

She started fully awake when he pecked on the canvas side. "Time to get up, Sister."

Jerking upright, she checked her veil to make sure her hair was properly concealed. Moments later she lifted the flap aside, wrapped the blanket around her shoulders, and dragged herself outside. The biting winds snatched her breath as she straightened, pulling the warm blanket around her chin more tightly. Gingerly picking her way to the fire, she muttered under her breath as her shoes sank above her ankles into the deep snow that had fallen during the night.

Hershall glanced up, a smile lighting his features. "Good morning, Sister! I trust you slept well?"

"As if I were in Eden." Lifting her hands to the fire, she eyed the three plump birds roasting on the spit. "You rise very early."

"Oh, my, yes. Can't sleep your life away! Coffee?"

"No, thank you."

"Oh, but you must have some. We have a long ride ahead of us."

"I don't eat first thing in the morning."

"But you must. You'll be hungry within the hour and if you want to reach a town

66

we can't tarry." He poured a cup of coffee and wedged it between her hands with a curt, "Drink it." Turning quickly away, he stifled a sneeze.

"Catching a sniffle, Mr. Digman?"

"It would appear so."

It would be short of a miracle if he didn't come down with a roaring case of consumption. Guilt nagged her. He *was* her only hope of reaching that cemetery. She should be nicer to him. Seating herself on a rock, she held the hot coffee between her hands, trying to keep her eyes open.

"Drink your coffee. We'll have meat shortly."

She wished he would leave her alone. Her stomach rolled at the thought of eating a greasy old bird at this hour of the morning.

"Drink your coffee, Sister. It's getting cold."

She puzzled over his lightning swift moods. Eat, Sister. Drink, Sister! Are you comfortable? May I fetch you anything? Then silence. Stony silence.

Bringing the cup to her mouth, she took a sip. The strong chicory seared her throat. Choking, she leaned forward, spitting the bitter liquid on the ground. "For goodness sakes!" she blurted.

He turned. "Is something amiss?"

"The coffee," she strangled out, "is too strong."

He turned back to the fire. "Gets the blood pumping, doesn't it?" He stifled a second sneeze.

Setting her cup aside, she huddled deeper into the blanket and watched as he turned the spit. He wasn't a tall man; in fact, she'd bet he wasn't three inches taller than she. When they talked, he addressed her almost at eye level but beneath the seersucker suit, his shoulders were broad and his waist surprisingly trim. He appeared to be quite well proportioned. His hands were wide and strong, and his arms — poking from those ridiculous sleeves — appeared tan and masculine. If she didn't know better she'd think he was a fraud. A hopeless fraud . . . but she had no idea whom he'd be trying to dupe.

Hitching herself closer to the fire, she took another sip of the coffee. It was so awful it had a certain fascination about it. "Why is it so cold? My feet are numb."

"Weather's unpredictable." Removing the spit from the fire, he extended the birds to her.

She viewed the meat and her stomach churned. "I'm not hungry."

Calmly he removed one of the birds and

handed it to her. "Eat."

Flipping the hot bird from hand to hand, she reminded herself that they were on the trail, not in a dining room, so he could be excused for his appalling lack of social graces. "Can't I have a plate?"

"You don't need a plate. Eat up." Breaking one of the birds apart, he bit into the savory meat. "Best stop juggling your food and eat it, Sister. Could be we won't be lucky enough to have such succulent fare tonight."

Clearing a skiff of snow off the rock, she laid the meat beside her. "I'm hoping we'll reach a town today."

"No harm in hoping."

Picking gingerly at the bird, she tried to pull one of its scrawny legs apart. "It's raw." She heard the sigh but ignored it.

"Perhaps you'd prefer mine."

She shrugged. "After you've eaten off it?"

"Then perhaps the third one would be more to your liking." He got up and fetched the bird for her.

Skeptically picking through the second piece of meat, she shook her head. "No, this one's raw too."

"Then perhaps you would like a piece of jerky."

"Well . . ." She studied the half-raw bird,

then his nice, plump, brown one that looked for the world to her as if it were cooked to perfection. "Maybe I'll try yours again."

"I've already taken a bite of it."

"I'll eat the half you haven't slobbered on."

"Fine." He swapped birds and held his over the fire to finish cooking. "And for the record, I don't slobber on my food." His smile seemed charitable, but barely. "Just so you'll know for future reference."

Shrugging, she bit into the meat.

When the meal was over, Hershall began to break camp.

"Are we leaving? Now?" She glanced at the leaden sky.

"Yes, ma'am."

"But it's so cold — must we break camp?"

"I thought you were in a hurry to reach the next town."

"I am, but it's too cold to travel. Couldn't we wait until it warms up a little?" Digman sighed. Of the three women, why did he have to get stuck with the whiner?

"Perhaps instead of complaining, you might pray for sunshine, Sister."

She'd pray all right — but it wouldn't be to his likin'.

When the last cup was stored, he stepped to the small mirror he'd hung on the tree and set the tall bowler hat with its Petersham hat-band and sassy little curled brim upon his head and fussed with it, turning it this way, then that, trying to get it adjusted just so.

Abigail watched the fuss from the sidelines.

Turning from the mirror, he balanced one foot on a log and brushed at his ash-coated white spats. "You must ready yourself so we can be on our way, Sister."

She eyed him sourly. "At this hour of the morning, I'm as ready as I get, Digman."

"Digman?"

"Mr. Digman."

He straightened, his eyes running over the rumpled blanket she clutched to her throat, her wrinkled habit, and matted veil. "And a vision of radiance you are. Do you plan to wear the blanket as we ride?"

She clutched the wrap around her more possessively. "Yes."

"Then shall we be on our way?"

He helped Abigail into the saddle before he once again removed the map from the saddlebag. Kneeling beside the horse, he smoothed the parchment on his thigh to study it. "As near as I can tell, the closest way station is a full day-and-a-half ride."

"That far?"

"I don't design the towns." Swinging into the saddle, he picked up the reins.

"I still don't know why we can't stay here," she complained. "At least until the sun —"

He kicked the horse into a gallop and the cad *grinned* when she nearly swallowed her tongue.

Mid-morning a watery sun came out, providing little warmth for March. By now Digman was ready to hand Sister Abigail to the first Comanche war party he ran into.

Was it his fault the horse had a gait like a lame donkey? The animal's pace never bothered him.

Did he ask her to doze off and nearly kill herself when she fell off the horse?

Was he in control of the weather? No, he wasn't God. If he were, he'd have found another rider to take her off his hands hours ago.

"Really, Mr. Digman, wouldn't it be better to take a more traveled route?" She ducked another low-hanging branch but it slapped her in the face. "You are *deliberately* riding under low branches."

He pretended he didn't hear as he pushed the horse toward a thick grove of trees.

"Mr. Digman! Do you have any idea

where you're going?" she demanded a few minutes later as they turned down a narrow trail that wound through the woods.

"Sister, would you please leave the guess-work to me?"

"No! Not if it means you're going to get us lost."

"We are not lost."

"Then where are we?"

His hackles rose with resentment. "In the woods," he informed her.

"I can see we're in the woods! What woods? Why can't we take the main road?"

"Texas is close to martial law. No one travels without a pass — do you have a pass?"

"Of course I don't have a pass. I'm a nun."

"I don't recall a clause excluding nuns," he managed through clenched teeth.

"Well, there should be. We do, after all, travel on missions of mercy."

"Mercy," he muttered.

"What?"

"Nothing."

"Hold up. My veil is caught again."

He halted the horse for the tenth time that morning and waited for her to unhook her veil from a thorny limb.

"Look at that. Now I have a hole in my veil. Sister Jane won't be happy about this.

She's very meticulous about the way we look."

She grabbed for his waist as the horse set off in a bone-jarring trot.

By noon he was pushing the horse hard, ignoring Sister's constant muttering about the bushes that grabbed at her habit, the limbs that persisted in trying to rip her veil from her head, the roughness of the horse's gait, the cold, the wind. Snow. She was hungry; she needed a private moment; she needed another private moment.

Hershall shifted in the saddle. If he set her off now, in the middle of the road, he could be halfway to Louisiana before she caught up . . .

Six

Hershall E. Digman might be an insipid little shoe salesman, but he had proved his worth today. Abigail grudgingly admired a man who could put up with what she dished out and not desert her at the first possible crossroad. In her eighteen years she hadn't met many with his stamina. By late afternoon they'd stopped to make camp.

"Are you building the fire now, Mr. Digman?"

"I am. Just sit right there on that log and rest yourself," he called.

"I'm sitting, Mr. Digman." They should have reached some sign of life by now, but so far they'd passed nothing but barren fields and snowy glades.

Striding to a nearby log, she sat down to watch the shoe salesman cut cedar branches for the tent floor. *Let him get his feet wet. He has extra shoes.*

In mere minutes she was shaking her head

and mumbling under her breath. It was amazing how he could turn the simplest task into a full-blown disaster. There he was hacking at the limbs, repeatedly knocking his bowler off into the snow.

She groaned, diverting her eyes when his persistent bumbling caused a whole section of snow to collapse down his jacket collar.

Prancing and flipping snow out of his shirt, he fumed out loud, his breath frosty in the cool air. "Pesky tree!" He wasted a full five minutes before he composed himself enough to get back to work.

Tossing the piece of canvas over a low-hanging branch, he was grabbing for the support rope when he noticed the big knot that he'd jerked into the rope in his haste to break camp that morning.

Lifting the end of the rope, he peered at the snarled hitch and began trying to loosen it. Squinting over the bridge of his spectacles, he picked and worked, and worked and picked, his teeth worrying his tongue as it lolled his lower lip. His scowl deepened when the pesky knot, in spite of his efforts, refused to budge.

Clamping his teeth firmly atop his lower lip, he grasped the lump with both hands and twisted and pulled, determined to loosen the coil. Losing patience, he yanked it, jerked it, and then, in a complete fit, pitched it aside and tramped back to the fire to warm his hands.

"Having trouble, Mr. Digman?"

"It'll be dark soon; I'd best hunt for game. I'll tinker with the tent later."

Glancing up at the sky, she frowned. "Looks like it's going to snow again. Don't you think you should put the tent up first?"

"I can only do one thing at a time," he said shortly.

"I can help —"

"No!"

My, my, Hershall's getting downright testy. She smiled, content with her heckling. So content that she decided to let his snappish remark pass. Annoying him broke the monotony of the long ride and she was learning that he was impossible to argue with. Besides, he was pigheaded and unreasonable, so why waste her breath? Anne-Marie popped into mind and her smile faded. Her sister wouldn't approve of her sharp tongue — never had. She'd made her promise to be gentler and more loving. Of late, she hadn't worked very hard.

"You get started on your evening devotions." He reached for his gun. "I'll scare up a rabbit."

Stepping closer to the fire, she watched

77

him load the gun and fade unceremoniously into the stand of timber encircling the small clearing.

Something big with fluttery wings darted overhead, shattering the wintry stillness. She glanced uneasily over her shoulder, wondering how long it would take him to run down a rabbit. If his fire-building or tent-erecting skills were any measure, it wouldn't be soon.

Huddling closer to the fire, she waited for the encroaching darkness. She didn't like the dark, but she wasn't about to admit that to Hershall. Only Amelia and Anne-Marie knew about her phobia that she struggled to overcome with little success. When evening shadows deepened, a peculiar feeling gripped her insides.

Lifting her hands to the fire, she let the heat penetrate. She could steal the horse tonight and go on, but since they were so close to the town why borrow trouble? He would likely come after her and she'd had her fill of Hershall Digman. No, she would stay put; relief was surely around the corner. Tomorrow might be warmer and she could be on her way back to Mercy Flats, free of the shoe salesman. The thought of seeing Anne-Marie and Amelia elevated her spirits, even though snow was falling again. Tiny, swirling flakes, misting the air. The wind caught a spray of red embers and skipped them across the frosty landscape. Rubbing heat into her upper arms, she repressed a shiver. It was so quiet and lonely in the clearing. Water dripped from icy branches, and something mysterious rustled in the shadows.

She started, her heart springing to her throat when she heard a *snap.* She peered toward the underbrush where a small creature darted for cover. The knot in her throat grew more pronounced.

Settling back, she composed herself. She'd never been such a sissy. Her thoughts wandered. What were Amelia and Anne-Marie doing? Were they as lonely and frightened as she was tonight?

It was an almost-certainty that Amelia was scared. She was afraid of everything. Anne-Marie could take care of herself, but Amelia needed all the help she could get. It used to annoy Abigail that she had to stand guard over her younger sister but right now she missed Amelia so much that she would welcome the opportunity to protect her.

The tall, dark-haired man who had snatched up Amy and ridden off with her appeared to be the sort of man who could take care of himself. She could only pray that he would take care of Amelia. Her gaze swept the stand of timber.

The exact opposite of Hershall E. Digman.

And poor Anne-Marie. She'd been rescued by that — well, a savage. Chewing her lower lip, her gaze returned to the fire, angry when hot tears burned behind her lids. What if he was one of the savages who had chased the jail wagon? What if he had been the leader? What if right at this very moment — No, she wouldn't allow herself to think the unthinkable. Anne-Marie was fine, and so was Amelia. And so was she. Hershall wasn't the most adept at anything, but he was capable of providing protection. And thank the good Lord this would all be over shortly and she would be back with her sisters. Right where they all belonged.

She reached over to stir the fire and then snuggled deeper into the blanket. The three of them hadn't been separated from the day their parents died. Having no relatives to take them in, the girls had been sent to the mission orphanage and raised by nuns.

Abigail smiled when she thought about her growing-up years at the orphanage. She had to give the nuns credit; they'd tried. When they discovered the girls were a fright when teamed together, they'd tried separating them, but the three little girls raised such a ruckus that there was nothing to do but put them back together. Even then, they had been worse than a plague. What one hadn't thought of, the other two had. Even as young girls they'd shown a talent for trickery. To fill time they'd learned to "imagine." They'd formulated stories that won them cookies from the cook and pesos from strangers, and they'd become most adept in finding ways to avoid evening prayers.

The games started innocently enough. Because the mission had been kind enough to take them in, the McDougal sisters decided that the order would never want for anything. And they'd kept that vow. In the years since, half of everything they'd gained from their endeavors had gone to support the mission. Assuming that their gifts of money were acquired honestly, the nuns were overjoyed whenever they received monetary favors from the McDougals.

As long as the nuns chose to believe that the three spirited girls were earning money forthrightly, the sisters agreed there was no need to tell them otherwise. The truth would only upset the older women and it was, after all, not a large fabrication, and their antics never really hurt anyone — except whatever victim they had chosen to deceive — and they took great pains to make sure that their prey could afford to take the loss.

At times Amelia fretted about misusing the nun's habit, but Abigail never gave it much thought. The masquerade, after all, was only a lark and they meant the cloth no disrespect.

Feeding sticks into the fire, Abigail glanced toward the woods. Where was that man and what was taking him so long? She could have snared four rabbits by now. Full darkness closed around her and he was still wandering around looking for something to shoot.

She couldn't hear a thing except the tiny scurrying of wildlife and water dripping from the barren tree branches. Shouldn't she have heard the gun go off by now? Did he even know which end of the gun to point? She should have gone herself. The meat would be hanging over the fire, all plump and brown by now . . .

"Uneasy, Sister?"

She started, nearly swallowing her tongue when his voice penetrated her thoughts. Glancing over her shoulder, she discovered he was standing directly behind her. How long had he been there — spying on her? Straightening, she glared at him. "Do you have to sneak up on a person?"

Lifting two plump rabbits, he smiled. "I'm hunting."

"I didn't hear the gun go off."

"Oh, my, my. I *never* shoot the furry little creatures," he chided.

She smiled. "I suppose you run them down and talk them to death?"

"No, but I do provide a merciful end," he assured her as he carried the kill to the stream.

"A merciful death?" She shook her head. Absolutely pitiful. "Can you hurry? I'm cold and starving."

"You should have eaten your breakfast."

She frowned, hardly able to miss the thinly veiled mockery. *You should have eaten your breakfast,* she silently mimicked, lifting her hands to the fire. The smell of sizzling meat permeated the night air when Hershall once again turned his attention to the tent.

Sitting back, she prepared for the show. Picking up the nub, he patiently worked the stubborn kink. How a man as inept as he survived in the wild . . . She could have gotten the knot free in minutes! But the more he worried with it, the tighter it got.

Stoically fixing her eyes elsewhere, she vowed that he wasn't going to upset her again. Anne-Marie was right about her:

Once she lost her temper, she wasn't responsible for what she said. Impatience would only hurt her cause, not help it. It was only a matter of time before he caught on to the fact that she was posing as a nun, and the knowledge that she'd tricked him could agitate him so that he might leave her by the wayside. Far better to sit still and keep quiet.

But her eyes refused to cooperate. In spite of all she did, they drifted back to his bumbling efforts. His spectacles kept sliding down the ridge of his nose, and he'd pause, patiently shoving them back up with his forefinger. As he bent closer, his front teeth worried his lower lip as he plucked at the knot.

Give him a few more minutes. He'll get it. Yet he managed, if anything, to make the knot tighter.

He'll get it. She fixed her eyes firmly on the roasting rabbits. Fat dripped into the fire and sizzled. She focused on the moment when she'd bite into the tender, hot meat.

Another ten minutes passed. The browned meat was near ready to eat. Hershall bent over the knot, picking, picking, his tongue resting on his lower lip anxiously.

He'll get it!

Pick, pick, pick, pick, pick, pick, pick.

Give him time. He's not exactly a bolt of lightning. Her eyes moved to the spit and she wondered if he intended to char the meat.

Pick, pick.

She'd had all she could stand! He was never going to get that knot out. That tent wasn't going up before Christmas and she was not going to sleep in the open because of his sheer idiocy!

Springing from the log, she bellowed. Her sudden high-pitched shriek sent Hershall reeling backward. She marched toward him, determined. "Can't you undo a simple *knot*?"

He struggled to right himself, fighting to adjust his spectacles that landed lopsided on the bridge of his nose.

"Give me that!" She snatched the rope from his hands, her eyes daring him to challenge her.

Stunned, he stared meekly at her.

"Honestly!" Whipping the skirt of her habit over her shoulder, she dug into the pocket of the dress she wore beneath and fished out a small knife. Flicking the blade open with her thumbnail, she slashed through the knot, tossing the piece of frayed rope into the fire.

Swiftly fashioning a new loop, she handed

the rope back. He gaped at her, slack-jawed.

"There! Now rig the tent!" Whirling, she stalked away, leaving a round-eyed shoe salesman in her wake.

Seven

Hershall sat paralyzed with the rope resting limply in his lap. Slowly but surely, the significance of her behavior sank in on him. Why, the little *conniver!* She was no more nun than he was priest! He slowly got to his feet.

Marching back to the fire, Abigail jerked off the dark veil and pushed her fingers through her hair.

"Hold on a minute, Sister." He stalked to the fire, grasped her by the shoulders, and turned her to face him. There wasn't the slightest hint of chivalry in his tone when he spoke. The ruse was over. She'd been playing him for a fool for two days! "Who are you and what are you trying to pull?"

"Why . . . nothing, Mr. Digman." Her head dropped. "It is positively inexcusable the way I've acted. I'll go into the woods and seek privacy, so that I may reflect on my sinful —"

His grip on her shoulders tightened. "*What* is going on?" His eyes raked her coldly, coming to rest on the hair that now swung free to her waist.

"Going on? Why I — please, you're hurting me —" Twisting free from his grasp, she drew herself up defensively. "*Kindly* remove your hands, sir!"

"You're not a nun."

She shrugged, clearly on defense now. "You don't know that . . . for certain."

"You're masquerading as a nun!" He was staggered by her audacity. "Are you even a Christian?"

"Yes, I'm a Christian," she spat back. "Are you a shoe salesman?"

"We're not talking about me! Your sisters? They're also posing as nuns?"

Her smile turned as glacial as his tone. "And if they were?"

"For what purpose?"

"I didn't say they were — but *if* they are, perhaps for safe travel?"

"Travel where, safely? Why would three young ladies posing as nuns want to roam through the countryside with a war in progress?"

Abigail heaved a sigh. "If you must know, we roam the countryside bilking strangers out of money." She met his eyes defiantly.

"*Male* strangers."

"Ohhh." His hand shot to his heart, about to swoon.

She heaved a sigh of disgust. "Don't look so stricken. It happens, you know. We don't hurt anyone. We take from the rich and give to the poor."

"But that's utter blasphemy," he accused.

"The money we take goes to the mission. If it wasn't for our work, the two remaining sisters couldn't or wouldn't have survived the past two years. The sisters are aging and they can barely feed themselves, even with our financial contributions. Months go by and we don't encounter anyone to . . . anyone who might contribute to a worthy cause."

"Contribute!" Her euphemistic rationalization appalled him.

"Now, now, settle down, Mr. Digman."

He lifted reproachful eyes. "Do the sisters know how you acquire this money?"

"Heavens, no. They assume we earn it honestly."

"Of course."

"Mr. Digman, I would have preferred to have kept my disguise. Now that you know the truth, though, I hope you'll excuse me." Bending forward, she caught the hem of the habit and yanked it up and over her head.

Underneath she wore a plain calico dress.

He should have never given her the castigating look. In a fit of pique, she wadded up the material and threw it at him. The bundle hit him squarely in the face.

Grabbing for support, he righted himself, stunned by the transformation he was witnessing. While Abigail McDougal had been lovely before, she was now stunning. Wild blonde hair, those strange lime-colored eyes . . . Coming to his feet, his eyes locked with hers. "Who are you?"

"I told you. Abigail McDougal." She bent and ran her fingers through the tangles in her hair.

"You were in that jail wagon because you'd been caught in one of your swindles!"

Straightening, she met his gaze. "Maybe."

"Maybe? There could be no other reason. But posing as nuns!" The sheer sacrilegious nerve of her actions rendered him speechless. One did not treat the cloth lightly. One did not *mock* His Church. Apparently this floosy would dare anything. "Miss McDougal. You have a severely misplaced sense of making a living."

She met his censuring glare. "Enough! Now that you know who I am, you have to take me to Mercy Flats."

He brought his hand to his forehead. "I

most assuredly do not. If I refused to take you when I assumed you were a nun, I certainly won't take you now that I'm aware you're an imposter! And might I add — a heathen imposter!"

"Oh, don't be so dramatic."

Folding his arms, he stared at her. She beat all he'd ever seen — and he'd seen sights one could only imagine. The audacity of this woman staggered him.

"It seems we've reached an impasse, Mr. Digman."

"You couldn't be more mistaken. I'm going to Shreveport and you can go . . ." Pausing, he drew a deep, controlling breath. "You can go anywhere you'd like as long as it isn't near me."

Lifting her brows, she repeated, "I'm going to get to Mercy Flats."

"Then I suggest you get started."

"I don't have a horse." They were nose to nose now, features flushed with anger.

"Perhaps you should have thought of that before you had your temper tantrum, Miss McDougal."

"Perhaps I did consider the possibility that my true identity would upset you, Mr. Digman. And I don't care! I will find the means to take me there." Her eyes were flat, hard, and filled with contempt as the underlying

91

meaning of her words sank in on him.

"You," he warned in a harsh undertone, "keep your hands off my horse."

"I haven't touched your horse, but I will if you don't take me to Mercy Flats."

He straightened, shrugging off the threat. In all of his thirty-one years he had never had the misfortune to meet such a woman. Jerking the sleeves of his jacket into place, he struggled to contain his anger. The very idea of her posing as a nun and milking innocent victims out of money infuriated him — as did her assumption that she could get away with it. What was this world coming to? "Under no circumstances will I take you to Mercy Flats."

"All right, then. Give me the money, and I'll take the old stage."

"Absolutely not."

"But you have to! You can't just leave me out here alone!"

His lifted a brow. "Oh, really? Just watch me."

Panic flooded her features. "But . . . but . . . !"

"Ha! *I'm* the culprit? I'm not the one —" He broke off, waving his hands, helplessly at a loss for the proper term. The woman's mettle knew no limits. "I'm not the one defiling the cloth."

"Defiling the cloth!" She raised her hand to smack him, but he blocked the reflex in midair, his gaze narrowing menacingly.

"I wouldn't do that if I were you."

"You take me to Mercy Flats," she demanded.

"When pigs fly."

A sob tore from her throat and he saw her icy exterior slowly thaw. She melted into a frightened child. "Please, I'm sorry I misled you. I didn't ask you to rescue me — that was your choice. We can solve this dispute easily. Take me to meet my sisters and you'll be done with me," she pleaded.

"Your getting to that cemetery is not my problem. The horse is mine and I'm going to Shreveport."

"Your shoes can wait. I can't."

"You aren't my concern. Selling shoes is."

"You wouldn't leave me out here alone and helpless!"

"Oh, wouldn't I?" He turned to walk away. "Helpless," he muttered. "About as helpless as a cat stalking a hummingbird."

"I could be killed, or worse," she reminded him.

"I'm not taking you."

"Please!"

"No. You're sorely getting on my nerves." Whirling, he faced her. "What *is* your name, anyway?"

"I told you. Abigail McDougal."

"Abigail." He sniffed. "I had a cranky teacher by that name. Never cared for her." Turning a deaf ear on her pleas he walked to the fire. "I'll be leaving early, Miss Mc-Dougal. I'll try not to disturb you."

"Oh!" She bent, picked up a stick, and hurled it at him.

Ducking the assault, he straightened his bowler. "You should do something about that temper. It doesn't become a nun."

She picked up a bigger stick and flung it at him. "I don't even know where I am!"

"Oh, you seem like an enterprising enough young lady. I'm sure it won't take long to discover your direction."

"You're the most infuriating person I have ever met!"

She wanted to call him names, did she? So be it. "So are you."

"I won't have this," she called to his retreating back. He heard what sounded like feet defiantly kicking the discarded habit to one side. Pure *sacrilege.* He stepped to the spit and calmly removed a piece of meat, ignoring her.

She grabbed the habit and ran to the fire. Before he could stop her, she flung the dress and veil into the flames. "There," she said with a touch of smugness when the disguise went up in smoke. "Now you'll have to take me. I don't have a disguise anymore. A woman can't travel these parts alone."

Pouring some coffee, he handed the tin mug to her dispassionately. "Take a load off, Abigail. You've got a long walk ahead of you in the morning."

She snatched the coffee from his hand and slammed the cup down on a nearby rock.

Settling beside the fire, he began to eat, unmoved by her tantrum.

"Then give me money for the stage fare."

He laughed.

Striding close, she jerked his glasses off, threw them down on the ground, and stomped on them.

His jaw dropped as he stared at the mangled debris. One earpiece lay to one side while the other stuck straight up in the air.

"Abigail McDougal!" Meat spilled down the front of his trousers as he heatedly sprang to his feet. Desperate or not, she had no call to stomp his glasses!

Whirling, she marched off as he snatched up the spectacles, anxiously examining the mangled rims. He couldn't believe she'd do such a thing! After scraping dirt off the lenses he irritably settled the specs on the bridge of his nose, trying to adjust the cracks to where he could see around them.

The sooner he was rid of this pest the better!

The moon lit up the sky, casting shadows on the ground.

Abigail hadn't wandered far before her temper cooled and reality set it. What would happen now that Digman knew her true identity? He wouldn't dare leave her to travel alone, would he? If only she had controlled her temper one more day — just one more day and they would have reached a community, a settlement. Something. But no. She'd erupted, burned her disguise, and alienated the shoe salesman forever. Carrying her cup of coffee to a nearby rock, she sank down and sat broodingly, watching him fuss with his glasses. She was glad she'd broken them.

Guilt assuaged her. No, she wasn't happy — or proud — of any of her actions of late. Drawing a deep breath, she willed herself to calm down. Now wasn't the time to compound her mistakes. She must get to the cemetery and now that she'd broken Digman's spectacles, he'd never help her.

A deep baritone interrupted her musing. "I've changed my mind. I am going to take

96

you to the nearest town and once we're there, I'm going to alert the sheriff to your little games."

She glanced up to find Hershall glaring at her with a self-righteous expression, his glasses askew. The sight so inflamed her that she let rage take control. In one quick gesture, she dashed her coffee in his face.

Spinning on his heel, he stalked back to the fire with coffee dripping off his shattered lenses.

His threats didn't intimidate her, and he wasn't taking her anywhere.

Because by morning, she'd have helped herself to his horse and be long gone. He wouldn't know what hit him.

EIGHT

She was going to steal his horse. Hershall knew that as well as he knew the time of day. She was waiting for the right moment, and then she'd take the horse and leave him stranded — or at least that's what she thought.

But he thought otherwise. She wasn't about to pull anything funny on him.

There she was, huddling on her side of the tent, watching the wind whip the canvas flap, innocent as a good deed. Once he drifted off, she'd creep out of the tent and be long gone. The map indicated there was a small community coming up anytime. When she found it, she'd connive a way to get enough money for a stage ticket. She'd be back in Mercy Flats before he could spit. Her plan was so predictable that he almost laughed.

As if he couldn't find Mercy Flats and set the authorities on her and her thievin' sisters.

Long after the shoe salesman snuffed the candlewick, Abigail lay listening to the wind keen through the tree branches. It seemed a long time before Digman's breathing regulated. Tempted to move quickly, she squelched the urge and bided her time, waiting until she was sure he was fast asleep. Undoubtedly he would try to out-smart her. She smothered a laugh. As if he could.

Close to an hour passed before she quietly sat up and carefully eased the blanket aside. Scooting a couple of inches, she glanced over her shoulder, listening to see if his breathing had altered. When it appeared that it hadn't, she grabbed his saddlebag, stuffed it beneath her shirt, and scooted faster.

Easing the flap aside, she got to her knees, about to crawl out when a hand suddenly clamped around her ankle.

"The sun isn't up yet, Abigail."

Blast his rotten hide! He was on to her now. "I need to make a trip into the bushes," she murmured.

"You just did, not an hour ago."

"Need-to-make-a-trip-to-the-bushes," she repeated.

"I'll go with you."

"No!"

His voice held more than a twinge of irritation. "Miss McDougal, I couldn't let you go out there alone and unprotected."

"I won't be gone long — I'll hurry." If she moved fast enough she could grab the horse and ride bareback; she didn't need a saddle. She shoved the flap aside but the hand tightened its grip on her ankle. "I'll go with you. There are coyotes running around and we wouldn't want you getting hurt, now, would we?"

"It's really not necessary . . ." *Think fast, Abigail. Don't let him walk out on you.* "I don't feel well. It must have been that undercooked rabbit." Affecting a gag, she clapped her hand over her mouth and tried to look deathly ill.

"Queasy stomach?"

She nodded, rocking back and forth as if she were experiencing stabbing pains. "Please, Mr. Digman. I'm not lying. If you don't let me go I fear we'll both regret it."

"I wouldn't think of letting you suffer. I'll go with you."

Burying her face in her hands, she broke into tears. Soft sobs at first, and then becoming more exuberant as water rolled from the corners of her eyes. Rocking back and forth, she cradled her stomach, her

100

wails more pronounced.

"Your theatrics are noteworthy, but you're wasting them on me. If you leave this tent, I go with you," he told her, clearly unimpressed by her caterwauling.

"I would rather *die* than have you watch me," she said, sobbing.

"Don't be concerned. I'll turn my head."

Tears dripped off her chin. "You'll still hear me."

Sitting up, he jerked the blanket off his legs. "If I let you go alone, you're not to get fifteen feet away from this tent, is that clear? I don't buy your arguments but I would like to get a few hours' sleep!"

"If I stay that close you'll still hear me."

"Twenty feet, and not a foot more." His tone said that he was beginning to despise her. Good. She didn't like him either.

She hurriedly scrambled out of the tent on her hands and knees, fumbling for the saddlebag.

"You'd better be back in a few minutes," he called.

The moment the flap dropped back into place, he reached for his shoes. He didn't trust that woman as far as he could throw her. His gaze shot to the bedroll and he saw his saddlebag missing. "Why — the little wench!"

Before he could get his left shoe on, he heard the sound of hooves breaking through the underbrush.

Bolting into black night, he heard hoof-beats bearing down on him. Jumping backward, he stumbled and pitched forward. Grabbing the tent for support, he groaned when the canvas gave way and he collapsed on top of the heap.

Rolling to his feet, he shoved the spectacles back into place, shouting after her, "Bring that horse *back* here!"

Abigail's jeering laughter seared his dignity. "See you, Mr. Digman!"

He stood for a minute, listening to the sound of fading hoof-beats. See him? She could bet on it. If it weren't for his saddlebags, he would let her go and hope a rattlesnake got her, but she was smart enough to realize she couldn't survive without the jerky he kept inside the bags. Little did she know she'd just stolen any hope of the Confederates winning a crucial battle.

Breaking camp, he fashioned a backpack with the canvas and rope and then struck off on foot, determined to hunt her down.

Abigail raced along the snowy road, kicking the horse into a full gallop. A spiritless moon now lit the pathway as beast and rider sprinted along the winding lane. Pushing the horse harder, she hoped to put as much distance as possible between Hershall and herself. He wasn't a threat on foot, but he had shown a peculiar assertiveness tonight that warned her not to take any unnecessary chances.

The moon slid behind a cloud, forcing her to slow the animal down. She frowned when she noted that the horse *did* have a rough gait. And she'd accused Digman of being an inferior horseman. Riding more slowly now, she prayed the clouds would pass. At times, she could barely see her hand in front of her face.

The horse shot noisily along the dirt road, the sound of its hooves echoing eerily in the darkness. Forcing back the lump of fear suddenly crowding her throat, Abigail assured herself that she had done the right thing. It would be daylight before long; there was nothing out here to harm her if she didn't stop. Her hands gripped the horse's mane tighter.

She was an excellent horsewoman, and the animal was sure-footed albeit rough to ride. The horse could outrun a wild animal — if it wasn't too big and if it was absolutely necessary.

The ride turned surreal. She was out here alone. Completely alone.

An owl hooted, and she pressed closer to the horse's neck. Maybe she should have waited until sunup to make her escape.

This is a fine time to think about that, Abigail. Anne-Marie's censuring voice echoed in her mind. *Where's your common sense? You should have waited until daylight.*

The horse carried her swiftly through the fallen snow. Abigail prayed they'd come to an intersecting road so she could get her bearings. If the moon came out soon she'd have nothing to worry about, but the weak moon slid behind a bank and the night turned black as ink. She could barely make out the lay of the land, much less decipher north from south.

She'd ridden over an hour before conceding that she was hopelessly confused. She didn't have the slightest idea in what direction she was traveling.

She reined the horse into a clearing and stopped to consider her options. If she was going north, then all she had to do was veer to the left and she'd be headed to Mercy Flats. If she'd gotten turned around and was riding south, on the other hand, then she would undoubtedly run into Hershall trying to make his way to the nearest town.

Nudging the horse's flanks, she started off again with uncertainty plaguing her.

Dawn streaked the sky when she spotted a stream ahead. She slid off the winded horse and allowed him to drink while she stretched her cramped muscles.

When she was able to feel her limbs again, she knelt beside the stream and cupped her hands to drink of the cold, sweet water.

Her stomach growled, reminding her that she had eaten little in the past twenty-four hours. She dreaded the thought of more jerky, but it was better than going hungry.

While the horse drank, she rummaged through the saddlebags, wishing she hadn't been so impulsive and burned her habit. Traveling alone would be easier — and safer — with the disguise.

She needed to be careful now to avoid others who might be on the road. Besides soldiers, there were any number of miscreants who might accost her, and she had no weapon to defend herself. She'd begged Anne-Marie to let her carry a gun hidden in her boot, but her sister refused, saying that she was worried that Abigail would shoot herself — or one of them.

After removing the jerky, Abigail unwrapped the cloth and stared at the leathery meat, wondering if she could bring herself to eat it. She tore off a strip and stuffed it into her mouth, and then dug deeper into the saddlebags. Hershall's map was in there. If she could understand it, she could figure out where she was.

She couldn't believe the collection of junk the man carried. The contents of his saddlebags were worse than an old maid's dresser. A jar of pomade, a shoe catalog, a knife, a pair of dark glasses, an extra pair of white spats, a comb, and a mirror. But no map.

Moving to the opposite side of the horse, she dug into the other bag and unearthed a man's shirt. Laughing, she imagined his consternation at losing his shirt to a woman. She tossed it into the bushes.

When she was about to close the bag, her hand brushed an object she couldn't readily identify. Frowning, she dug deeper, pulling out a small brown leather packet.

Curious, she untied the string around the fat folder. The packet was stuffed tight as a tick with papers.

Unfolding them, she hoped they were territorial maps. She experienced a keen sense of disappointment a moment later when she saw they weren't maps at all; they were just a bunch of writing that didn't appear at first to make a lick of sense.

Wondering why Hershall had kept them,

she removed a pack of matches and then sat down on the creek bank. The stench of sulfur filled her nostrils when she struck a match, squinting in the dim light to study the papers.

The first sheets were copies of messages from General Ulysses S. Grant. One paper was addressed to General Butler. Her eyes skimmed the page quickly. Apparently, Grant had been given a commission to organize the Northern armies, which, until this date, had operated independently. From what Abigail could discern, Grant was now busily creating a unified effort against the Confederate army.

His message to Butler was, in effect, to take all the forces that could be spared at his command and move to the south side of the James River. Her eyes widened. Richmond would be his objective.

The match sputtered; she tossed it away and lit another. Her eyes moved to the second page, where there was another like message, this one addressed to General Sherman. *It is my design, if the enemy keeps quiet and allows me to take the initiative in the spring campaign, to work all the parts of the army together and somewhat toward a common center . . .*

She read on, realizing that Sherman was

being told to move against Johnston's army, to break it up, to get as far into the enemy territory as possible, to inflict all the damage he could against the resources of the Confederacy.

Frowning now, she read on. The third sheet was a copy of a message which directed General Meade to stick to General Robert E. Lee.

Wherever Lee goes, there you will go also.

The fourth sheet appeared to be a directive to General J. Kirby Smith, commander of the trans-Mississippi department of the Confederacy. The message warned General Smith that General Banks and his Union troops were marching from the east to take Shreveport. Smith was directed to immediately gather all forces to repel the attack.

Stunned, Abigail let the pages flutter to the ground as she stared into the water. What was Hershall, a shoe salesman, doing with — ?

Tossing the match away, the answer to the puzzle suddenly hit her.

Hershall E. Digman wasn't a sappy shoe salesman; he was a Confederate spy — posing as a sappy shoe salesman!

Springing to her feet, her eyes narrowed with fury. Spit on his worthless hide! He'd lied to her. Lied to her! She couldn't believe it. She began to pace back and forth, driven by anger. He hadn't been avoiding the roads because he was stupid, or because he didn't have a pass. He'd taken the hard way because he was afraid of being discovered by Union soldiers!

Why, the worthless toad! He'd been so indignant about her posing as a nun, while all along he was nothing but a low-down, conniving sneak!

She paced more furiously. How dare he pull such a stunt on her? How dare he! She snatched up the sheets of paper and shoved them back into the leather packet. Swinging back on the horse, she kicked it hard, sending it off in a full gallop.

Daylight broke. Rays of pink and orange streaked the east as Hershall walked down the road, shifting the saddle from his left shoulder to the right one. His shoes were rubbing a blister on his heel, and the bowler kept falling off. He knew he should throw the thing away, but he wouldn't.

When he got his hands on Abigail McDougal, there wouldn't be enough left of her for the buzzards to fight over.

The sun's warmth melted the small skiffs of snow littering the ditches. He flinched as his ankles sank into another muddy rut. When he found that woman he . . . Glancing up, he heard the sound of approaching hoofbeats.

Darting swiftly into the bushes, he listened as the sound grew closer. The riders appeared to be a large contingent. All he needed was to get caught by a patrol —

Crouching behind the row of heavy thicket, he watched a company of Confederate cavalry come down the road at a fast clip. From the lather on their horses' necks and the number of wounded in the saddle, it was obvious that the men had been involved in recent battle.

As the lead horse drew close enough for him to get a good look at the rider, his face broke into a relieved grin. Parting the thicket, he stepped out into the center of the road, waving the company to a halt.

The lead rider reached for his pistol when Hershall called out, "Captain Broder, sir!" He executed a mock bow.

Frowning, Les Broder slowed his horse, astonishment overcoming his drawn features. "Drake?"

"In the flesh."

Swinging out of the saddle, Les grasped his hand. "Barrett Drake! Good grief, man, what are you doing dressed like some fancy tinker?"

Flashing him a tired grin, Barrett clasped his friend on the back, relieved to see a familiar face. "That's what I am, Les — for all practical purposes." He glanced at the soldiers, who were so exhausted that they seized the chance for a momentary doze in their saddles.

"A tinker on foot?"

"Well, that's a different story. One I don't care to explain at the moment."

Grinning, the captain shook his head, his eyes on the rumpled seersucker suit. "You look like a hard night on the town."

"I feel like one," Barrett acknowledged. The two men slapped each other's backs affectionately.

"It's good to see you." Les had aged ten years since Barrett last saw him a year ago but the war had a way of doing that to a man.

"We just fought one mother of a battle." Les's smile faded when he turned to assess his company. "Fourteen men gone. I've got a bellyful of this war."

Barrett glanced at the row of exhausted riders. "Could you spare an old friend a horse?"

The captain's eyes moved to the back of

the company, where fourteen riderless horses followed, the fallen soldiers' gear still tied to their backs. "Take your pick," he offered in a voice that suddenly sounded very tired. Drawing Barrett aside, Les asked quietly, "What's going on? The last I heard you were with Smith in Texas."

"I'm still with Smith," Barrett admitted. "I'm doing a little work on the side." He left unspoken the fact that he was carrying messages for the Confederacy, but Les picked up on his meaning.

"I thought they left that up to civilians."

"Not this time."

His friend's eyes darkened. "You're taking a pretty hefty risk, aren't you?"

Barrett shrugged. "Someone has to."

"Things are moving quickly. What do you think?"

"Honestly? I don't know." Barrett didn't want to admit what he thought was going to happen. The South was losing the war. "You know Grant's received his commission from Lincoln."

Les frowned. "Where we've been you don't hear much news."

"Lincoln has told Grant to organize all the Union armies. From what I hear" — Barrett paused, unable to share all that he knew — "Meade still commands the Army of the Potomac, but Sherman is heading up affairs in the West. Johnston's in trouble, and maybe Smith. If the North can open a way between the Atlantic coast and Mobile, they'll divide the Confederacy north from south, like the conquest of the Mississippi parted it east and west. If that happens, the Confederacy is in serious trouble, Les."

Drawing a deep breath, Les lifted his face to the sun and breathed deeply — as if he couldn't get the stench of war out of his nostrils. "It can't be over soon enough. I want to go home," he said, his voice growing softer, his drawl more pronounced. "I want to sit on the veranda sippin' a tall glass of tea with a breeze comin' in off the river. I want Kathleen by my side — dear sweet Lord, I miss her. There's times, if I think hard enough, I remember the way she smells and the feel of her lying next to me. Sometimes I think back to the days before all this started, and I think about how innocent we all were. I thought I'd never leave Georgia, thought I'd just inherit my papa's place and farm it, grow tobacco and cotton and be happy." His smile closed. "I was a fool, wasn't I?"

"God doesn't fault a man for his dreams, Les."

"Last I heard the farm had been burned

down. Daddy's gone. Momma's gone to live with her sister in Atlanta. When I hear the ignorant things people say about the war, about it all being over slavery, I want to shout that it isn't. It isn't that at all. Remember when we were back at the Academy, when war was just rumor? Remember how patriotic we were, how blind we were? Why, we believed it was going to be over in a matter of months. Now it's gone on for years, and there's no letup in sight."

"Hold on a little longer," Barrett encouraged softly. "Just a little longer. We're in this because the South should be able to govern itself, the way we always have."

"The Northerners don't know anything about us. Why should they tell us what we can and can't do? We're not traitors. We love our homes and our land, just like they do. And we're not politicians lining our pockets with war profits. We want the freedom we're due. And because we're willing to fight, we're losing everything we've got. It doesn't make sense." Les studied the ruins of his company, his eyes sick with regret. "Not a lick of sense."

"Not now, but we have to hope it will someday."

Lifting his hand, Les motioned to a young

corporal. "Jackson! Bring that bay over here."

A moment later, Barrett had a horse beneath him again. "Can't thank you enough, Les. Hope I can repay the favor someday."

Lifting his eyes, Les said wearily, "You know how to stop a war?"

"No."

Walking back to his horse, the captain swung into his saddle. "Me neither." He shifted to look back over his shoulder to the riderless horses. "But I wish I did."

NINE

Brittlefork, Texas
Population 86

Abigail studied the weather-beaten marker with a sigh of relief. *Brittlefork.* It was a stage town near the Texas-Louisiana border, if that man on the road had informed her correctly. And he'd also said the transportation came through on Thursdays. Today. Kneeing the horse forward, she entered the small burg.

Like most east Texas communities, weather-beaten storefronts lined the main street. The livery stood at the edge of town, surrounded by corrals. There was the usual mercantile, dress and millinery shop, dry goods store, boardinghouse, eating establishment, hotel, barber shop, and inevitable saloons. The saloon keeper of the Gold Nugget was outside this morning, sweeping the sidewalk as Abigail rode past, smiling.

The door of the livery stable creaked as

116

the owner shoved it open. Slowing the horse, she waited until the owner glanced up at her.

"Mornin'," he said, nodding to her.

"Good morning." Sliding off the horse, Abigail followed him into the shed's cool interior. Swain Hollister was a scant little man with a trim white beard and twinkling blue eyes. His stooped stance belied the quickness of his step, making it hard to tell his age.

"Is it true the stage comes through Brittle-fork?" she asked.

"Yessum. Stops at the saloon around noon. Or afternoon. Depending on what the soldiers do." He reached for a pitchfork, momentarily distracted. "Sorry, didn't catch your name, little lady."

"Betsy Ross," she said, recalling hearing something about a woman making a flag or something. Stripped of her disguise, she was forced to use another ploy.

Turning, Swain tipped his hat congenially. "Pleasure, Miss Ross."

"The pleasure is mine. I'll be buying my ticket and leaving today. Would you like to buy my horse?"

"Not really," he conceded.

"I'll sell it cheap."

Squinting, he studied the animal. "She

looks like she rides rough."

"Well — I won't fib. She does, but she's from prime stock."

They stared at the saddleless bay, silence overtaking the conversation. Finally, "How much do you want?"

"Enough for a stage ticket."

"Sold. I'll fetch yore money."

"Thank you. I'll tie her around back in the shade if you can spare a piece of rope."

"Help yourself." He motioned toward a pile of hemp lying on the floor. "Water trough is in back."

"You're ever so kind."

Once the mare had drunk her fill of water, Abigail led her around the building and tied her in the shade of a large tree. The smithy returned with the coinage and she smiled. "Pleasure doing business, kind sir."

"Just tie her around front when you're through."

Rummaging through the saddlebags, she removed the leather folder and messages. She glanced around to make sure no one was watching her, and then she folded the papers and slid them down the front of her shirt. Fishing back into the bags, she took out the pair of dark glasses and stuck them into her pocket.

When she came around the corner of the

building, she saw that the livery owner was preoccupied with a customer now. The two men were bent over, examining a horse's hoof.

Quickly stepping inside the livery door, she waited a moment for her eyes to adjust to the dim interior. She could hear Swain and the customer talking as she moved deeper into the shadows.

A moment later, she heard a horse trot away and Swain enter the livery again. Whistling off-key, he moved up and down the hallway, mucking stalls and pouring grain into bins.

With practiced ease, Abigail's eyes took stock of the livery. A plan was slowly forming in her mind that would allow additional funds, but she would need specific articles for the ruse. She quickly located the hat and blanket that had been thrown across the grain bin.

As Swain bent to inspect the horse's leg, she quietly stepped from the shadows and gathered the two items and then snatched two nice red apples from the peck sitting on the floor as she tiptoed out the doorway.

Hurrying behind the building, she shook out the musty blanket and headed toward the alley. Taking a quick look over her shoulder, she ducked around the corner, tucking her hair beneath the pilfered hat as she approached the back of the cafe.

Easing the screen open, she peered inside. The cook's hands were shoved into a pan of hot, soapy water, washing dishes. He seemed oblivious to the world as Abigail's hand crept between the screen and door frame and snatched one of the tin cups he'd just washed.

Continuing on down the alley, she stopped at the mercantile next. The store was open, and she was relieved to see two women inside, discussing the merits of the bolts of new fabric that just arrived. The owner shuffled in and out the back door, carrying in supplies as he complained to his wife about the cat trying to trip him.

Tossing aside her apple core, Abigail stepped inside, pretending to study the saddles on the back rack. When she was certain that the two women were immersed in gossip and that the owner was distracted by the cat, an oak cane joined the tin cup beneath her blanket. She made a mental note of all her theft — when she rejoined her sisters she would send the amount to the livery and ask the owner to distribute the money for her pilfered items. She should change; she would change. Starting now. She wasn't a thief at heart — at least not

Welcome to Crookston Public
Library
You checked out the following
items:

....

1. Sisters of Mercy Flats #1
   Barcode: 33500011004488
   Due: 6/26/2023

....

CROOKSTON 6/5/2023 10:15 AM
You were helped by CIRC-Jane

that kind of thief. These were poor, hard-working folk. The men she helped bilk were . . . men.

Casually sauntering out the door, she darted down the alley. Only when she'd distanced herself three stores away from the mercantile did she dare to release the breath she'd been holding.

Mid-morning, Barrett Drake rode into Brittlefork. Leaving his horse at the livery, he headed straight for the sheriff's office.

Since the war had begun, both it and the blockade brought about an economic revolution in Texas. The exportation and importation of goods nearly ceased. Limited trading could be done through Mexico and by blockade runners, but goods were still precious and hard to come by. The absence of most able-bodied men threw the burden of providing the necessities of life upon the women. Having been raised in a household where ladies were protected from the rigors of daily life, to Barrett the sight of women picking cotton and working in the fields disturbed him. The war changed everything, and he hated it. It wasn't an uncommon sight to see women selling extra produce from their gardens or butchering to put up their own meat. Some had been known to

121

sell their cattle, chicken, and hogs to the army.

Barrett spotted the sheriff's office at the end of the street and his step quickened. A child darted out, and in Barrett's attempt to sidestep a young mother and her two small children, he nearly stumbled over a blind beggar sitting next to the jail entrance.

After steadying himself and then the mother, he tipped his hat to the young woman pleasantly. "Have a good morning, ma'am."

The woman nodded, hurrying her children along the walkway.

He started into the sheriff's office when the beggar's cane shot out to block his entrance. "Alms. Alms for the blind."

He fished a coin from his pocket and tossed it into the beggar's tin cup.

"Thank you. God grant you a blessing, kind sir."

The sheriff turned when Barrett entered the room, his gaze measuring the shoe salesman quizzically. "Yes sir. What can I do for you?"

"Hershall E. Digman, at your service." Barrett bent from the waist, extending a hand of greeting. "I have a bit of a problem that I hope you might assist me with."

The sheriff's eyes traced the man curiously. "I'll try. You're new in town, aren't you?"

"Passing through." The two men shook hands cordially.

"What seems to be the problem?"

Barrett turned a wooden chair toward the desk, lightly dusting it with his handkerchief. "Well, you see, Sheriff, I sell shoes. And while on my way to Shreveport" — he paused to sit down before continuing — "I stumbled into a most troubling encounter."

"You don't say. What might that be, Mr. Digman?" The sheriff grinned. "Female woes?"

"Well," Hershall leaned forward, lowering his voice, "I met a woman who seemed to be in some distress. I offered to escort her wherever she needed to go just as soon as I had finished my sales rounds." His serious blue eyes met the sheriff's, seeking understanding.

"And?"

"And all was going well — you understand, swimmingly well." Hershall cleared his throat. "But apparently the woman wasn't satisfied with the arrangement, so she stole my horse."

Sheriff frowned. "Stole your horse?"

"Stole my horse. Now, the animal isn't my main concern. I can purchase another horse, but the female ran off with my saddlebags. They contain personal possessions that I don't intend to lose."

"So you want me to find the woman?"

"That's right. I wish to press charges."

His eyebrows rose. "What charges?"

"Horse theft."

"You said the horse didn't matter."

"It doesn't, but my saddlebags do."

"Well, now, Mr. Digman." The sheriff stood up, obviously considering the request. "I can see where that'd upset a man, but don't you think maybe you're jumping the gun a bit? Surely the woman had a good reason . . ."

"Those saddlebags are irreplaceable, and she's guilty of horse theft," Hershall reminded the sheriff. "I believe there's a law against horse theft."

"True, but I'm willing to bet once she cools down, she'll realize the gravity of her rash decision and turn your horse loose. When she does, someone will find it and bring it into town. Leave your name and where I can locate you, and I'll see that the saddlebags are eventually returned to you."

Well, won't that be just dandy! thought Hershall. If she turned the horse loose and it wandered around with the saddlebags containing the messages, his efforts to prevent a battle would be in vain. Maybe she had already found the papers and read them. There wasn't a doubt in his mind that if she knew that he wasn't Hershall Digman but actually Captain Barrett Drake, she'd lose no time informing authorities. Time was running out. His only hope, though slight, was the hope that she was somewhere nearby and that the sheriff would track her down quickly. As it was, he'd have to ride hard to reach Shreveport in time to warn Smith that Banks was approaching with a large force of Union soldiers.

Drifting to the stove, the sheriff poured a cup of coffee. "Coffee, Digman?"

"No, thank you. I want my saddlebags."

"Won't do no good to get yourself worked into a lather. Me and my boys will do what we can to help." He took a sip of coffee.

"There's one other thing you should know about this woman, Sheriff. She's a con artist. She and her sisters have been posing as nuns to bilk unsuspecting men out of their money."

Bushy brows lifted with surprise. "Nuns, you say?"

He nodded. "Nuns."

"That's low," the sheriff conceded.

"I have reason to believe that she may be near Brittlefork, and if she is, she's going to pick your town like a banjo. I think she'll try to take the stage out of here. She's anxious to reunite with her sisters in Texas. When do you expect the stage to arrive?"

"Around noon today — if it makes it. Got a lot of thievery going on these days. They waylay our drivers faster than we can hire 'em, and it's impossible to get a shotgun rider these days."

"Mark my word, she's headed this way."

"What do you plan to do in the meantime?"

"I'll keep an eye out for the stage if you'll organize a posse. It is imperative," Barrett said, stressing the point again, "that my saddlebags be found and returned to me expeditiously."

"I'll do what I can, but I can't promise anything. There's a lot of territory out there a woman can hide in if she takes a notion."

"Yes, and this one's wily," Barrett noted. *Mean and wily,* he silently added.

The sheriff stood up and walked to the gun cabinet. "I'll get a couple of men together. We'll scout the area. What's the woman look like?"

"Pretty, light hair, eyes an unusual shade of green."

"Green?"

"Lime. Height, five three or four." He

126

wasn't positive. "Probably doesn't weigh a hundred pounds soaking wet." All he knew for certain — she could look him straight in the eye and tell a lie. No decent woman could do that — at least none he'd met. A *nun.* Ha! And he'd bought it hook, line, and sinker! "I'll be at the hotel if you need me."

"What do you want me to do with her if I do find her?"

"Having my bag returned and seeing her behind bars will be sufficient."

When Barrett left the office, he nearly tripped over the beggar who was sitting directly in front of the doorway now.

"A penny for the beggar?"

He peered sanctimoniously at the pauper over the rim of his spectacles. "You're blocking the doorway."

"Alms for the less fortunate?"

"I've already given you a coin."

The figure swathed in a blanket and large hat lowered his head and tapped his cane beseechingly.

Dropping a second coin in the cup, Barrett stepped around the pathetic soul and set off with a jaunty step in search of a hot bath and a few hours of sleep.

TEN

Six hours passed, and still no sign of Abigail McDougal. Around four that afternoon, Barrett decided to join the official search. The sheriff, while appearing cooperative, failed in his efforts to find the little thief.

Barrett stepped out of the hotel and tipped his hat at a passing lady, smiling at her dismissive glance. When Hershall Digman, women overlooked him. Continuing down the sidewalk, he turned up his shirt collar against the brisk wind. He'd give everything he owned to be back in uniform. The collar choked him, and the undersized jacket was nothing short of fashion murder.

No sight of the stage yet. He'd watched from the window of the hotel room, but as of yet, the Wells and Fargo proved as elusive as Miss McDougal.

He crossed the street and it occurred to him that Abigail might not have stumbled onto Brittlefork. She could have become confused and ridden in the wrong direction, or she could have simply outsmarted him and ridden until she came to a way station. If she chose that route, then it was possible that she would turn the horse loose with the saddlebags intact. Cold fear gripped him. The only thing worse than her discovering the papers would be for her to turn the horse free to roam. Anyone could find his personal effects. The female gave him indigestion!

The sheriff glanced up when Barrett entered the stuffy office.

"Howdy."

"Afternoon. Just wanted to see if you'd heard anything about the woman."

"Nope."

"Are you looking for her?"

"Yep."

"Do you have a posse working on it?"

"Yep."

"Have they seen anything of her?"

"Nope."

He reined in the senseless conversation. "Since you aren't having much luck, I thought I might join the search."

Rising slowly to his feet, the sheriff moseyed to the stove, carrying his cup. "Don't much like anyone interfering in my duties, Mr. Digman."

"I don't plan to interfere in your duties; I'm merely offering my assistance." At this rate Abigail could be three counties away.

The sheriff's stubborn stance made it clear that he didn't want any help. "You're gonna have to give me and the boys more time. You're in too big of a hurry."

"I have shoes to sell. I need to be on my way."

"Then be on your way." The sheriff walked back to the desk and sat down. "I told you, leave me your name and address and I'll see that you get your bags if they show up."

Annoyed, Barrett turned, about to leave, when the sheriff's voice stopped him. "I wouldn't be doin' anything foolish, Mr. Digman. Here in Brittlefork, I'm the law, and I don't take lightly to a man disputin' my authority. You give me time; I'll find your horse."

Barrett nodded, undaunted, and closed the door behind him. The sheriff's thinly veiled threats didn't bother him. If Abigail McDougal was still in the area, he'd find her. He strode to the opposite side of the street and entered the livery stable. Swain came out of one of the stalls, smiling. "What can I do for you?"

"Do you have a carriage I might lease? Considering the sunny day, I thought I'd take a ride into the countryside."

"Sure do. A real nice one with brass fixtures. Got a fine animal to pull it I can let you have for next to nothin'."

"That will do nicely."

"Yes, sir, a fine rig for a pleasant ride. How long would you be needin' it?"

"A few hours, I'd imagine."

"Sure thing. Take me a few minutes to harness 'er up. Take a load off your feet." He pointed to a hay bale. "Have a seat."

Ignoring the offer, Barrett walked outside and leaned against a hitching rail to study the main street of Brittlefork, watching each female who walked by for signs of that vile woman in disguise.

"Here she is."

Barrett paused and noted the horse. *His* horse. Oh, she was here all right. He paid the man and then climbed into the rig. "Did you purchase the horse recently?"

The smithy paused. "What makes you ask?"

"The animal looks familiar — did it come with saddlebags?"

"Nope, the owner took them."

That didn't surprise him. Giving a whistle, he drove the rig down Main Street, stopping at the cafe long enough to purchase a hot coffee.

131

Continuing on his way, he nodded amiably at passersby.

The sheriff had moved from behind his desk to the shade in front of the office. He sat with his chair propped against the wall, balanced on the back two legs, his feet resting on the hitching rail.

Barrett nodded curtly when he passed.

For the remainder of daylight, he drove the buggy up and down various roads and trails leading out of Brittlefork, looking for any sign of Abigail.

Cold and discouraged, he reined up toward dusk beneath a big tree. Time was running out. If he didn't locate her soon he would have no choice but to ride on, hoping he could remember enough details about the message content to assist Smith.

Darkness overtook the buggy and he grew desperate. He widened his search, but each time he came up empty-handed. Several times he stopped and tied the horse to a tree to investigate the heavily wooded thicket, searching caves, approaching several empty cabins, hoping to discover signs that she might have been there. But she eluded him.

The night was as black as pitch when he started back to Brittlefork. He let the horse set his own pace while his mind reviewed the odd set of events that had taken place since he'd first seen the jail wagon with its strange cargo. A new, more disturbing thought occurred to him. What if the little fool had gotten herself killed? The McDougal sisters were a brave lot when together, but alone Abigail would be prey to any unfortunate character she met on the road. He didn't know why he found the thought disagreeable, but he did.

By the time he returned the rig to the livery it was late, and he was hungry. He walked to the café, located a table, and ordered. As he drank a cup of coffee, he found himself listening to the talk surrounding him.

The cafe was active tonight, filled with locals and travelers. Some were upset that the stage had been delayed again.

"The durn stage is late because the driver's seat come loose from the main body!" a man reported.

Some hooted at the information.

"Anyone hurt?" another thought to ask.

"Unfortunately, the driver had been on the seat at the time," the first man noted. "Old Mort's agility just barely saved him from being dragged to death behind a running team. Rumor has it, the stage will be

133

delayed another day until a new seat can be built."

The observation between two men sitting directly in front of him caught Barrett's full attention.

"I don't think the South can last much longer, not after the whippin' they been takin' lately."

The second man lowered his tone. "You heard what happened in Sherman's raid a few weeks back."

"I've heard the talk. Some say it'll be over before long, but talk's cheap, Will, just like blood. Real cheap."

"I know, but they say Sherman's been whippin' it on those Yankees lately."

"Like I say, talk's cheap. There's no end to the suffering. I've seen enough war to last me a lifetime, and just because people say the South can't hold out much longer don't make it so."

"At least Lincoln's boy is servin' now."

Barrett knew that Robert Todd Lincoln, oldest son of the president, once divided his time between Harvard University and the nation's capital and never felt the impact of the 1863 Conscription Act. Young Robert had long been the target of widespread gossip and criticism for not serving his country, especially when Illinois was conspicuously eager to fill its quota of young, able-bodied men.

"Yeah," the man said, laughing mirthlessly. "He's servin' as official escort to commanders and notables, including his father. That's not quite the same as having your boy on the firing line, now, is it?"

"No, but I hear his mother, Mary, couldn't bear the thought of losing the boy. You know the president and his wife lost their son Eddie when he was a small lad and then eleven-year-old Willie three years ago."

Barrett heard the rumors that Mrs. Lincoln had been so inconsolable after Willie's death that she'd taken to her bed for days whenever anyone made mention of Robert entering the war. Finally, in an act of desperation, Lincoln penned a letter to Grant, a man whom he had made general-in-chief, asking if it would be possible "without embarrassment to you or detriment to the service, to arrange for Robert Todd Lincoln to go into your military family with some nominal rank."

Grant complied with his president's wishes and suggested that Robert, who had no prior military training or experience, should enter the army with the rank of captain, with the anticipation that he would be made an assistant adjutant general on the headquarters' staff.

"I know all about the president's troubles." The voice retained its affability, but the tone changed. "Me and my Martha have lost two boys, and a third is still fighting, so I find it hard to sympathize with Mary Todd Lincoln, especially since many of us feel this is her husband's war. What mother wants to lose her son?"

"None," the other man agreed. "Not any mother, Will."

Signaling for his check, Barrett finished the last of his coffee and then paid his bill, disturbed by the men's conversation and Abigail's strange disappearance.

He stepped outside, absently drawing a cheroot from the inside pocket of his suit coat. Cupping the match against the March breeze, he lit the smoke, drawing deeply as he mentally prepared himself for the worst. The way things looked, the sheriff wasn't going to find her —

His thoughts were interrupted when he felt a light tap on his shoulder. Turning, he found a young Quaker woman looking at him.

"Ma'am?" His eyes suddenly narrowed when he recognized the intruder. "You!"

"Don't *you* me, you beast!" His head snapped back when she slapped him smartly across the cheeks with the leather folder. "How dare you lie to me! You conniving, no good, sneaky, lowdown, lying, miserable, traitor!"

"Me?" Barrett glanced up and down the near empty street to see if she was drawing attention. "That's like the pot calling the kettle black, isn't it, Sister Abigail?"

"You're a Union spy!"

"Lower your voice!"

She smacked him across the cheeks again.

His hand caught hers. "Stop slapping me with that pouch!"

"You traitor!" She whacked him again, hard.

Grabbing her wrists, Barrett dragged her into the alley behind the café where they'd be less conspicuous. If she wanted war, she was going to get it. "You listen to me, woman. I *work* for the Confederacy."

Her eyes widened, and she ceased her struggle. When he noted that he'd gotten her attention, he repeated himself. "I work for the South, and if you don't give me those papers you alone are going to be responsible for an entire company's death."

ELEVEN

"I don't believe you." Abigail whirled to face off. "Prove it." She whacked him again.

"You wallop me with that pouch one more time . . ." Barrett grabbed for the leather, but she managed to smack him again.

"I've been looking everywhere for you!" she accused. Twisting free of his grasp, she glared back at him, rubbing her wrists. "Brute!"

"Liar." His eyes skimmed her plain gray dress, shawl, and matching bonnet. "Now you're a Quaker? Have you no shame?"

She calmly retied the strings of a sheer cap before adjusting the white scarf folded about her throat. "None. How else could I travel? Because of you, I burned my habit."

Shaking his head, he noted, "I would be hard pressed to name one woman — or man for that matter — with more heretical audacity. There is no stopping point to how far you'll go to accomplish your mission, whatever that mission might be. If it's money you're after, you're barking up the wrong tree. I have savings, but I don't carry them on me." Skimming her apparel, he sighed. "First a nun, now a Quaker. If God doesn't strike you dead, I'll eat my hat."

"Which, by the way, would be doing us all a favor," she allowed, eyeing the bowler. She snatched his shattered lens off and peered through them. "Exactly as I thought. These are nothing but clear glass — one more reinforcement to defraud the innocent."

He snatched the spectacles back and put them on, leveling his gaze upon her. "You are, without a doubt, the most irritating woman on earth."

"Well, well, well." She crossed her arms. "Does my dress offend you? That *is* like the pot calling the kettle black. You're traipsing around the country posing as a shoe sales-man, when in fact you're a spy for the Union army!" She whacked him across the shoulders with the pouch.

Grabbing her hand, he stilled her attempts to flog him again. "What I am is none of your business!"

"You're a spy!"

"Keep your voice down." Barrett glanced at the entrance to the alley. "You'll have us both in jail! Give me those papers."

He tried to snatch the pouch out of her hand, but she held it over her head, out of his reach.

"Never."

"You'll give them to me or I'll turn you over to the sheriff so fast it will make your head swim."

"Try it. And I'll inform the whole town who you are and what you're doing." Shielding the packet behind her, she backed against the building and firmly planted her feet.

"Give them to me," Barrett repeated.

"No. You're a miserable, malicious spy. You call me a thief, but you're a bigger one."

Their eyes locked. "Give me those papers, Abigail."

"No."

"Keep your voice down. I do not work for the Northern sympathizers."

"*You* say."

"I say it because it's the truth."

"Why should I believe you?"

"At the moment you don't have a choice. You can either take my word or have the weight of a nasty upcoming battle on your conscience, a battle that's bound to make a huge difference in the war effort. No doubt you read the papers in that pouch."

"Maybe not."

"So I'm sure you know there's a message in there for General Smith."

Doubt flickered in her eyes and then faded. The little sneak *had* read the papers.

She raised her voice two octaves. "Don't you want everyone to know who you really are, *Mr.* Digman?"

He grabbed for the packet, but she shoved his hand away. "Help, oh, someone please help me!"

Clamping his hand across her mouth they struggled for control. She stomped his foot but he only tightened his grasp on her arm and tried to wrestle the pouch away from her.

"Let go of me!"

"Give me that pouch!"

"I'll die first!"

The two locked in a stubborn duel. Screaming, she yanked his hair but his strength overtook her. He had the leather packet almost in his fingers when she wriggled away from him.

He caught her arm and jerked her back, quickly sidestepping her vicious kick. He flipped her around so that her back was to him. Trying to hold her was like trying to hold a sackful of furious cats. Legs and arms flailed in all directions, nails scratched, feet lost footing.

Screeching she hurled herself headlong at him. He caught the full brunt of her weight and almost toppled to the ground, nearly taking her with him. "Give up, McDougal. I'm gettin' those papers!"

The warring couple fought, unaware of the two men who'd stepped out of the café and were heading down the alley now.

"Get off me!" she shouted.

"Not until you give me those papers."

"Get your finger out of my eye!"

"Get your foot out of my throat!"

All of a sudden she spotted the men. "Someone's coming." A hand clamped over her mouth, preventing her from calling out.

"Don't say a word," Barrett warned in her ear. She threw a right hook, catching him in the nose. Blood spurted and his hand came up to stem the flow when she belted him again.

"Help! Help me!" Scrambling away, she took off running. Barrett grabbed for her, snagging the hem of her skirt as she yelled louder. "Help! Oh, please, someone help me!"

"Here now! You unhand that woman!" The sound of thundering boots coming down the alley drew closer. Groaning, Barrett drew back into the shadows. How was he ever going to explain why a shoe salesman was wrestling a Quaker woman in the alleyway?

"Oh, please, help me, sirs!" Abigail cried. "This man — this beastly cad — is a lunatic!"

Dragging a handkerchief from his pocket, Barrett brought it to his bleeding nose, clearly waiting for the inquisition to begin.

"What's goin' on here? What do you think you're doin', mister?" The largest man snatched him by the scruff of his neck and jerked him roughly to his feet.

"Just a little disagreement, gentlemen," said Barrett. Abigail stood back as Barrett forced a wheezy laugh, trying to make light of the incriminating circumstances. "Nothing serious, I can assure you. Her father doesn't approve of me, but I told her I wasn't thinking of marrying her father —"

He turned when he heard Abigail feign a faint behind him.

The second man quickly stepped over to support her wilting frame. "Oh, I thank thee, kind sir . . . it was so horrifying . . ."

"Are you hurt, ma'am?"

"I don't believe so — but I've hardly had time to assess my injuries. I cannot thank thee enough for rescuing me from this . . . this brute."

"She's lying through her teeth," Barrett

said tightly. "She —"

Before he could finish the rebuke, the first man grabbed his arms and slammed him against the wall. Wincing, she turned away. When next she looked, he was flat on the ground with a knee planted firmly in the middle of his chest.

"Listen — she's misleading you. I can explain."

When his vision cleared, he found himself looking down the barrel of a Colt .44 pistol. Abigail gasped when she saw it. The second man soothed her, asking her quietly to turn away. She faced the opposite direction with her hands folded and her eyes downcast.

"Are you sure you're not hurt, ma'am?"

"Maybe you should let him go . . ."

"It's dangerous for a woman to be out after dark without a man's protection," he chided kindly. "We'll take care of the matter."

"My mother is most ill, sir, and she needed medicine so badly that I ventured out on my own. I had no idea that a man like this" — she cast a dark look in Barrett's direction — "was allowed to roam the streets at will. But perhaps he's learned his lesson." She dusted the dirt from her shirt, faking a few tears. She almost felt sorry for the spy now. Almost.

"Now now. Don't cry. You're safe with us."

"I thank thee, sir." She smiled brightly. "Thou art most kind."

"What do you want us to do with this piece of dung, ma'am?" The man quickly realized his slip of the tongue. "Pardon my salty language, ma'am. That just slipped out." Barrett tried to lift his head but the heel of a boot smashed it back to the ground.

"Sirs! Please." She stepped up, blocking the men's path. "I cannot tolerate violence. If you would, please release this man."

"But ma'am, he accosted you."

"Release him. I bear him no ill will."

"Ma'am . . ."

" 'Twas nothing more than a . . . dispute. A simple misunderstanding."

The smaller man scratched his head. "I thought you folks . . ."

"We too are weak in nature, kind sir." And to prove it, she nudged the bigger man's boot aside and planted her foot in Barrett's back. "My life is simple and I believe in peaceful ways, so I cannot, in my heart, permit any man harm. Jail would be most agreeable. Perhaps a few days behind bars will allow this man to rethink his evil ways."

"Well, it's up to you, ma'am. If you want him in jail then so be it, but I'd beat the thunder out of him."

"Oh, I thank thee for coming to my rescue and for thy kindness. I will pray for thee." Kneeling, her gaze locked with Barrett's. "And I will pray for this man as well. He needs it," she added.

"I'm going to hunt you down like a snake," Barrett said. "And when I do, you're going to regret the day you ever met me, Abigail McDougal."

Turning back to her rescuers, she rallied two fat tears to roll down her cheeks. "He speaks unkindly again."

Barrett's feet skimmed along the dirt as the two men dragged him from the alley toward the sheriff's office.

"Have a pleasant evening." Turning, she struck off for the hotel. She'd collected enough money as a beggar to treat herself. And now that Hershall E. Digman, or whoever he was, was out of her hair, she planned to take full advantage of her good fortune.

When she entered the lobby, she met the clerk's curious look with the sweetest smile she had. "I'd like a nice room, please. A front one, if possible. And could hot water for a bath be brought to my room by six tomorrow morning?"

"Certainly, ma'am." He turned the regis-

146

ter around toward her. "Just sign here."

She smiled, accepting the pen. "A lovely day was it not?"

"Yes, it's been right pleasant, even with the snow we've had."

Bringing the pen to her chin, she thought for a moment, and then, in a flourishing hand, wrote *Prudence Penn.*

She handed the pen back to the clerk and waited for the key.

The clerk read her signature and scratched his head. "Penn, huh?"

"Yes. My father is a direct descendant of William Penn, the man who established the colony of Pennsylvania."

"Is that a fact?" The clerk looked adequately impressed. "That Penn, huh? That's real interestin'. It's not every day that we get such a notable guest. If you need anything you just sing out."

Reaching for the key, she warned him firmly, "Please, treat me as thou wouldst any other guest."

She turned, aware she'd told yet another lie. The habit was starting to wear on her. Once her stories were larks — fun and creative imaginations. This afternoon, witnessing the clerk's kind and helpful services, they were what they were. Lies.

TWELVE

"Digman! Roust yourself."

Barrett sat up, swinging his legs off the cot. The sheriff stood outside the cell, peering through the bars at him. The key slid into the lock and a moment later the cell doors swung open. "Ten dollars and you're a free man."

"Ten dollars!" The fine seemed excessive, even if it was for assaulting a Quaker woman.

"Any man who'd abuse a woman, and a God-fearin' Quaker woman at that, is lower than a rat's belly in my opinion. But I can't hold you longer than twelve hours," the sheriff conceded, "or I would."

Wincing, Barrett reached for his suit jacket, disregarding his splitting headache.

"Men in Brittlefork don't pick on defenseless women," the sheriff continued. "Or aren't you aware of that, Mr. Digman?"

"I understand that . . ."

"I don't want to hear it!"

Barrett walked out of the cell, pulling on his coat.

"Them Quakers are peace-lovin' folk, or don't you know that?"

"I do know . . ."

"I don't want to hear it!"

Barrett realized that it was useless to argue. He'd tried for over five hours to convince the sheriff that the "Quaker" woman was the one who'd stolen his horse, but he just stared at him.

In short, Abigail McDougal had him right where she wanted him: in one fine mess. Not only him but the whole South.

"The fine is highway robbery," Barrett grumbled when he followed the authority to his desk. Bending over, he tried to brush the wrinkles out of his seersucker trousers. "The whole incident is a misunderstanding."

"Mister, I don't want to hear it."

The sheriff unlocked the safe and Barrett stepped to the mirror to adjust his bowler. Handing Barrett his personal belongings, the sheriff started in on him again. "Why a man would want to hurt a woman just don't make good sense. Wrestling a Quaker like she was some big old man? We don't act that way here in Brittlefork, Digman."

"I understand, but I'm trying to tell you that she's the woman —"

"I don't want to hear it! Now I want you out of town by noon, clear enough?"

"Perfectly." Counting out ten coins, Barrett paid the outrageous fine. "I still think this assessment is highway robbery."

"I could hang you, if that'd suit you better."

Stepping out of the jail, Barrett glanced up and down the street. With his luck, Abigail McDougal had disappeared again. She could be a priest by now.

Well, she could run as long and as hard as she liked, but when he found her — and he would, if it took him the rest of his life — she was as good as dead. Because of her, his credibility in Brittlefork was ruined. By noon everyone in town would have heard how Hershall Digman, the shoe salesman, had attacked a young Quaker woman and wrestled her "like a big old man." No one was going to believe that she lied about his attacking her. It was hard enough for him to conceive.

Not a man in town would be willing to help him now. In fact, he was lucky that he hadn't been ridden out of town on a rail.

He leaned against a post to think. Yessir, she had him in one fine fix. She'd stolen his horse, so now he was a Southern spy riding a horse clearly marked with an army brand. The only clothes he had were the ones on his back and for him to continue to pose as a shoe salesman in Brittlefork would be about as worthless as teats on a stallion.

He'd spent his last dollar on the fine, and here it was seven o'clock in the morning and he didn't have the vaguest idea where to go. And to top it off, the McDougal woman still had his papers.

It was hard to believe how simple his life had been a short forty-eight hours ago.

He glanced up when the door to the jail opened. The sheriff walked out, carrying his rifle.

"Thought I told you to move on, Digman."

"I'm going. I just —"

"I don't want to hear it." The sheriff hefted the gun and started firing at Barrett's feet. Springing off the porch, he raced through the center of town in a dead run.

Dodging bullets, he danced his way to the city limits, vowing that he would get even with Abigail McDougal if it killed him!

Coming awake slowly, Abigail stretched, thoroughly enjoying the luxury of having slept between clean sheets for the first time in weeks. Outside her window, birds chirped and the sun's rays fell across the wooden floor. It was going to be a glorious day!

Languidly stretching again, she listened to the sounds of Brittlefork coming to life as a balmy breeze fluttered the lacy curtain at the window. The mouthwatering aroma of frying bacon drifted through the open window.

Rolling lazily onto her side, she frowned when she remembered the murderous look on Hershall's face when he'd been hauled off to jail last night. Still, if he was the best the South had going for it — and she wasn't sure she believed that he *was* working for the Confederacy and not the Yankees — no wonder they were losing the war. Her mind wandered and she idly wondered if his name really was Hershall Digman or if he'd lied about that too.

A tap sounded at the door and she groaned. "Who is it?"

A woman's voice answered. "The maid with your bath, ma'am."

"One moment." She pulled herself out of bed, wrapped the blanket around her shoulders, and padded barefoot to the door. Opening it a crack, she found the maid with two large buckets of steaming water sitting on the floor beside her.

"Hot water, for your bath, ma'am."

"Yes, come in."

She opened the door wider and waited as two young boys carried in a copper tub and set it in the middle of the floor. For the next several minutes the boys worked to fill the tub with the buckets of steaming water.

When they left the room, the maid turned back to Abigail and curtsied. "If you be needin' anything more, just pull the cord above your bed."

"Thank you. Have you any word about the stagecoach?"

"No, ma'am. Nothing."

"Will you please notify me when it arrives?"

The young girl curtsied again. "Yes, ma'am."

The door closed and Abigail tiptoed to the tub. Closing her eyes, she sighed deeply and dipped her fingers into the warm water. A real bath. She could hardly wait to sink into the mound of steaming bubbles.

An hour later she was still leisurely soaping herself, humming beneath her breath. If the rumors floating around were true, it could be hours or days before the stage arrived. Apparently getting a new wagon seat wasn't as easy as expected, but she felt no pressing need to hurry. Digman was tucked in jail and likely to spend a few days cooling his heels. Ducking her head beneath the water, she rinsed the last of the soap out of her hair. She had nearly forgotten how good it felt to be so wondrously clean.

As she toweled dry, she said a prayer of gratitude. The citizens of Brittlefork had been uncommonly generous to the "blind beggar" sitting in front of the sheriff's office. Guilt reared its ugly head. She didn't like the way she earned her keep, but she wasn't given much choice. God would forgive her iniquities. The convent sisters were so compassionate, so honest . . . but they were also naïve. Money was hard to come by and Abigail had no legal way to earn coins. Education was limited — yet the sisters said that if God provided for the sparrows He would surely provide for His children. If it weren't for her, Amelia, and Anne-Marie's efforts she feared the sisters would go cold and hungry — though never once had she or anyone at the convent sat down to an empty table or suffered a cold room.

Even that dratted Hershall had been kind. Before she'd known it, she'd garnered enough coins to pay for a few necessities at the mercantile and board and bath, and she had enough left over to buy herself the delicious ham and egg breakfast she was about to enjoy.

If, by any stroke of luck, the stagecoach came through today, she'd hop on it and be free of any threat by Hershall E. Digman after tonight. Besides, he might stay in jail for weeks. She hoped so — or maybe she didn't.

Frowning, she decided to stop by the jail and leave enough to pay Hershall's fine. That little she could do; after all, part of it was his money . . . though he didn't know it.

She dusted herself lavishly with the scented powder she'd purchased with part of her financial windfall. The other coins were safely tucked away for the convent and Digman's fine. In a few days she'd be back in Mercy Flats and all this unpleasantness would be behind her.

She reached for her new hairbrush and absently drew it through the thick, wet tangles in her hair. Her eyes fell upon the plain gray dress lying on the floor where she'd left it last night. She'd bet that the lady who owned the garment would be surprised to find it missing from her wash line this morning.

The dress was a little big for her, but it didn't matter. She was used to making do.

Abigial had always counted that as one of her strong points — making do. But she did wish that the dress was clean. If the stage failed to come by noon, she'd have it washed and ironed, so it wouldn't feel so stiff and sticky over her new muslin undergarments, which she also purchased with her tidy little profit.

She had just finished pulling on the dress when heavy boots suddenly kicked open the wooden door.

She whirled, the brush clattering to the floor. Giving a gasp of astonishment, she shrieked when she recognized the intruder. "Hershall Digman! You get out of here!"

Barrett leveled his finger at her, his eyes pulsating with outrage. "I am going to throttle you," he said succinctly. So succinctly that her heart pumped like a steam locomotive.

She started easing backward toward the bed. Hershall didn't look like himself this morning. His nostrils flared and his eyes glazed like a wild animal's.

"I am going to *personally* strangle you with my bare hands," he said.

"You wouldn't dare." He wouldn't dare — would he? She felt the blood drain from her cheeks.

"My dear lady, where you're concerned, I

will dare anything. I've had to *hop* out of town like a hare to escape with my life, and you are going to pay for my humiliation. Oh, you are going to pay."

She noted the clothes that he was wearing and snorted with contempt. "Why are *you* dressed as a Quaker?"

"We shop at the same clothesline, dear lady."

"You *thief*."

"Ha!"

This was Hershall all right, yet there was something different about him this morning. The silly little bowler was gone, and so was the seersucker suit. He no longer wore the wire spectacles, and the spats had been replaced by plain, but highly polished, brown leather boots.

Shock and anger flooded her when she stared at his drab, collarless suit and broad-brimmed hat. Though he was only a few inches taller than she, the new Hershall exuded a confidence that the old Hershall could never have pulled off.

She thought she'd detected something different about him while she'd been masquerading as the beggar in front of the sheriff's office yesterday, but until this moment she hadn't tried to identify the change. Now it hit her. It was his commanding air and his wicked good looks. The broad shoulders, slim hips and the play of muscles rippling across his shoulders quickened her pulse until she felt positively giddy. And his hair! She was speechless; the greasy pomade had been washed out and now soft brown waves that fell to his shirt collar gave him a roguish air. Hershall had transformed into a strikingly fine-looking male.

Coming to her senses, she tried to slam the door in his face, but she was no match for Barrett's newfound force.

Setting her aside, he stepped into the room. Lifting her chin a notch, she met his gaze defiantly. "Leave before I scream."

"Scream all you want." He closed the door and turned the key in the lock. "You set those well-meaning protectors on me again," he said, his eyes arrogantly meeting hers, "and this time I guarantee, lady, I'll deserve it."

For the first time since she'd met him, he alarmed her. She had never considered him dangerous, but now she wasn't so sure. She drew a quick deep breath and started to scream, but he clamped his hand over her mouth. "You're not getting away this time, McDougal. Where are those papers?"

"Muummmmph!"

"I want those papers!"

She tore his hand away from her mouth and spat in his face.

He wiped the spittle away. "Who raised you? Heathens?"

She clawed her nails down the length of his cleanly shaven face before he trapped her wrists. "Let go of me!"

"You're not going anywhere until I have those papers." His grip tightened until she feigned weakness. "Where are they?"

"I won't tell you."

"You will, or I'll march you straight to the police station and show the sheriff what you really are."

"He'll put you back in jail and throw away the key."

He toughened the grasp on her arm, ignoring her threats. "That only works once. Now give me the papers and I'll be on my way."

"All right," she grunted. "I'll get the ridiculous papers, and then I don't want to ever see your face again!"

"Oh no you don't," he said. "I'm not that mindless. Tell me where the papers are and I'll get them."

"*I'll* get them. They're not in the room."

"Then forget it. The minute I turn you loose you'll run out on me again. I'll get them. I don't trust you to walk across the room, let alone leave it."

Clearly, they'd reached a standoff. Abigail knew that if she told him where the papers were, he could easily take her money and stage ticket, and then she would be detained another whole day trying to regain financial solvency. Her lips firmed with stubbornness. "You're not going to get them," she said.

"Then we'll pay the sheriff a little visit."

"And I'll tell him that you're a Yankee spy. You'll be shot before sundown." Though she'd never personally witnessed a man's execution, she would stick around to watch this one.

"But you'd be wrong and I can prove it. I work for the South. Look, I'll level with you. I have to get those papers to Shreveport by the end of the week. I know you don't care whether the North or the South wins this war, but it matters to me, and to thousands of men who are right this minute giving their lives for something that you and your sisters take for granted — freedom. Freedom, lady, to go and do and be what you want. Not everyone has it."

The logic in his tone and the grave set of his features reasserted how important the papers were to him. He wasn't just angry that she had outsmarted him; he was actually desperate to get those papers to their intended destination. She wasn't immune to logic, nor was she immune to the horrors of war. She'd seen women sobbing when their men marched off to fight, and she'd heard babies crying for their fathers. War was ugly, but she hadn't started it and there wasn't anything she could do to stop it.

Except . . . maybe there was. "I don't like the war any more than you do. And I would give you your old papers, but how can I believe you?"

His gaze sobered. "Just like spiritual convictions, you have to take this on faith."

She didn't like it when he made sense. And she didn't relish being on her own. The world was a whole lot bigger — and darker — than she'd realized. And she wasn't accustomed to traveling without her sisters, so until she could get back to Amelia and Anne-Marie, she would have to trust that Hershall — or whatever his name was — wasn't playing her for a fool. That was going to take a bushel of trust.

"Abigail," Barrett sighed wearily, "I can't personally take you to Mercy Flats. I work for a man who has thousands of men under his command. Those men are facing imminent death unless I get those papers delivered by the end of the week. The man is a Confederate commander. Getting those papers to Shreveport could make the difference in ending this war. And I don't know a person — Confederate or Yankee — who doesn't want that to happen."

She rubbed her wrists as she studied him. "And if I trust you and you're not who you say you are, I'm endangering Southern troops even more."

His eyes drifted shut. "You make a valid point; you can only take my word. Have I done anything to you that would make you question my integrity?"

"Kicking the door open didn't help your case."

"Besides kicking the door open."

"No. You've been gentlemanly — in most instances."

"Then trust me. I won't leave you here. You have my word. I'll personally arrange for an escort back to your sisters."

"Personally?" She wanted to believe him. It would make life much easier to think that he would help her, but he'd fibbed so convincingly about being a shoe salesman. Why should she believe he would suddenly keep his word?

His patience teetered. "Can't you get it through your head? I don't have the *time* to take you anywhere! I've wasted too much time as it is."

"See! It's exactly as I thought. You'd be nice to me until you got those papers, then you'd be gone!"

"Give me those papers!"

"No."

Marching to the opposite side of the room, she jerked a curtain in place and began pulling the blankets on the bed into place. He muttered something, but she ignored him. "The way I see it, we're stuck with each other, Mr. Digman, until we can figure out a way to get rid of each other. I can't trust you and you can't trust me. We're in a fine fix."

Barrett groaned. Drawing a breath of resignation he finally lifted his head and quietly yielded. "You win."

She frowned, waiting for the *but*. When the word didn't come, she prompted hesitantly. "And?"

"We're stuck with each other. Since I'm going to Shreveport and since you refuse to give me the papers, it looks like we'll make the trip together."

"Only if you'll sign a paper agreeing to take me to Mercy Flats once your documents have been delivered." She didn't fancy the arrangement, but he left her little recourse. It was obvious that both had met their match; he was as mean and stubborn as she.

"All right, but as God is my witness, I'm agreeing to this only because of duty to my country."

"Sure, sure," Abigail muttered. "The same goes for me. But the papers stay with me until we reach Shreveport."

"That isn't —"

"It's that way or not at all."

"Agreed. You keep the papers — but you'd better guard them with your life."

"We'll travel as man and wife," she decided. "No one will be likely to ask a Quaker couple to show a pass."

"We'd better hope they don't, but I'd suggest you don't fly into me or give me a tongue lashing in anyone's presence."

"Agreed. And you keep your distance. Understand? I may be feisty but I am a virtuous woman."

"Granted. Your virtue stands out like a diamond."

"There's no need for sarcasm." She hurriedly stuffed personal articles into her newly purchased reticule.

"We'll need money," he said.

"I have money."

Sitting up, he looked at her. "How did you get money?"

She turned, smiling. "I earned it." She wrapped her hair into a coil at the base of her neck and jabbed a pin through it. "One more thing. Is your name really Hershall Digman?"

Standing, Barrett affected a mock bow. "Captain Barrett Drake, at your service."

"Well, Captain Drake," Abigial said, jerking the strings on her bonnet smugly, "you'd better behave as a gentleman on this trip or you won't live to make major."

He turned dispassionate eyes on her. "And you're to do the same, Miss McDougal. I'm warning you."

Well, honestly, Abigail seethed as she trailed him out the doorway. *Does his bloated male ego actually think I should be impressed by him?*

THIRTEEN

The monotonous clatter of steel against track did little to still Abigail's anxiety the following morning. She squirmed on the narrow train seat, trying to find a comfortable spot.

"Sit still," Barrett chastised from the corner of his mouth. "Are you intent on disturbing everyone sitting around us?"

The train was crowded this morning. The only empty seat was next to a heavyset woman by the name of Wanila Knob. She was traveling to meet her husband, who had been injured during a battle and was hospitalized in Louisiana.

Squirming again, Abigail switched sideways, causing Barrett to turn again, frowning. "Will you sit still?"

"I don't have any room," she complained. She glanced at Wanila's generous bulk hanging over the seat and her lips puffed resentfully.

"Don't say it," he warned.

She glared back at him, wondering how he could read minds.

"Move over. It's so close in this stuffy old car I can hardly breathe."

"Forget it. Everyone makes sacrifices."

Abigail gritted her teeth, trying to make the best of a bad situation. She'd wanted to ride on horseback to Shreveport, but Barrett had insisted that they go by train to make up for the time she'd squandered.

She wiggled edgily, aware of the infant in the seat behind them. The child was fussy and had already cried for hours.

I don't blame you, baby. I'd cry too. No one dared open a window because of the black soot and smoke belching from the engine smokestack three cars ahead. But even soot would be preferable to the haze rolling from two men with cigars who sat across the aisle, deeply engrossed in a conversation about buffalo.

"If my Darnell don't get to come home, I don't know what me and the young'uns will do," Wanila bemoaned. Abigail tried to be sympathetic, but how could she sympathize when she was so uncomfortable? She could see the older woman studying her from the corner of her eye. "Your kind don't believe in war, do they?"

Lifting her chin, Abigail dabbed perspiration from her neck. "The Society of Friends believes that war is contrary to the life and teaching of Jesus," she murmured.

Barrett bent closer and whispered in her ear. "And how would you know that?"

"I know my faith, Mr. Drake. I am a woman of God."

"Right."

"I am. Often one does what one must to stay alive and simply hope that our Father understands."

"Our Father is full of grace," said Barrett, "but there's only one hitch. A person must truly believe to accept that grace, and repent of his ways."

"I believe."

Wanila leaned close. "You call yourselves the Society of Friends? Why is that, honey? I thought you was Quakers."

"Quaker is but another name. We are called Friends because that is our philosophy. We believe there is good in everyone. If thou believest in living day by day with family, neighbors, and everyone thou meetest, thou art a friend, is that not correct?"

Wanila shifted, jamming Abigail more solidly against Barrett. "Seems to me one name would do."

Exchanging a pained glance with Barrett,

Abigail continued, "The name was acquired when our founder, George Fox, was arrested and put in stocks. When the judge was about to send him to jail for six months, Friend Fox became defiant and shouted, 'Thou shouldst quake at the name of the Lord!' The judge roared, 'Quake! Thou, sir, art the quaker!' Then the crowd chanted, 'Quaker, Quaker.' " Abigail mopped at her chin again. "So that is why we are called Quakers."

"You're making that up," Barrett accused quietly.

"I am not. Read once in a while." Anne-Marie had made her study all religions in case the information should come in handy, like right now, for instance.

The train lurched, throwing the passengers in the car violently forward. Screams erupted in the car, confusion.

Abigail's nails clawed Barrett's leg when she grabbed on to him to keep from being thrown to the floor. Women and children babbled over the high-pitched, squealing brakes. "What in tarnation is going on?" Barrett cried out.

The passengers' necks were whipped forward and then jerked painfully backward as the train slid to an ear-splitting, spark-shooting, screeching halt.

Silence turned deafening. Travelers took stock, patting down their bodies to discover if anything was broken, and then bedlam broke out. Children's cries filled the car as the passengers picked themselves up off the floor. Female voices babbled in confusion.

The conductor raced down the aisle toward the door, calling for calm.

Abigail met Barrett's anxious features. Travel papers. They had none. They were in trouble again.

"Oh, Lord help us! We're going to be scalped!" Wanila moaned.

Straining to see over the woman, Abigail tried to catch a glimpse out of the window. "What is it? Indians? I can't see anything!"

Barrett helped Abigail and Wanila to their feet seconds before the door to the rail car burst open. Two masked gunmen entered, their six-shooters leveled on the group.

"Everybody sit real quiet and nobody gets hurt," the one in front ordered.

Abigail felt Barrett tense beside her.

"What do we do now?" she whispered.

"Whatever he says," Barrett acknowledged quietly. For the first time since they'd boarded, the train car fell silent.

The men were an intimidating lot. The leader wore filthy clothes, a hat pulled low over his eyes, and a handkerchief covering the lower half of his face. The second man looked equally nasty, his eyes cold and menacing. Experiencing a quiver of fear, Abigail scooted closer to Barrett.

The outlaws moved down the aisle, their eyes sweeping through the car, evaluating each passenger. The barrels of their guns moved over the travelers threateningly.

Pausing in front of Barrett, the leader motioned for him to step into the aisle. "You there. You and your wife step out."

"My wife and I mean thee no harm," Barrett said.

"Git out here!"

"Now just a minute —" Abigail blurted.

Barrett laid a warning hand on her arm. "I pray thee, gentlemen, we mean thee no harm."

The barrel of the gun centered on Barrett's temple. "Git out of that seat, mister."

Barrett and Abigail sprang to their feet simultaneously, crushing Wanila's toes in their haste to comply.

Wide-eyed, Wanila watched, stuffing her handkerchief deeper into her mouth.

Barrett discretely eased Abigail in front of him. She felt his hand resting in the middle of her back as the two men started herding them down the aisle.

"Where are the papers?" Barrett whispered.

"I have them," she whispered back.

"Well hidden?"

"You don't see them, do you?"

"Make certain they don't leave your body," he warned.

Well, sure, Barrett. I'll fist-fight both of them if they try anything.

"Where do you think they're taking us?" she asked softly.

"I have no idea."

"Don't you find this odd?" She felt color flood her face. He couldn't possibly find it normal.

She found his hand resting in the center of her back comforting as they marched toward the back of the train. A hundred thoughts raced through her mind. Who were these men? Why did they choose Barrett and her? Surely they looked like the least-threatening couple on the train. If they killed her, what would happen to Anne-Marie and Amelia? They would never know what had become of her. She blinked back the hot tears that stung her eyes. This was awful.

When they stepped out onto the platform, they saw a third masked man waiting astride

172

his horse and holding the reins to three others.

"You and your woman mount up," the leader told Barrett.

Abigail glanced up at Barrett. He nodded at her, silently urging her to comply. Lifting her skirt slightly, she made her way slowly down the uneven grade.

"If you're a praying woman, I'd start now," Barrett said quietly. He boosted her into the saddle and then mounted behind. "Above all, stay calm and do what they say."

"I'm frightened."

"So am I."

The train was moving again. Abigail spotted Wanila's face pressed to the window, gawking at the scene playing out before her. Abigail tried to take comfort in the knowledge that at least someone would know they'd been taken captive, not that it would do them any good. No one knew who they were. They'd introduced themselves as Mr. and Mrs. Levi Howard, a Quaker couple on their way home from visiting family in Texas.

The three men lowered their masks and kicked their horses into a gallop. The leader was a despicable-looking animal, lean and hungry in appearance. Wind whipped back his long brown shaggy hair, and his eyes were black and unreadable.

The other two men didn't look much better. Abigail wondered if they were brothers or if they looked alike because they all were dirty and had the same belligerent manner. Everything about the men was worn and faded, but their gear was neat and their horses showed good care. Still, their faces lent no clue as to who they were or why they'd taken her and Barrett captive, nor did it help allay her fears of what they planned to do to them.

The party rode hard for over an hour. The outlaws, one riding ahead, two behind, kept quiet. The men's grim expressions revealed nothing as they preserved a strained silence.

When Barrett would allow their horse to fall back, one of the men would move up alongside them, his dark look warning Barrett to keep pace.

During a brief rest stop, Barrett was allowed to escort Abigail into the underbrush under the pretext of her needing privacy, but the men's guns remained trained on them.

"What could they possibly want with us?" Abigail agonized when they disappeared into the heavy thicket.

"We'll find out soon enough."

"You don't think they know who you

are . . ."

"No."

She shivered.

"Keep those papers well hidden."

"I will. I'll do all I can to protect them, but the situation could easily get out of hand."

His features sobered. "It goes against my grain to put you in danger like this. Give me the documents —"

"No. I don't mind danger."

Taking her by the shoulders, he turned her to face him, his eyes grave now. "Listen to me closely. When we get to where they're taking us, I'll distract them long enough for you to get away. Take one of the horses and ride like the wind. It shouldn't take more than a couple of days for you to reach Shreveport. Go directly to Kirby Smith — no one else. Ask around. Someone will show you where he's camped. Do you understand?"

She nodded, for the first time fully aware of the danger they faced.

"Can I trust you to do this, Abigail?" The gravity in his eyes once again told her how important it was that the papers reach their destination.

She nodded, her pulse hammering in her throat. She prayed that it wouldn't come to that, but if it did, she'd get the papers to Smith — one way or another.

"You two. Get out here!" one of the outlaws shouted.

"Barrett . . ." It was the first time she had called him by his given name, and strangely enough, she liked the sound.

"Yes?"

"If it turns out the other way — you know, if you should get away and I don't, will you tell my sisters —" She broke mid-sentence, powerless to face the prospect of never seeing Amelia or Anne-Marie again. "Will you make sure my sisters know what happened to me?"

He reached for her hand and held it for a moment. Their eyes met. There was no longer any animosity, just a mutual need to offer comfort. "That's not going to happen."

"I know, but if it should . . ."

He squeezed her hand reassuringly. "If it does, I'll personally inform your sisters of your tragic demise." Giving a small smile, she bit her lip to keep it from quivering as they walked from behind the bushes and mounted the horse once again.

It was late afternoon before the riders reined up. When Abigail saw the deserted-looking shack, she glanced apprehensively at Barrett. There wasn't a sign of life anywhere. They had ridden for hours and not seen another soul.

The leader reined in and quickly dismounted. The other two men followed suit, gesturing for Barrett and Abigail to do the same.

The boss bounded up the set of rickety steps, kicked the cabin door open, and entered. The two other men walked behind Barrett and Abigail, nudging them up the steps and into the overheated room with the barrels of their guns.

Abigail's eyes gradually adjusted to the cabin's dim interior and she saw that it was little more than a pit, hardly fit for pigs. The incredibly dingy room had a table and chairs, a broken cabinet, and a crude fireplace fashioned against the south wall. A wooden baby crib sat beside the fireplace and Abigail could see an infant sleeping there who looked to be no more than a year old. To the left was a closed door, which Abigail assumed was a bedroom.

The leader strode to the closed door and opened it a crack, peering inside the dim interior.

"Hattie Mae?"

The tenderness that suddenly lit his voice shocked Abigail.

"Luke? Luke, is that you?" a woman's

voice returned.

Abigail glanced at Barrett, whose face remained expressionless.

"It's me, honey. I got us some help."

Luke turned, his black eyes pinned to Abigail. "You've gotta help my woman."

Leaning forward, Abigail tried to see around him into the bedroom. "What's wrong with her?"

"She's been sickly the past few days. Been coughin' real hard. The baby's startin' to come and it ain't time yet."

Abigail's eyes moved to the child sleeping peacefully in the crib and then, quizzically, back to Luke.

"The new baby," Luke said shortly. "It ain't supposed to get here for another three months, but it's actin' like it's comin' anyways."

Abigail wilted with relief. "This is why you brought us here?" Luke, assuming that she was a Quaker, must have reasoned that she would know about these things. Gripping fear overcame her initial relief. She couldn't tell him she wasn't a Quaker without explaining why she and Barrett were dressed as such.

She glanced at Barrett, debating whether or not to tattle on him. If she told this nasty-looking man that Barrett was a spy, then he

178

might help her get to Mercy Flats . . .

Her gaze slid to Barrett and then back to her kidnapper. No. She couldn't do that to Barrett. "I don't know anything about delivering a baby," she confessed.

Luke's hand moved to his holster, and his eyes narrowed. "All females know about those things."

"No. I'm telling the truth," Abigail promised. "I don't know anything about delivering babies. I don't know anything about babies, period." The closest she'd been to a baby were the occasional foundlings left on the mission doorstep, and there hadn't been one of those in years.

Luke frowned. "You're foolin' me. You're a female, ain't ya?"

"Yes, but I've never given birth and I've never been around anyone who has," she assured him.

Calmly stepping behind Barrett, Luke rested the gun barrel at the base of the captain's neck. "Your man don't have much to say, but I'd shore bet you wouldn't want to have to bury him afore you learned something, now would you, Quaker lady?"

Barrett glanced at Abigail as Luke pressed the gun tighter against his neck.

Meeting his distraught gaze, her answer came easy. "What do you want me to do?"

The captain was growing on her; she couldn't just let him die. Who would get her to Mercy Flats then?

"I don't rightly know — that'll be for you to decide." Luke tapped the gun prophetically against Barrett's temple.

"You'll have to give me a moment." She started to pace, knowing that she was prolonging Barrett's agony. It was the least she could do to pay him back for all the misery he'd caused her.

"You're wasting time, Quaker lady. My woman's not gittin' any better."

She racked her brain. Hot water. Sheets — clean sheets — not likely to be found in this cabin. She'd heard talk in passing that these items were essential to birthing.

"Abigail," Barrett said quietly. The minutes were ticking past. "You could start by praying for Hattie Mae."

"Yes, I could pray for Hattie Mae," she complied. "I could pray extra hard."

Luke nodded. "I ain't a religious man, but whatever it takes to make my woman well."

"Luke!" Hattie Mae's agonized screams shattered the silence and Luke shoved Barrett toward the bedroom doorway.

Dragging her feet, Abigail entered the dim bedroom behind the men. The sisters at the mission had meticulously avoided mentioning anything about "birthing babies." Luke believed that a Quaker wife must know something about midwifery, but since Abigail wasn't a Quaker, she was as ignorant as a rock about such things. Anything could happen to the new mother — and if the worst happened, Luke would hold her responsible.

She heard the outlaw's ominous voice affirming her pessimism from behind her. "Just so's you don't get any funny notions, I'll keep your man with me. If anythin' happens to Hattie Mae or th' baby, well . . ."

The outcome was implied. Abigail clearly understood the silent threat. *God help us all.* She approached the bed where a young woman was writhing in agony.

If the men were expecting her to save Hattie Mae, they were all in for a big disappointment.

"Sit." Luke gestured for Barrett to take a chair at the kitchen table. Abigail had ordered the men out of the sickroom. "Spook, you and Roily might jest as well make yoreselves comfortable," he told his two friends. "This here could take awhiles."

The two outlaws stripped off their hats and hung them on a peg beside the cookstove. They drew two more chairs up to the table and sat down. Luke took a bottle of cheap whiskey out of the cabinet and set the bottle in the middle of the table.

Roily reached inside his coat pocket, dug out a pack of cards, and began shuffling the deck while Spook lit the lamp and turned up the wick.

It wasn't long before the three men were absorbed in a game of cutthroat.

Barrett noticed an odd-sounding thump at the front door. When the thump persisted, Luke, still sorting his hand, pushed back from the table and went to unlatch the door allowing a skinny, liver-colored hound to sidle into the room. The dog yawned widely, dropped in front of the fireplace, and shut its eyes.

"Hattie Mae don't like for the dog to be in the house," Spook reminded Luke.

"What Hattie Mae don't know ain't gonna hurt her," Luke mused absently. He poured three glasses of whiskey and then glanced questioningly at Barrett. "Don't guess you folks imbibe?"

Barrett shook his head negatively.

"Didn't figure so."

Barrett's gaze focused on the door to the bedroom as the three men played a couple of hands. There was no sign of Abigail. He could hardly imagine what she was doing in there. Now was probably the one and only time she'd told the truth: She didn't know how to deliver a baby. But nature had a way of taking command. If the baby was coming, it wouldn't be stopped. All she'd have to do was catch the infant and cut the cord.

His gaze switched to the three outlaws. Apparently the men played poker together often. The cards were dispensed about as fast as shared drinks from the bottle of whiskey.

"Got a run a' luck there, Roily." Luke sat back, taking a swig from his glass when Hattie Mae's brother dragged in another pot. Tossing down the last of the liquor, he poured more.

"Lady Luck always did like me," Roily bragged.

"A mite too well," Spook muttered. "My highest card the last two hands has been a ten."

Luke's eyebrows raised a fraction. "You complainin'?"

"Nah, just deal."

Luke glanced toward the bedroom. Everything had been quiet for some time now. "Wonder what's going on in there?"

"Don't know. At least Hattie ain't screaming no more," Roily noted.

"Yeah, noticed that."

The dog lifted his head, giving a wide, whiny yawn.

"You'd better git that dog outta here afore Hattie hears it," Spook warned Luke a second time. "She don't like that animal."

Luke dealt another hand.

Roily was on a hot streak, winning the next two consecutive hands. Luke's features grew tenser when Roily continued to rake in the pile of money from the center of the table. Luke seemed to take the losses in stride, but his foot rhythmically twitched against the leg of the chair, making Barrett uneasy.

Barrett's eyes kept moving back to the bedroom door, wondering what was taking so long. The almost eerie silence coming from the bedroom was getting on his nerves.

The hound got to his feet and moseyed over to the table.

"Git!" Spook said sharply when the hound licked one of his boots.

Roily grinned. "One thing ole Spook cain't stand is a dog a lickin' his boots. Makes him sick."

When the hound persisted in nosing around his feet, Spook's left boot shot out and sent the animal flying across the floor.

Yelping, the dog limped back to the fire and lay down on the dirty rug.

"Don't kick my dog, Spook." Reaching for the liquor bottle, Luke refilled his glass.

"He ain't your dog. He's a stray come wanderin' around Hattie Mae, and she was silly enough to feed him."

Luke's eyes narrowed on Hattie's brother. "Don't give a hoot how I got him. He's mine, and I don't want you a-kickin' him."

Spook, having swallowed his share from the bottle, held firm. "Well now, the way I see it, if the dog licks my boots, it's gonna get kicked, no matter who it belongs to — and it sure ain't you, Luke. That dog don't belong to nobody."

"I feed her."

"Don't make her your'n."

"Makes her more mine than yours." Luke called the dog back over to the table and kicked it himself.

Yelping, the dog whipped back to the fire and lay down, shooting a desperate look at both men.

The matter was getting out of hand. "Gentlemen," said Barrett with a small cough. The men had had too much to drink and they were getting abusive. "Why don't I let the dog out?"

Luke fixed his eyes belligerently on Barrett. "You jest stay where you are, Quaker man. It's my dog and if 'n I want him to go outside, I'll take him outside."

"Ain't your dog, Luke," Spook said.

Luke's eyes turned steely. "Spook, you're steppin' on my nerves now. It's my dog."

"Gentlemen," Barrett warned.

"Spook, let it pass," Roily said. "Don't matter whose dog it is. Deal the cards."

"No." Spook laid his hands on the table, his jaw fixed obstinately. "Ain't his dog and I ain't gonna say it is."

Luke sprang to his feet and grabbed the whiskey bottle, sending the cards and money scattering across the room as he broke the bottle across the table. "Now looka here! It's *my* hound!"

"Ain't neither!" Spook jumped up, jerking his revolver free of his holster.

Whether he intended to shoot Luke or the dog, Barrett was never certain. But before he could stop the fight, Luke had whipped out his gun. Scrambling out of his chair, Barrett stumbled over the dog that was rushing to get out of the way. The hound darted under the table and cowered.

A shot rang out, the explosion echoing throughout the cabin. Spook slumped over the table and a splash of bright red spread across his chest.

Jumping to his feet, Roily pulled his gun.

"Luke! You got no call to shoot Spook over a dog!"

A second shot rang out and Barrett dove under the table to join the dog for cover.

Luke fell to the floor, his gun still smoking in his hand. A second later, a third shot sounded. The bullet Luke had shot with his dying breath caught Roily in the chest. Dropping to his knees, the outlaw pitched forward and sprawled face-first on the floor. Lifeless eyes met Barrett.

Easing from beneath the table, Barrett slowly got to his feet, dumbfounded.

Luke, Spook, and Roily lay on the floor, dead as doornails.

He stared at the carnage, shaking his head. If this wasn't a fine mess.

FOURTEEN

The bedroom door flew open. Abigail stood in the doorway, round-eyed. "I heard gunshots," she said over the screams of the baby.

Barrett shook his head. "Well, they shot one another."

She stared back at him vacantly. "Shot one another?"

He nodded, staring at the three bodies.

"Over what?"

"The dog."

Abigail found the information impossible to believe until her eyes located the three men sprawled haphazardly on the floor. "All three of them?"

"It's the craziest thing I've ever seen. One minute they were playing cards, and the next minute they jumped up and shot one another."

Another wail punctuated their conversation.

"Oh shoot," Barrett murmured. "I don't

know what to do about that child." The baby pulled itself up in the crib, its face red and streaked with tears.

"He wants you to pick him up," said Abigail.

"Shoot," Barrett muttered again. Turning to Abigail, he asked, "Hattie Mae?"

Abigail shook her head. "Neither she or the baby made it."

"I'm sorry to hear that."

"Not five minutes after I went into the room," Abigail confessed. "I've been sitting in there wondering how to tell Luke."

Her eyes shifted to Luke's lifeless form sprawled next to the table. "Boy, this just gets worse, huh?"

Barrett glanced at the child, and then back to Abigail. "Let's get out of here. What do we do about it?" he asked, pointing to the baby.

Abigail stepped to the crib and lifted the child out, trying to hush him. "There, there, baby. You must be hungry." She turned with the child in her arms. "He's hungry, Barrett. What do we feed him?"

"Milk? I don't know anything about babies."

"Yes, milk. And he'll need a clean cloth nappy." Abigail searched for the items and Barrett paced the small cabin.

"Well, if this isn't a fine state," he finally said. "Now we have an infant and four folks to bury. On top of that, it's still a two days' ride to Shreveport, which means if I'm going to reach Smith in time, we should be leaving right now."

"It's our Christian duty to bury them," Abigail unpinned the baby's soiled nappy. "Barrett!"

He whirled. "What?"

"Look!"

Stepping across the room, he peered over her shoulder. "What?"

"It's a boy."

Once he stopped screaming, the child was adorable. Abigail decided he couldn't be much older than a year. He had a bright thatch of red hair and big blue eyes. He grinned, showing off his two bottom and two upper teeth. He was about the cutest thing she'd ever seen — and the tiniest. Crooking her finger, she laughed when he grasped onto it, trying to wedge it into his mouth.

"I'll see if there's a shovel around." Barrett walked to the door and paused with his hand on the knob. "It'll take me awhile to get them all disposed of."

"Want me to help?"

"No." His gaze focused dispiritedly on the baby. "It'll be morning before we can travel. You figure out what to do with him."

She turned back to the baby and it suddenly occurred to her that both his mother and father were gone. "Oh, Barrett, what *will* we do with him?"

Shaking his head, he opened the door. "I'm out of answers; I have been for the past three days."

Five horses, a raw-boned cow, and a few scraggly chickens in the barn, but no shovel. After searching for over an hour Barrett hadn't come up with anything but a fork with a missing prong. The best he could do was lay out the bodies and cover them with straw. When he walked back to the cabin, thunder rolled in the distance. *Wonderful.* To top off the day, he'd have to wade through mud up to his ankles.

It took awhile to drag Luke, Roily, and Spook to a small clearing behind the barn. He gently carried Hattie and the newborn, laying mother and child in a soft mound of fresh hay. At first glance, the ground behind the barn appeared to be the best place to lay them to rest.

The work didn't take long. Finally, he studied the results of his efforts and then bowed his head.

"God, I'm not much good at eulogies — You know that from the battlefields — but I'd be much obliged if You'd have mercy on these souls."

Abigail stepped to the front door to open it and look out. Barrett was beside the barn, standing ankle-deep in mud. She began to feel sorry for him. It occurred to her that he hadn't asked for trouble; he had just been trying to do a good thing when he rescued her. She had to wonder how much simpler his life would have been if he had ridden away that day without coming to her aid.

No doubt he'd questioned that judgment more than once.

She leaned against the door frame, conscious of the strange feelings that he provoked deep within her heart. He'd stirred warmth and caring in her lately . . . and she wasn't sure what to do about it.

Barrett Drake was an attractive man — there was no denying that. Though their situation was anything but romantic, something about him energized her. She'd heard women giggle about being drawn to a certain man but she'd always laughed and said there wasn't a man alive who could make her feel anything but indifference.

Now, standing here watching Barrett pray in the growing twilight, she was curious. What was Captain Drake really like? A charming man or caustic enemy?

Closing the door, she tiptoed over to check on the baby. He was asleep, his little bottom curled up in the air adorably. Poor child. Both mother and father gone. Like her, the child was an orphan now. Though she barely remembered her folks she knew well the ache in her heart when someone mentioned they had both a mother and father. Deep down, she suspected that would be a blessing.

She reached for the lantern, lit it, and then carried it to the barn.

"Hello."

Grunting, Barrett stepped away from the makeshift grave site. "Hello."

"I baked a pan of corn bread. There was a pot of beans on the stove, so you can eat anytime you want." She peered inside the barn and then looked away.

"I'll be up in a few minutes. Better go back to the house. Another storm's brewing." Snowclouds swirled in the distance. She turned and started back to the cabin.

Barrett fed the stock as the wind picked up. He trudged slowly back to the cabin, oblivious of the storm going on around and inside of him. What was he supposed to do with Abigail and a baby? How could he take care of them and deliver the papers in time?

Entering the cabin's warmth, he found Abigail asleep on a pallet in front of the fireplace. The baby lay on his stomach, curled up against her.

He moved to the fire to warm up, his stomach knotted from hunger, but he was too cold and too weary to eat. He reached for the thin blanket that she'd laid out for him and wrapped it around his shoulders. He returned to the fire to hang his wet clothes over the back of a chair to dry. He had to admit that Abigail had done well under the circumstances. The cabin was warm, the dishes were washed, and the infant was sound asleep.

His eyes reluctantly returned to the floor, where she and the baby lay sleeping. Her hair was loose, spread out across the pallet in a silky tangle. Exhaustion shadowed her features but she slept peacefully, her arm protectively cradling the small bundle beside her. He'd yet to figure out what made her tick. In the beginning, it hadn't mattered. He'd wanted free of her — still did, didn't he? His eyes rested on the bottle she'd fashioned — a simple contraption that the baby could suckle. The device took longer to appease the appetite but it would work. His gaze returned to the young woman cradling the babe.

For one insane moment, he wanted to hold her. The desire was so intense that it startled him. Sinking onto the pallet, he stretched out beside her, studying her in the firelight. She looked so very young. She *was* young, Barrett realized. Ten years his junior or more. A smile touched the corners of his mouth as he gently reached out to touch a strand of her hair. Closing his eyes, he brought the silk to his nose, breathing its scent.

She was beautiful, all right. Too beautiful.

The baby awakened sometime during the night. Abigail fumbled and pulled the baby to her, tenderly stroking its soft cheek.

Barrett stirred, listening to her soothe the child. "You're already getting attached."

"Nonsense." She lifted the infant to her chest and patted his back. "Go back to sleep."

The snow outside had turned to rain, by the sound of it on the roof, but the thick bed of coals in the fireplace kept the room dry and comfortable.

"Did you get everything — taken care of?" she murmured. She had been so exhausted she hadn't heard him come in from the barn.

"I did."

"Did you eat anything?"

"Too tired," he murmured, rolling to his side and dozing off again.

Twice more before dawn, the baby woke and cried for his mother. Each time it took Abigail longer to quiet the infant. By morning, both she and Barrett were exhausted and the baby's fretting had turned constant.

When it was finally daylight, Barrett got up and sat at the kitchen table as Abigail rocked the fussy infant. Her long hair hung limp around her face and her shoulders slumped with weariness. For the first time, her spirit seemed shaken.

She rocked slowly, back and forth, back and forth; patting the baby's back, blinking back tears of frustration. She didn't know what to do. She had no notion of how to calm an infant.

"You want me to rock him?"

"I don't think he'd let you," she returned wearily.

"He's hungry, and he wants his mother. Hattie Mae undoubtedly nursed him. He's barely getting enough to eat through that milk soak rag."

Sighing, she whispered, "I'll soak the cloth again."

"I'll get fresh milk."

The cow eyed Barrett balefully when he entered the barn. Bending over, he ran a hand down her side. Her udder was full, but it had been many years since he'd milked stock. As a child, he entered the warm barn before daylight and milked several head before sunup.

He took a bucket off a nail and scooted the stool closer with the toe of his boot and then spoke to her in reassuring tones. "All right, girl. I'll be gentle with you if you'll be gentle with me."

The heifer glanced over her back.

Tucking his head into her flank, he grasped two teats and pulled.

The cow jumped, knocking the bucket aside.

Barrett moved the stool, positioned the bucket again, and grasped two teats.

The animal shifted and he shadowed her movements around the stall, determined to gain the upper hand.

Trapped against the side of the stall, the cow finally settled down. Within a few minutes, Barrett had a steady stream of milk flowing into the pail.

As he was stripping the last teat, the cow's

tail suddenly whipped to one side, catching him on the cheek with a ball of matted cockleburs. His cheek stung like fire and he grabbed for the bucket before it tipped over. "Steady, Bossy," he murmured.

The heifer steadied, and Barrett finished up. Relieved, he had just stood up when the cow calmly lifted her hoof and stomped the bucket, toppling it onto its side. Half of the milk spilled out of the bucket onto the ground before Barrett managed to grab it.

"This had better be enough," he told Abigail when he stepped into the cabin with what was left of the milk a few minutes later. "I'm not waltzing with that heifer again."

Abigail viewed the offering with mild curiosity. "You've been out there an awfully long time to have come up with no more milk than that."

Setting a plate of biscuits on the table, she motioned for him to sit down. "I found a can of sorghum. It's almost turned to sugar, but it still tastes good."

He sat down at the table, grateful for anything that would make his stomach cease its rumbling.

The baby was still fussy, angrily waving his fists in the air.

She pulled the rocking chair closer to the

table and put the child on her lap, dipping the end of a cloth into the bucket of milk. When she offered the cloth to the baby, his mouth puckered tight. Gradually, she coaxed his mouth open with a little pressure on his lower lip and he managed to get a taste of the milk.

Smacking his lips, the baby hungrily suckled the cloth.

Over the next hour, Abigail coaxed nourishment into the child so that he was content enough to fall asleep. For the first time in hours, the cabin was blissfully quiet. Outside, rain fell and thunder rumbled in the distance.

Barrett ate six of the twelve biscuits and drank two cups of milk as he stared through the dirty windowpane. He had exactly three days to deliver the messages.

"I'll hold the baby so you can eat," he told her when he'd swallowed the last of his meal.

Abigail transferred the tiny sleeping bundle into his arms, smiling her gratitude.

Awkwardly, Barrett adjusted the child in the crook of his arm and settled into the rocking chair. Gazing at the boy's shock of fiery red hair, he smiled. "Kinda cute, isn't he?"

Abigail smiled and slathered sorghum

between two fat biscuits.

"Abigail?"

"Yes?"

He met her gaze. "Don't get too attached to the boy."

She smiled away his concern. "I don't know where you'd get an idea like that. Don't worry. I won't."

He studied the child's chubby features. "It'd be easy to do," he admitted. "Real easy."

"I've never given thought to babies or husbands, if you're worried."

By the time she'd finished her third biscuit, Abigail's eyes were heavy. "I've been thinking about what we should do with him," she said sleepily.

"Come up with anything?"

"He must have kin, but I wouldn't begin to know where to find them."

"I've thought of that. The shack is isolated."

She pushed her plate aside, folded her arms on the table, and rested her head atop them. "Since we don't have time to look for relatives, we'll leave the boy at a mission. If the baby does have kin, they'll surely make an attempt to find them. We'll leave a note here explaining what happened and what we plan to do with the child. If we can find a mission, I'm certain that the sisters will take good care of him." She glanced up.

He was smiling, the baby lying snugly against the width of his chest.

FIFTEEN

A clap of thunder shook the shanty. The reverberating boom repeated over the hillsides. Abigail focused on the small windowpane. Rain fell in torrents, and the wind savagely battered the tops of the trees.

A flash of lightning split the sky, followed by another thunderous blast. The sound vibrated the floor of the cabin as Barrett got up and carried the baby to the crib. The child momentarily roused and whimpered but he gently patted its back until he drifted to sleep.

Abigail rose from the table and began to round up the baby's articles in preparation for leaving. "I'll only be a minute. The baby will need his belongings at the orphanage."

Barrett moved to the window and looked out, his eyes grave as he viewed the worsening weather. "We can't take the child out in this storm."

Abigail moved about the room, packing

essentials into a pillowcase she'd found. "It'll let up before long." But when the storm continued to rage with no end in sight, hope began to fade. Hours later, they were still sitting at the table, waiting.

She watched Barrett from the corner of her eye, concerned about the grave set of his features. Reaching over, she rested her hand on the sleeve of his shirt. "Don't worry; it has to let up. Once it does, we'll ride hard and make good time. We'll meet your deadline."

"I don't know, Abigail." Barrett studied the baby, whose blue eyes stared innocently back at him as he stuffed bits of food into his mouth. "It looks like it's set in for the day."

The minutes ticked slowly by. He paced the shanty floor, looking out the window as the storm raged on. The roof was leaking in a dozen places, and they'd set cups and buckets here and there to catch the drips.

By mid-morning, he put on his heavy coat. "I'll be back shortly. I'm going to poke around and see if anyone in the area is able to shed light on Hattie or Luke's relatives."

Abigail watched him go with a tight knot forming in the pit of her stomach. She couldn't help but wonder if he'd be back. Had he made a decision to ride on without her? He knew enough details about the messages to alert Smith to the pending attack, even without the papers.

He was gone for over an hour, during which she grew more and more frantic. When she heard the horse trot up, she went weak with relief. Smiling at the baby, she said softly, "See, I told you he'd be back."

"Have any luck?" she asked when he came into the cabin. Water streamed from the hem of his slicker.

Shaking his head, he strode to the fire to warm his hands. "There are no neighbors."

"Did you ride far?"

"Far enough. These folks lived in isolation. Who knows where their kin might be found?"

When night fell, the couple sat at the kitchen table, listening to the storm rage. Rain lashed the windowpane and thunder and lightning streaked the sky with disheartening regularity.

Barrett reached for the milk bucket, his features fixed in resolve. "I'll be back shortly."

In spite of herself, Abigail let a giggle escape.

"What is it?"

"Nothing. Just the sight of you standing there, so serious. It struck me as funny."

He stared at her. "It's good to know that you can laugh."

"I've laughed before," she said, defensive.

"I know — but usually at me."

She pictured the little sensitive shoe salesman and grinned. Drake was far from sensitive in most areas, but he was confident and more important, steadfast. She hadn't realized how she admired the trait until now. They smiled, and their morbid set of circumstances suddenly held more promise.

"Well, guess I'd better get the milk." He glanced at the baby. "He'll be hungry soon."

"I'm sorry you have to get wet. I can . . ."

"I'll go. You're better with the child."

She glanced away, embarrassed. "I'd help if I could."

"I want you here, with the baby."

Abigail turned to thoughts of dinner. She felt uneasy about being in another woman's kitchen. There were signs of Hattie everywhere. Her bonnet hung on the peg; her shoes were in the corner by the fireplace; her hairbrush was lying beside the washstand. No one would ever guess that her remains were at rest beside the shed, neatly covered with hay.

On the way back from the barn, Barrett paused and sniffed the air. *Drake, you're los-*

ing your grip. You're so hungry you're smelling food where there isn't any. He could have sworn he smelled chicken frying.

When he stepped inside the cabin he stopped and stared at the domestic sight before him. The baby crawled on the floor, while Abigail bent over an iron skillet turning pieces of nicely browned chicken. The smell of biscuits wafted from the oven.

His gaze fixed on the sizzling meat. "Where did you get that?"

"Oh, I found a couple of old hens out by the barn. Since no one is going to be needing them anymore, and we need a solid meal, I decided to wring their necks. I used the last of the flour to coat the chicken and make a batch of biscuits. The meat could be a little tough — big birds are better boiled with dumplings — but . . ."

"I'll eat it if it's tough as a leather boot." Setting the pail of milk on the counter, he relished the mouth-watering smells drifting from the stove. "I can't remember when I last ate fried chicken."

She flashed a smile. "Dinner's almost ready. Better clean up."

While he washed, she heaped mounds of fried chicken on a plate. Taking the biscuits out of the oven, she called, "I realized that this was about as close as I've ever come to looking after a man."

"Yeah? Think you might take to married life?"

"Actually, my sisters will never believe it when I tell them, but this isn't so bad." She straightened, her cheeks rosy. "It's sort of nice." She paused a moment, considering. Hershall Digman hadn't been married, but she wasn't certain about Barrett Drake. Was there a Mrs. Drake waiting at home for her handsome captain? Her pulse quickened. It was clear he had a liking for children. She shook her head, unwilling to let her thoughts wander further.

"I don't know when I've ever smelled anything so good," he admitted when he pulled a chair up to the table.

"I didn't know I could fry a decent-tasting chicken," Abigail admitted as she set the baby on her lap. They began to eat, sharing a compatible silence as she absently tore off small bits of biscuit and fed the baby.

"Look, Barrett. He eats well for his age, don't you think?"

"He does all right," Barrett admitted, "though his table manners need work." The child had thrown a biscuit at Barrett twice.

"I wish I could have done something for Hattie Mae," Abigail mused.

"What went wrong, exactly?"

"I'm not sure. Her forehead felt very hot to the touch, and she was coughing real bad."

"Did she say anything about the husband or child?"

Abigail thought back to the last moments of Hattie's life, and she slowly shook her head. "No. She just rambled on about nothing, mostly. Nothing I could understand."

Reaching for another piece of cornbread, Barrett frowned. "Luke mentioned that she'd been sick for a few days."

"I remember at the orphanage, we were taught to pray for healing. Sister Agnes had a weakness in the joints. They pained her something awful. The sisters told us if we'd pray for her, she would get better, but I didn't believe it would help." A smile lit Abigail's eyes. "But her condition improved," she went on. "After my sisters and I prayed about all we could, she told us that she was better." She glanced at him. "Do you think prayer works?"

"It has for me. Many times on the battlefield — and often at other times when I needed Him." He paused, his knife in midair. "Never met an atheist on a battlefield."

"Sometimes I wonder. I mean, I prayed for Hattie, and she and the baby still died."

"We can't explain His ways. I just know they're not like ours."

Thunder continued to rumble in the distance as Abigail began to clear the table. She peered to the north, silently wishing that it would rain for a week and she could stay in the little cabin with Barrett and the baby. But then . . . she didn't want him to miss his deadline. The papers were important. There seemed no end to the bitter struggle, but maybe those papers could help. "Still raining," she reported. "If we ride hard tomorrow, we can be in Shreveport by late Friday night."

He shook his head, clearly wary of her prediction. "If I don't get those papers there . . ."

"You will," she promised. "If the weather hasn't cleared by daybreak, we'll leave anyway. I'll wrap the baby tightly and we can just get soaked. Clothing will dry."

"How can we travel with a baby? It was hard enough when it was just you and me."

"The baby won't melt." Handing the child another bite of bread, she smiled when he stuffed it in his mouth hungrily. "He's a good boy."

"Good boy or not, we can't have him coming down with pneumonia."

Dropping back to her chair, she broached

the subject she'd been dreading the most. "About finding a foundling home and leaving the child there . . ."

"It's sensible," said Barrett. "We can't take him with us, and we don't know if Luke or Hattie Mae had family. I rode for miles this morning and I didn't see another cabin. I can't recall any orphanages this side of the line, but there could be something closer to Louisiana."

The baby threw his biscuit on the floor, and Abigail bent to pick it up.

Barrett grinned and stood. "Guess I'd better get a fresh bucket of water for washing up."

She glanced up to see his eyes twinkling devilishly. There it was again — that little twitch in the pit of her stomach. "Would you like extra water for a bath?" he asked. "I spotted a tub hanging in the barn. I can fetch it while I'm out. I'll take the baby and wait outside while you bathe."

"A bath would be sheer heaven." She focused on the dirty dishes, afraid to look up for fear he'd see the color rising to her face. No man had ever embarrassed Abigail McDougal, but here Barrett Drake offered to bring her a simple bucket of water . . . and he had her blushing like a schoolgirl!

When the door closed she hurriedly wiped

the table and swept the floor. By the pile of dirt she came up with, it was evident that Hattie hadn't swept much — or ever. The baby played around her feet, banging a pan and a lid together.

She paused to stare. Tiny fingers, tiny toes, and the tiniest hands she'd ever seen.

"You'll be taken care of," she promised when she picked the child up and hugged him. "Captain Drake and I will see to that."

The door to the cabin swung open and Barrett came in dragging a galvanized washtub. "Here you go, my lady," he said. He dragged the bathing apparatus across the floor and set it in front of the fire.

"A bath! I hadn't dare hope for such luxury. Thank you!"

"Thank you? Abigail McDougal telling a man *thank you*?" He grinned. "When you're through I believe I'll have me a good soak too." His eyes met hers briefly, and then quickly moved away. "I'll get the water now."

Abigail banked the fire to heat the stove and warm up the water. After completing several trips, Barrett had the tub half-full.

"You go first. The baby and I will wait on the porch," he said.

"He's fine; he can stay." They focused on the infant, who sat in his crib chewing on a rag doll. "Unless you just want to hold him?" she offered.

"No that's all right."

When the door closed behind him, she whirled to search for soap in the boxes of odds and ends stacked in the corners of the cabin. She rummaged for over five minutes before she finally found a piece.

She stepped out of her clothing and sank into the water up to her chin. Closing her eyes, she savored the feel of the steaming warmth. She knew she shouldn't dally, that Barrett was waiting outside the door, but she couldn't remember when she'd enjoyed a tub of hot water more. Or a certain person's company. Was this the Abigail McDougal who'd had no regard for men a scant few days ago?

She lingered for over fifteen minutes before she made herself climb out. Reaching for the large blanket that she'd laid across the back of a chair, she wrapped it around her body and tucked the ends snugly against her chest.

"Barrett?" she called.

"Yes?"

"I'll only be a moment longer. I'd like to wash my clothing."

"Take your time."

Smiling, she quickly washed out her dress and petticoats and hung them to dry on a line in front of the fire. Not so long ago she wouldn't have cared about her appearance around him but something had changed. She wasn't sure why, but she'd developed respect for him. Even though the porch roof protected him from the rain, she'd heard him sneeze twice that day and the last thing she wanted was for him to catch a chill because of her.

Still wrapped snugly, she hurried to the front door. "You can come in now!" When she found that he wasn't on the porch, she closed the door and walked slowly back to the fire. The baby babbled to her, and she unthinkingly returned his meaningless gurgle. "He's around somewhere. Don't worry."

She wasn't sure that she appreciated this sudden dependence upon him; she was beginning to feel almost as secure with Barrett Drake as she did with Amelia and Anne-Marie.

Easing to the floor in front of the fire, she combed her hair with her fingers and exchanged gibberish with the baby. And that was how Barrett found her when he returned to the cabin.

Stepping into the room, he paused, surprised at the transformation. Golden hair spilled down her back. His breath caught in his throat. Had he ever seen a woman so lovely? When he closed the door behind him, she glanced up in alarm.

"Sorry. I was getting cold out there."

"I'm finished. I called, but you didn't answer."

"I'd walked down to the barn."

She smiled at him. "There's fresh water boiling on the stove. The baby's almost asleep, so I'll sit on the porch while you have your bath."

"No need to do that. I can string a blanket for privacy," he said crisply.

"I don't mind — no need to go to all that work. We'll be leaving in the morning." She absently brushed her fingers through her drying hair. The gesture drew his eyes when he stepped to the stove. Hefting the heavy pan, he poured additional water in the tub. *Keep your eyes and mind on your business, Drake.*

"Ever had a beau, Abigail?" Unless his eyesight was going, that was color he saw in her cheeks. He seemed to be making her blush a lot lately.

She glanced up. "No."

"Ever want one?"

"No."

"No? Why not? You're a pretty young

woman. You've surely had your share of suitors." Steam rose from the second bucket of hot water he poured into the tub.

She visibly shuddered. "I never wanted one."

Chuckling, he set the buckets aside. "I thought all women wanted a husband and family."

"Not all women. Not me. I don't need a man in my life. I have my sisters. That's enough."

"Ah, but your sisters can't take the place of a man. Someone to grow old with, to share your life — your dreams."

"My sisters do that. Once we reunite life will go on as usual. My life is very happy. I don't need what other women want." Her gaze focused on the baby.

"How do you know? Have you ever *wanted* a beau?"

She bristled, drawing up straighter. "I thought you wanted a bath."

"Answer the question."

"No, I haven't wanted a beau."

"I think you might have." Her air of innocence was comical, despite the bravado she wore on her sleeve like a red flag of challenge. Barrett strongly sensed that Abigail McDougal would be a good woman for the right man — a spirited man, one who wasn't afraid to take on challenge. For an unbidden moment, he compared her to Ramona: the flash of her smile, a turn of phrase, a certain look in her eye . . .

But right now, there was nothing about her that reminded him of his wife. Ramona wouldn't have cared for the child; she would have expected Barrett to care for it. Ramona took; she never gave. She expected; she never asked. And she didn't have the logic to try to bluff her way out of a subject the way Abigail was trying to do without success.

"There, that should do it." He set the bucket aside. "I'll string that blanket. You can't sit on the porch in what you're wearing."

She turned an ear to the window where rain drummed against the pane. "You did, so I wouldn't mind."

"It'll only take me a minute to string a wire and you can stay where you are."

Sighing, she smiled. "The warmth does feel good." He set to work locating a thick blanket and stringing a rope across the room.

"We were in Texas one time," mused Abigail as Barrett worked, "and a man stopped and picked Amelia a whole bouquet of wild flowers because he'd overheard her say that she thought they were pretty. Anne-Marie and I looked on with envy because we'd never had a man do anything nice like that for us." Barrett disappeared behind the blanket and she huddled closer to the fire. "Then there was the time when we were picking peas," she said. "There was this man who owned a neighboring farm. Late one afternoon, out of a clear blue sky, he stopped by to bring some ears of corn to the mission but he gave the produce to Amelia. Just left Sister Agnes and Sister Lucille standing there in the pea patch looking at him as if he'd lost his wits." She laughed, her voice clear and pleasant. "Amelia just stood there in the patch, smiling real pretty at him. He smiled back, telling her how lovely she was and how it was too hot for anyone as pretty as she to be working in the sun. That made Anne-Marie angry. She said later that Amelia looked awful — all sweaty, with her hair hanging down in her face and her dress dirty from kneeling in the garden. And the sun was just as hot boiling down on us as it was Amelia."

"But none of you ended up with the man?"

"None of us liked men."

"And now?"

Seconds stretched before she answered.

"Barrett? May I ask a very personal question? By now you know I'm not the ordinary woman. The sisters taught us etiquette but I've never been very good about it. I say what's on my mind."

"Nothing wrong with curiosity as long as it doesn't hurt anyone."

"Are you married? I mean, Hershall wasn't . . . but you . . ."

"I was. Once. My wife's dead."

"I'm sorry. She must have been young."

"How old are you, Abigail? Seventeen? Eighteen?"

"Eighteen. How old are you?"

"Old enough to know better than to play question and answer games."

"You sound as though — perhaps you're still in mourning?"

"Mourning?" She detected the resentment in his tone. "No, I'm not in mourning."

"I think you are. You avoid her name. If you weren't grieving you would talk about her."

"Why would you say that? We haven't been sharing about our personal lives, have we?"

"No."

"Being the honest soul that I am I will say her name: Ramona. There. Ramona."

"I didn't mean to pry."

"Ramona." He was talking to himself now. "The lovely Ramona."

They fell silent as a log in the fire broke, sending a shower of sparks through the grate. She hadn't meant to offend him. The way he spat the name out meant that he couldn't have loved her without end. His tone held too much bitterness. Umbrage. She relaxed.

His voice drifted from behind the curtain. "You be honest with me. You never dreamt of having a husband and children some-day?"

"Never. My sisters and I made a pact when we were very young that we would never be apart. If one should marry then we risked the chance we would be separated."

"That's a pretty serious pact. You and your sisters are older now. You can say and do a lot of things when you're young. With three women as pretty as you and your sisters, some man is bound to come along one of these days and change one of your minds."

Her tone softened. "I'm older now, but the pact holds. We won't be separated — not by a man."

"Well, you never know," he murmured.

"What about you?" she asked.

"What about me?"

"Do you plan to marry again? Surely a

man your age wants a wife and children someday."

"A wife is the last thing I want," he said with a finality that sounded almost gruesome.

Later he emptied the tub and then leaned it against the porch before he came back inside. When he stepped into the room, he saw the tail of Abigail's blanket disappearing into Hattie and Luke's bedroom.

She'd mentioned over supper that she had stripped the linens and put two old blankets on the bed. "It won't be as nice as sleeping on fresh sheets, but it appeared that Hattie had nothing more, so the blankets will have to do. They look moderately clean, and the bed will be more comfortable than sleeping on the floor."

"You take the bed; I'll sleep on the floor. Again," he offered dryly when he stood at the bedroom door, watching her tunnel beneath the blankets. For once the baby was sleeping like a baby.

Her sleepy voice came to him through the rumpled covers. "That's most nice of you. Rest well."

"Yeah." He closed the door, picturing his back in the morning after a few hours on a wood floor. "You too."

SIXTEEN

"Shoo! Get, girl!"

Barrett whacked the cow across her rump when he turned her loose the next morning. Walking by the chicken coop, he opened the door and propped it open. The last few chickens would have to fend for themselves.

Selecting two of the best horses, he saddled them and then turned the others free. Rain had slowed to a drizzle, and thankfully all the snow had melted away, but the low-hanging clouds promised the storm wasn't over.

Inside the shanty, Abigail fed the baby by candlelight. The lantern spit the last drop of kerosene, and the can was empty. She'd washed two of Hattie's threadbare petticoats the day before and hung them to dry by the fire. While Barrett saw to the stock, she'd torn the material into diapers for the little boy. Extra blankets were bundled behind the saddles for use at night, but even with those, the dampness and chill would make traveling uncomfortable for the child.

Packing the last of the chicken and biscuits into the pillowcase, she paced the floor, holding the infant and trying to still his fretting.

Barrett returned, drenched to the bone. "I found a few pieces of oilcloth in the barn. We can use them." He removed a knife from the saddlebags and cut long slits to fashion makeshift hoods out of the cloths. He then slipped one over Abigail's head and a smaller one over the baby's.

"This should help, but by the way it looks, we're still going to get wet," he warned.

"I don't mind." She tucked the chicken and biscuits into the saddle-bags, yawning. "What time it is?"

"Early. Let's get going."

She stripped the blanket off the bed and wrapped it snugly around the baby. "We're ready."

The last twenty-four hours had been about as bad as they could get, but Barrett had yet to hear her complain. "Do you want the baby to ride with me?"

"I'll hold him awhile. He's cranky this morning." Smiling up at him, she said lightly, "Lead the way, Captain Drake. Your troops will follow."

When the horses rounded the barn, she turned, looking back over her shoulder at the four fresh piles of hay. "Barrett, could we stop for a moment?"

He followed her gaze and reined up. Taking the baby from her arms, he helped her down. They stood silently at the foot of Hattie's and Luke's graves.

Water stood in puddles on the stacks, making the sight even more dismal. Though she'd never known Hattie Mae, Abigail felt an indelible bond with the woman whose child had been entrusted to her care. She bowed her head. "Forgive them, Father, and have mercy," she said in a quiet voice. "Grant me wisdom to find the proper home for the son they've left behind."

A moment later, they remounted the horses and disappeared in the heavy mist.

"Don't worry, Hattie Mae," Abigail called softly over her shoulder. "I'll see that your baby is taken care of."

An unexplained sadness came over her when the old shanty slowly blended into the dense underbrush. The shack was filthy and most people would find it barely habitable, but those pitifully thin walls had given her a sense of belonging. In the few hours spent there with Barrett and the child, for the first time in her life she'd felt like she had a real home.

Huddling deeper inside the oilcloth, she and the baby rode on a roan behind Barrett's scarred bay. The sky, overcast and gray, lightened shortly after dawn.

Mid-morning, she realized they hadn't seen a sign of human life anywhere. There were no neighbors and they passed no other travelers on the road.

The baby cried out several times, and Barrett quietly soothed him. The boy was tucked in front of Barrett now, his oilcloth shielding him from the brunt of the rain. Noticing how good Barrett was with the baby, she wondered if he'd been raised in a large family.

Twice they stopped and he filled a cup with milk from his canteen. While he held the boy's head, Abigail tried to coax the child to drink from the cup, but he refused, twisting his head and screaming with rage. Knocking the cup away, he wailed.

Several cups of milk were lost, a precious commodity now that they no longer had the cow, but finally the child's hunger won out. Eventually he settled down and began to greedily gulp from the strange object.

"There's no use stopping at noon," Barrett called as the horses set off again down the muddy road. "The way this rain's coming down, I'd never get a fire going."

"We can eat as we ride," Abigail offered. "You don't mind?"

"I don't mind. Prefer a thick steak and potato but the chicken and biscuits don't sound bad."

By late afternoon Abigail was exhausted and the baby was howling again. Even worse, they hadn't passed a cow in miles. Kicking her horse into a trot, she moved up beside Barrett.

"We've got to find a cow."

"I know. I've been watching but I haven't seen anything that even resembles a cow."

"Then a goat. Anything." The baby's continual crying had her nerves near the breaking point.

"Are there more biscuits?"

Wearily wiping the rain out of her eyes, Abigail shook her head. "No. He ate the last one hours ago."

Barrett sneezed. The sound startled the baby and he wailed all the louder. She took the child from his arms and rode beside him for the next few miles, holding the baby close, trying to soothe his sobs as her eyes frantically scoured the countryside for cattle.

By dark, cries had faded to pitiful whimpers. The infant lay against Abigail's chest, drained and lifeless now. Her heart wrenched every time he looked up at her with those wide, questioning blue eyes.

Barrett's cough was more pronounced and she feared he was going to be sick before they found shelter for the night.

"Are you sure you're all right?" she called for at least the fifth time.

"Just a tickle in my throat," he assured her. "There's a barn up ahead," he noted when thunder rumbled.

"Thank goodness." If there was a barn, there might be a cow.

They reined up on the far side of the building and she held the horses while he crept around the structure to make sure it was empty. She flinched at the squeal of a protesting hinge, praying that no one heard it.

"We're in luck."

She jumped at the sound of Barrett's voice when he approached from behind. "The barn's empty, except for a heifer. Doesn't look like anyone's home. We'll have milk for the boy." He took the child from her and then helped her off the horse.

"Is it clean?"

"The hay's fresh. We'll feed the baby, get a few hours' sleep, and then be on the road before sunup."

Trailing him into the warmth of the barn, Abigail relished the dry, pungent heat. Barrett spread a blanket and lay the baby down as Abigail took off her makeshift rain gear and hung it on a nail. He stripped off his oilcloth and hung it beside hers. And then he set to work milking the cow.

The child drank two cups of milk as fast as Barrett could fill them. Once the hunger was temporarily appeased, he handed Abigail the cup. "This is all she'll give for now."

"We'll share it." The warm milk tasted so good Abigail could have gladly drunk every drop, but she made herself stop when the mug was half empty. Handing it back to Barrett, she smiled. "That'll hold me until morning."

He accepted the offering, his gaze lightly tracing her. There wasn't a dry thread on her. Water ran in rivulets off her hair and trickled down her cheeks. The dark circles beneath her eyes gave silent testimony to her remarkable courage. She'd sipped a half cup of milk for supper and acted as if it were pot roast and gravy. "I'm sorry," he said gently. "I wish I could make this easier on you and the child."

She nodded and sank wearily to her knees. Crawling up beside the baby, she rested her head beside his on the hay. "We'll be fine. We're just a little tuckered . . ." Her voice trailed off as she closed her eyes and wriggled deeper into the nest.

Thunder rolled in the distance. Barrett drank the last of the milk, and then sank down on the hay beside her. His arm instinctively drew her closer and he smiled when he heard her sigh and snuggle closer. She was becoming a habit for him, one he wasn't sure how he'd break.

"Your cough is getting worse," she murmured. "Can't get sick . . . need you . . ."

"I won't get sick."

But by morning Barrett's cough was more pronounced. Abigail watched as he saddled the horses. His face was flushed, and his eyes were unusually bright.

"Maybe I should go on and let you stay here with the baby until the rain lets up," she suggested. She offered the baby a second cup of milk. "Tell me where to find your contact and I'll deliver the papers."

"Stop worrying. It's only a cough," he dismissed shortly. Too shortly. He was cranky and that wasn't like him. "Sounds like the rain's let up."

"Let's pray it stays that way." A watery sun struggled to start the day. The three of them rode for over two hours before they met a traveler, who greeted the Quaker couple cordially.

"Mornin', Friend. Looks like the rain jest might be tryin' to let up for a spell."

"Would be most welcome," Barrett returned. Abigail noticed he sounded hoarse. "Perhaps thou couldst be of help to us, sir."

The man halted his buggy, breaking into a grin when he spied the baby. "What's that you got there? A wee little one?"

Abigail returned his smile and lowered the blanket so the man could have a better look.

"Right good-looking child you got there. Must be real proud of him."

"Yes, he is a fine lad," Barrett agreed. "We are not familiar with this area. Is there an orphanage or a mission nearby?"

The man's brow furrowed in thought. "Orphanage?"

"The child is not ours. While on the road we happened across a woman who was delirious with fever. In spite of all we could do for the child's mother, it was the Lord's will that she pass on. We have done for the child what we can, but we cannot keep him . . ." Barrett broke off, coughing.

Abigail listened to the dry hack, her concern for him growing. The cough sounded much deeper.

"It would be most kind of thee, sir," she continued for Barrett, "if thou couldst help us."

"The tot's mama died, huh? Sad. Sad indeed. Good thing you two happened along, though. I'm afraid there's nothin' around like an orphanage. Not much but a little loggin' goin' on around these parts, and I wouldn't leave a dog in those camps, much less a child. Wish I could help."

"We thank thee," Barrett said. "Godspeed, sir."

The man touched the brim of his hat in response to Barrett's blessing, and then continued down the road.

"I don't like this." Barrett's jaw firmed and he kept his eyes on the road.

"What? Posing as man and wife?"

"Posing as anything. It goes against my beliefs. You may like misleading people but I don't."

"Isn't that a little like the pot calling the kettle black? You pose as a shoe salesman."

"For my country — and I'm not partial to the idea. But the Good Book says to uphold the law and I'm bound by duty. Once I leave the service, pigs will fly before I mislead anyone again." He stiffened. "It goes against my grain."

"Well." She shifted uneasily. "I can't say

that I'm all that fond of the lifestyle myself. The ruses used to be fun but now . . . now they seem like lies."

"Maybe because they *are* lies."

"God forgive me."

He glanced over. "Is that true repentance or duty?"

"True repentance. When this is over I'm going to lead a quiet life. I'm going to plant a vegetable garden, grow flowers, and learn to cook. A lady can change if she sets her mind to it."

His gaze slid to her again and a slow smile crossed his features. "Yes, ma'am. A lady can — *if* she sets her mind to it."

As they drew closer to Shreveport, the road became more populated. Stopping each traveler they met, they asked the person if he knew of a mission orphanage or found-ling home where the child would have good care. Each person shook his head, admitting that he knew of no such place.

Toward late afternoon, a man and woman approached in a wagon. Halting their wagon, the couple nodded, listening sympathetically as Barrett explained their situation.

"Oh, the poor babe," the woman crooned, looking at the tearstained face of the little boy who peered out sadly from the blanket.

"Dost thou know of a mission orphanage where we might leave the little one for safekeeping?" Abigail inquired.

"Well, not close by," the woman said pensively, "but I hear tell there is one further down the road — how far I don't know, but they say you just keep riding straight and don't take the bend in the road you'll come across it."

Relief flooded Abigail, and she hugged the little boy closer.

Gazing up at her, he murmured, "Mama."

Stunned, her heart momentarily twisted. She whirled to face Barrett. "Did you hear that? He called me *mama!*"

Barrett averted his head in a fit of coughing.

"Caught you a chill, did you?" the stranger asked.

Nodding, Barrett took his handkerchief out and held it up to his mouth.

"The orphanage is run by nuns, I'm told," the man offered. "Of course, with the war and all, I understand they have their hands full, but I know they wouldn't hesitate to take the child under the circumstances. He's a fine lad, he is. Why don't you and your wife keep him?"

Barrett tried to speak around his coughing, but Abigail settled her hand on his arm protectively. "My husband is ill, and we cannot care for the child."

"Oh, I understand." The man looked at Barrett, suspicion creeping into his eyes. "I hope it isn't anything catchin'."

I hope it isn't either, thought Abigail. "We would keep the child, but we can't." It hurt to say the words; she'd wish nothing more than to take this baby and raise it. She could — she could carry the child back to Amelia and Anne-Marie and they could care for the infant together. The McDougals could give this child a good life.

Her hopes fell. She had no means to provide even milk for the infant, and Barrett wouldn't permit her to risk the boy's life to deliver the papers. War raged and with it danger loomed from every corner.

"Well, keep to the road and you'll see a sign just this side of Shreveport," the man offered. "The orphanage is off the road — I've only been by it once. You'll have to watch close. The sign is a little faded."

"Thank you for the information. God bless thee."

"And you," the couple returned. The man slapped his team across their rumps with the ends of the reins and the wagon rattled off.

"Well, it sounds like what we're looking for," Barrett said.

Brushing the little boy's hair back from his face, Abigail gently kissed his forehead. "Yes, it sounds exactly like what we're looking for."

Later that afternoon he set up the small tent and made a pallet for the infant. Milk was more plentiful now. Small farms dotted the countryside, and Barrett had learned to skim a fence and milk a cow before she could count to twenty.

"One more night," he promised after supper. Wrapping a blanket around his shoulders, he squatted closer to the fire. The baby was asleep and the camp was peaceful. Overhead, stars dotted the evening sky. "This time tomorrow night, we should be enjoying Smith's food and hospitality."

"I wish we had meat." She sipped a cup of milk, unable to think about the time when they reached General Smith's camp. She realized that the messages they were carrying were vital and that delivering them in time could determine the outcome of a battle. However, by the time they reached Smith they would have left the child at the orphanage, the papers would have been delivered, and shortly afterward, Barrett would be taking her to Mercy Flats.

She wasn't sure how she felt about that anymore. In the beginning all she'd wanted was to unite with Anne-Marie and Amelia, but it wasn't so bad having Barrett around. He'd been good to her, and she felt happy with him — happy and content.

"You think the baby's getting enough to eat?"

She smiled down at the infant sleeping beside her, grateful that his ordeal was nearly over. "Do you realize we don't even know his name?"

"Hattie Mae didn't say?"

"No, she wasn't rational."

Moving closer to the fire, he drew the blanket around himself more tightly and she noted the chill that shook him. He had a fever now, but he didn't want her to know. True, if he told her the truth she would try to coddle him . . . and he was having a hard enough time completing the journey.

"He needs a name." Abigail thought for a moment. "I'd like to name him something from the Bible."

"Like what?"

"Like Matthew or Mark — something brave and daring. Maybe Daniel."

"I have an Uncle Daniel. He's mean as a grizzly and twice as ornery."

"I don't want to name him something

mean. I want a name that he can be proud of. Joshua is nice, or Nebuchadnezzar. He was the king of Babylon and conqueror of Jerusalem, you know."

Barrett glanced up. "You'll name that child Nebuchadnezzar over my dead body."

"Well, maybe Nebuchadnezzar is a little grandiose."

Coughing again, he leaned closer to the fire.

"If I remember my catechism classes, the biblical Daniel was brave and strong. He was thrown into the lion's den and came out without a scratch."

"Well, there you go. If his namesake can socialize with the lions and come out in one piece, he ought to do all right in life."

"Then Daniel he is."

They sat hunched in blankets, listening to the night sounds — the howl of a coyote, the hoot of an owl, the twittering of a night bird.

She broke the silence. "Do you ever think about what you'll do when the war is over?"

"Go home and see what's left."

"Where's home?"

"Georgia."

"Are your parents there?"

"No, my mother died and my father followed a few years later. I have a couple of sisters and some nieces and nephews. Haven't seen any of them in years." He reached for a stick and stirred the fire, his gaze focused on the shooting sparks. It was a long time before he continued. "About Ramona."

She sat up straighter, patting the baby's back.

Pitching the stick into the fire, he leaned back against his saddle, studying the stars. "I'm not still grieving over her, or mourning her. I'm not still in love with her. That ended long before she passed."

Abigail noted the telltale muscle tighten in his jaw. She'd noticed that anytime he was upset, a twitch there gave him away.

"Were you with her when she passed away?" She wasn't comfortable with the thought of another woman having a claim on him. Maybe he had a child being cared for by someone at home. That would explain why he'd been so patient with Daniel and so disinclined to marry again.

He laughed cheerlessly. "She ran off with a circus."

"A circus!" Abigail blurted. Then, seeing the flash of discomfort the confession had brought, she softened her comeback. "A circus? How awful. Do you care to talk about it?" Anything that serious surely warranted discussion. Now. A few days earlier the story wouldn't have made a difference, but somehow tonight it had become important.

"I don't know what I can tell you."

She knew a variety of things he could tell her. "Well — let's start with how you met." Actually she wanted to start at the end of the story, to know what had brought about their alienation at the end of her life.

"I told you her name. Ramona."

"Was she pretty?"

"Beautiful. And self-centered and spoiled. I was aware of the fact when I married her, but when you're nineteen those things don't bother you too much. Ramona and I had grown up together, and we sort of fell into marriage."

"An arranged marriage?"

"At first we both thought it was more than that, but it wasn't. Our parents fully agreed we should marry. She was seventeen when we tied the knot. She loved to sing, and she had a passable voice. She was the apple of her father's eye, and he was good at filling her mind with big dreams, telling her that she was good enough to go to New York and sing in one of those big symphony halls someday."

Abigail saw the smile playing about his

lips, and she was stung by jealousy. In spite of all he said, she was certain that he was still in love with the memory of his beautiful, ambitious Ramona.

"But when her father walked out the door, she'd sing bawdy tunes she'd heard from her brothers and dare me to stop her." His voice faded momentarily, and she waited for him to go on.

"We'd only been married a few months when a traveling show came to town. They were doing some sort of play and she wanted to go. We went, and she was enthralled. All she talked about for days was how the music excited her and how much better she could have sung the lead role. I thought she was excited because the experience had been new and different for her.

"I eventually got tired of hearing about the play and how she wanted to go see it again every time the circus came through town. We were in the middle of harvest, and I told her she'd have to wait until the crops were in before we could go. One day I came to the house for dinner, and she was gone. Just like that. She left me a note and ran off with the circus."

"What did the note say?"

"The note stated that she loved me, that she didn't want to hurt me, but that she wanted a chance to fulfill her dreams. She was joining the traveling show, and when she'd made a name for herself, she'd be back."

Both fell silent, lost in thought.

"Barrett?" she finally said.

"What?"

"She didn't run off with the circus." She felt obligated to point that out to him. Men could get things so mixed up.

"She did."

"You said a traveling show — there is a difference," she reassured him gently.

He turned to look back into the fire. "It's taken me years to get over the fact that I'd been deserted for a circus. Can't see much difference."

"Well, there is a difference. A circus is . . . a circus, but a traveling show, well now, that could turn any woman's head if she had a dream to sing. And it sounds to me like Ramona was young and full of life, and she didn't stop to think that maybe she'd hurt your feelings so badly that you might not be waiting when she returned."

"And I wasn't," he said, as though that somehow purged his part in the whole. He offered a shrewd smile. "I'll never marry again."

"So she did come back."

240

"In a pine box."

"Oh, goodness," she whispered, appalled by the story's outcome.

"I got word six months later that a brawl had broken out during one of her performances. Shots were fired, and Ramona was caught by a stray bullet."

The fire popped, sending another spray of sparks through the air as if in the deceased's honor.

"I'm so sorry."

He didn't answer but continued to stare into the fire, deep in thought.

Abigail wondered if even Barrett knew his deepest feelings. "Well, guess we'd better get some sleep," she said. She wanted to say more, and she would have, but she couldn't think of a single comforting thing to say to a man whose wife had run away to join a traveling show and gotten her fool self shot.

"I'll be along in a while."

"Don't sit out here too long." *And brood about her,* she silently added. "It's getting chilly."

She climbed to her feet and leaned down to take Daniel into her arms. If anyone asked her, Ramona had been just plain wrong to run off and leave a man like Barrett Drake.

But then . . . no one asked her.

Seventeen

Before noon the following day, Abigail spotted the mission's faded wooden sign. It was almost hidden by the overhanging limbs of a spreading walnut tree.

Slowing the horses, Barrett read the sign aloud. "All Saints Home for Children. This is it."

Turning the horse down the narrow lane, they rode toward the house, studying the dwelling that was barely visible through the treetops. While the structure appeared solidly built, it appeared to be in need of major repairs. There were massive barns in back, and several head of cattle grazed in the fields beyond. A large garden set off to one side, enclosed by a wire fence. Abigail knew from experience that the sisters raised most of their own food.

As the horses drew near, she saw a large number of children playing in the yard. A nun with a discerning eye stood watch over them.

The sister looked up as the horses approached, but her attention was immediately diverted by a couple of small boys who engaged in a tumbling match.

Barrett dismounted, then took little Daniel while Abigail climbed off her horse. "It looks nice enough."

"Yes, it looks nice enough."

She focused on the sister who prowled the playground from the corner of her eye, wondering if she was as tolerant as Sister Lucille had been. The answer was readily apparent: She wasn't. She could tell by the tension in her face even from this distance that she wouldn't be as understanding of childish pranks.

Balancing the infant on her hip, Abigail waited as Barrett knocked on the orphanage door. Daniel clearly had endured all he could of the tiresome ride.

A few minutes passed before the door finally opened. A sister appeared before them, her austere appearance sobering. "Yes?"

Nodding a greeting, Barrett said gravely, "Sister, we have a young boy who needs a home."

"Oh, my . . ." The sister's face fell with

dismay. "We are so very crowded . . ."

"Surely there is room for one more." Abigail switched Daniel to the opposite hip, trying to quiet his fussing.

Uttering a prayer, the nun ushered them into the darkened foyer. "I am the Mother Superior of this convent."

"Levi Howard and my wife, Abigail."

Abigail mentally flinched at the misinformation but she knew it was necessary. How did one explain their unusual circumstances? A clatter of feet erupted when several boys half-walked and half-slid down the steps from the upper story.

"Boys, you will walk like gentlemen! A demerit for each of you!" the woman reprimanded sharply.

"Yes, Reverend Mother," the boys intoned repentantly. They glanced at Abigail and Barrett curiously as they tiptoed along the hallway and out the back door.

Sighing, the Mother Superior turned back to the Quaker couple. "They're late for class again, and we're very strict about studies here. At times, the job is so overwhelming . . ." Her voice faded hopelessly.

Abigail hugged Daniel closer to her, picturing him a part of that long, strict, narrow line. "And when the children accumulate too many demerits?"

"A suitable punishment is chosen," the Mother Superior assured her. "Each child is aware of the rules. No infractions are tolerated."

Barrett glanced at Abigail. "How many children reside here?"

"Oh my. We've lost count. We do what we can but the war has left so many foundlings." She drew a ragged breath. "Unfortunately, we have the same number of staff that we had when we had twenty children. There must be over eighty now, but none as young as this one. We will make do, however. The Lord has always provided."

Abigail felt a sinking feeling in the pit of her stomach. This wasn't what she'd expected. The matriarch seemed so stern, so puritanical, and her eyes lacked the kindness that was always in evidence in Sister Lucille's.

The Mother Superior's eyes roamed puritanically over Barrett and Abigail. "You are not the child's parents?"

"No. The boy's parents are dead."

"And you and your wife do not wish to assume responsibility for the child?" Censure tinged her weary tone.

Lowering her eyes, Abigail bit back tears. "It isn't that we don't want to keep him," she murmured. The nun waited, her eyes

245

unreadable now. "We can't," Abigail finished softly.

"Very well." Daniel screamed when Mother Superior took him from Abigail's arms. "I'll see that the child is settled. You and your wife are welcome to stay for supper, Mr. Howard," she invited as she started up the stairway.

Scalding tears rolled from the corners of Abigail's eyes when Daniel's screams grew more hysterical. Holding his arms out to her, his eyes mutely begged her to rescue him.

Whirling, she ran for the door, the knot in her stomach tightening. Gripping the railing, she closed her eyes, trying to blot out the sound of Daniel's cries as they echoed up the stairway.

She heard the door open and close a moment later. Barrett stood behind her, hat in hand, his eyes uncommonly bright.

Without thinking, she stepped into his arms. "A Quaker man does not remove his hat," she said, sobbing.

"I know," he soothed, "I know."

He let her cry until the tears no longer came in a rush. Handing her his handkerchief, he said quietly, "We'll stay for supper."

"We are so short of time." She sighed. She

246

hated that she was making a difficult situation even more impossible by giving in to her emotions. Shreveport was still a long ride, and here she was, asking him for yet another delay when he had been so tolerant of her almost hourly interruptions.

"Another hour won't make a difference," he conceded.

"Thank you." Lifting her head, Abigail smiled at him through a veil of tears. "I know that time is precious . . . but if we could just make sure Daniel's settled in properly I'd feel so much better. He's so little . . . and so frightened."

He returned her gaze soberly. "Abigail, Daniel must stay. You must understand that. We don't have a choice in the matter."

"I know. I just want him to adjust — because he's so little, and the sisters are . . . different for him. Please understand."

"I understand," he said when she returned to his arms.

"Single file, children! Single file," a strident voice called from the hallway.

Abigail and Barrett watched children file through the doorway in a straggling line to take their seats at the three long wooden tables in a dining room adjacent to the kitchen.

The cook carried in large bowls of mashed potatoes and green beans and platters of roast chicken and set them on the tabletops.

A nun walked slowly up and down the aisles, overseeing the meal. There was none of the laughter and infectious whispering that would normally accompany such a gathering. A strained hush occupied the room as the children's plates were filled and set before them. After prayer, the children picked up their forks and began to eat.

The cook returned carrying two plates. Setting the food in front of Barrett and Abigail, she unceremoniously returned to the kitchen.

Abigail stared at the chicken, trying to swallow the lump crowding her throat. She could see Daniel strapped into a makeshift high chair across the room, being fed by a sister who was hurriedly poking food into his mouth. Abigail's appetite, which had seemed so intense only a moment earlier, completely disappeared now.

Mother Superior entered the room, the hem of her habit brushing softly over the wooden floor. Pausing behind Abigail's chair, she viewed her untouched plate and frowned.

"Is there something wrong with the chicken, Mrs. Howard?"

"The chicken is fine, Mother. I seem to have lost my appetite."

"Are you ill?"

"I must be coming down with my husband's cough." She hadn't felt herself all day. She'd been hot and then cold.

Mother Superior's eyes focused on Barrett assertively. "Your cough seems to be acute. Is there anything we might do to make you more comfortable?"

"I thank thee, but no. It isn't serious," he insisted.

"We have been traveling in the rain," Abigail explained, "and apparently my husband has caught a chill."

"Perhaps you should stay the night? Though the rain has let up, there is dampness in the air."

Abigail lowered her eyes. "Thine offer is most kind, but we must be on our way —"

Barrett interrupted. "How far is it to Shreveport?"

"Over a day's ride — less if you travel harder."

"No more?"

"No, but it is a long and most tiresome day's venture."

"Then my wife and I will accept thy generous offer." Meeting Abigail's disbelieving look, he said gently, "The rain has worsened my cough. Perhaps a night's rest in a warm bed will hasten my recovery."

"You have made a wise choice," Mother Superior agreed. "I will have Sister Louise prepare a mixture for your cough."

"Thou art most kind," he said.

Laying a hand briefly on Abigail's shoulder, the nun moved on.

Leaning closer to Barrett, Abigail whispered, "Thank you."

He casually lifted the fork of chicken to his mouth. "I'll think of a way you can repay me."

She poked him sharply in the ribs and the chicken on his fork flew, nearly hitting the stern-faced sister sitting across from them.

The hem of Mother Superior's habit whispered along the hallway when she led them toward the back of the house later.

"I'm sorry we have no provisions for married couples. Your beds are close, but we have nothing that is large enough for a man and his wife."

"It is quite all right," Abigail told her. She glanced at Barrett and grinned. "He snores and keeps me awake."

"Sister Mary Rebecca went to be with the Lord last month. She was a dear soul. This was her chamber," Mother Superior said as she inserted a key into the lock. The door swung open, and Abigail and Barrett focused on a small spartan room. The narrow cot was covered with a thin blanket drawn so tightly that the corners were strained. A square table, the only other piece of furniture in the room, contained a pitcher and bowl and a folded white towel. A crucifix hung on the wall above the bed.

"The beds aren't large, but they will be more comfortable than sleeping on the floor," Mother Superior acknowledged as they entered the room.

Barrett's eyes fixed on the single cot. "This will do fine. We appreciate thy thoughtfulness."

"We are a service order," Mother Superior explained as she opened an adjoining door where a second cot had been set up. "You will sleep here, Mr. Howard."

Mother Superior viewed the arrangement, her hands tucked inside the sleeves of her habit. "Our needs are simple. We have little communication with the people of the area. Whenever help is needed, we are ready and willing to serve. We see to the orphans' spiritual needs as well as their physical ones, and provide the discipline to make them responsible adults. Sister Mary Rebecca was particularly fond of children. She is sorely missed."

"Would it be possible to have a bath? I'll be happy to carry the water," Abigail assured her. She couldn't remember ever feeling so grimy. And hot water would ease her chill.

"I've requested water to be heated, and I will go through the clothing that has been donated to find a dress that might fit you." Mother Superior paused. "It might not be proper attire for you, but it will be dry."

"I thank thee. What about Daniel?"

Mother Superior's brows lifted. "Daniel?"

"The child," Abigail said, realizing that Mother Superior hadn't asked his name. She guessed there were so many children, names didn't matter. He was just one more mouth to feed. "If you'll permit me, I'll bathe him. Perhaps you might even find him something suitable and warm to wear." The child had only the bare necessities, and even those were pitiful.

"I'm sure we can find something — it might be large, but it will be adequate. The washroom is off the kitchen. The cook will be glad to show you."

Nodding, Abigail smiled at Barrett.

"The cook will bring hot tea and honey for your cough, Mr. Howard. I trust you will sleep well," Mother Superior called as she disappeared out the door.

When another nun returned carrying Daniel, Abigail eagerly reached for him. The infant drew back, solemnly staring, and then, upon recognizing her, he grinned and eagerly held out his pudgy arms.

Laughing, she gathered him close, marveling at how much she'd grown to love him in such a short time. It was hard to believe that a week ago she couldn't have found a male that she liked. Now she had two.

Carrying the baby to the washroom, she paused at Barrett's door, listening to his muted cough. Was it her imagination, or was there a rattle in his chest now? Fear gripped her but she pushed it aside, telling herself that his illness wasn't serious. He had simply been in the dampness too long.

The cook showed her the washroom. The cast iron tub was filled with steaming water and waiting for her enjoyment. Sitting Daniel on the floor, she tested the temperature and smiled when she found that it was nearly perfect.

She undressed the infant and then took him into the bath with her. Together they splashed and laughed, getting nearly as much water on the floor as was left in the tub. An hour passed before she finished drying and dressing him, and by then his eyes were drooping sleepily.

She hurriedly wiped up the water on the floor and then carried the baby back to her room. A short candle burned on the table, illuminating a note from Mother Superior that said the child could sleep with Abigail if she preferred.

Abigail preferred. Before she had Daniel settled beneath the covers, he was fast asleep.

After blowing out the candle, she sat down on the side of the bed, gazing down at him. Moonlight streamed through the small window, beckoning to her. Though she was exhausted, the moment was too inviting. There were so many thoughts troubling her tonight. What would she do without Daniel? What would she do without Barrett?

She slipped outside a few moments later and drew a deep breath, savoring the smell of rain-washed air. Coolness swept her, but the sky was a canopy of twinkling stars. *Thank You, God, for this wildly unexpected adventure.* He was a God of mystery — and of intrigue. A month ago she wouldn't have dreamed she would be in love with a man and a child. Now she had both.

Strolling along the flagstone walk, she idly wondered if Barrett was sleeping. She'd seen the cook fixing tea that would ease his cough before she and Daniel had bathed. It would be nice if he were with her now. They could walk together and talk about the day and how it hadn't gone as they had expected. Nothing had gone as they'd expected from the day they'd met, but he had been patient with her. Was it possible that she'd fallen in love with him? Deeply, irrevocably in love. Her pulse raced and that knot formed in the pit of her stomach. She couldn't. She just couldn't! Her life had been so neatly settled until he came along. What would she do about all the plans she and Amelia and Anne-Marie had made? They had planned to be independent, answering to no one but God — granted, they would have their share of questions from the Almighty One.

Had she fallen in love with a man whose heart might still belong to a dead woman? A woman who had traded his heart for a singing job? She shuddered. Could she wrestle a ghost for the man she loved? Anne-Marie taught her many things, but she'd never mentioned a thing about ghosts.

And then there was Daniel.

Just thinking about riding away and leaving him in the morning brought an ache to her heart. Yet she had to. She couldn't take care of a baby. Someone who loved children would happen along and take a small baby into their home. Someone who could provide in a way she couldn't.

The aroma of tobacco drifted to her. Drawn to the familiar smell, her pulse quickened when she spotted Barrett standing in the moonlight, one boot propped on a low stone wall as he gazed out at the quiet hillsides.

Drawing a deep breath, she casually sauntered toward him. She didn't want him to think she was eager to see him.

"Hello."

"Hello."

"Lovely night isn't it?" She drew the shawl closer.

"I thought you'd be asleep by now," he said, straightening. He tossed the thin cigar into the darkness and the breeze caught the sparks and sent them into the night.

"I put the baby down and I was too restless to sleep." Edging closer to him, she gazed up at the stars, heaving a sigh of contentment. "It's so beautiful here." She drew in fresh, rain-washed air.

"It is, but you should be asleep. We have a hard ride tomorrow." He effortlessly shifted his stance, putting a little more distance between them.

"I know. I'll go shortly."

They gazed at the heavens, sharing a

relaxed silence. She wondered at times if he was blind. Couldn't he see how she was beginning to feel about him? It was in her eyes as plain as the nose on her face every time she looked at him.

"Daniel settling in?" he asked.

She leaned against an oak trunk, studying him. "He's fine. Sound asleep."

"He can put away the potatoes and chicken for a little fella."

She laughed. "He's a growing boy." Pushing away from the tree her eyes fixed on his when she moved a step closer. "Did the cook bring you tea?"

"Yes, a while ago."

She paused in front of him. Sliding her hand up his arm, she whispered softly, "It has been a strange few days, hasn't it?"

He groaned. "What are you doing? Haven't we got enough complications?"

She gazed into his eyes. "Complications? I'm simply inquiring about your health."

"When are you going to stop making up stories? It's time you grew up, Abigail. You and your sisters."

Stiffening, she realized he spoke the truth. It was past time that she grew up and acknowledged that fabricating stories wasn't innocent fun. She was telling outright lies. *God, forgive me for my lies. From this mo-*

ment on, I will speak only the truth — if it kills me.

"All right, I'll tell the truth. I want you to kiss me." She had never been so brazen in her life.

He set her back a step. "You ever been kissed by a man, Abigail?"

Feeling a little fearful, she slowly shook her head. "A boy kissed me once, but I gave him a black eye."

Drawing her closer to him, he gazed down at her. "Then maybe it's time we remedied that. I'm not asking for a black eye, you understand, and chances are you're going to come down with my cough. Still want me to kiss you?"

Her answer was swift and imploring. "Yes. Very much so. Will you kiss me, please?" She'd been adolescent for too long; she longed to experience what other women found so fascinating.

His eyes devoured her. "Yes ma'am. If you want to be kissed then I'm more than happy to be the first man who has that pleasure."

She cocked a teasing brow, suddenly hesitant with dread. What if she didn't like his lips on hers? What if he read more into the kiss than she could deliver? "Perhaps I am being a bit too uninhibited, Barrett Drake."

The hue of his eyes darkened, and she wondered about the wisdom of her actions. "There's no doubt that you are."

"But you see," she said as their mouths drifted perilously close, "that's my problem. I'm not sure I should let you, even though I have provoked this. You'll go all preachy on me and say nice women don't kiss men."

He chuckled, and it sounded to her as if he found her comment amusing.

"Any advice before we proceed?"

"Nice women don't kiss men."

Her eyes widened, both enchanted and frightened by the expectation. "My intentions are most proper."

"They'd better be." His mouth lowered to take hers.

She flushed, and then went cold. Then giddy. She'd never dreamed a man could make her feel so alive. His lips tasted faintly of tobacco, lemon, and the night air. Her arms tightened possessively around his neck and he caught her up in his arms.

Trepidation — and realization of her overwhelming need for him to hold her — made her turn and flee for her room like the child he accused her to be, made her ignore his voice when he called after her. The kiss was no longer a folly — a game. Emotions she was ill-equipped to handle spiraled.

"Abigail, come back here."

Tears rolled down her cheeks and she blindly ran down the flagstone walk. By taking the initiative and inviting him to kiss her, she had hoped to prove to him that she could be as worldly and refined as any other woman he found desirable; instead she had succeeded in showing him what an innocent, brainless child she was.

"Abigail!"

Sobbing now with weariness and just plain dismay, she climbed the steps to her room, wondering how she would face him in the morning.

Slamming the door behind her, she told herself that her misery was her own fault, as usual! She should never have fallen in love in the first place.

EIGHTEEN

"Your cough is of great concern to me, Mr. Howard. Are you certain you feel up to traveling?" Mother Superior inquired during breakfast the next morning.

"We can delay no longer, Sister, but I thank thee for thy compassion." Barrett's voice was little more than a hoarse whisper.

Abigail scrutinized him closely as he picked at his food, convinced that he was feverish today. Leaning across the table, she whispered, "The cough does sound worse, Barrett."

"I'm fine. Eat your breakfast."

"But you look terrible," she insisted. His forehead was a sickly white, and two round crimson circles dotted his cheeks. She had heard him cough most of the night.

"Thank you. You've made me feel considerably better."

She absently pushed a piece of ham around her plate, worried about him and

Daniel. She knew that they would be riding out immediately after breakfast, but knowing didn't make it any easier to accept. She awakened that morning to Daniel lovingly patting her cheek.

She'd set him on the floor to try his walking skills. Clinging to the covers, he had cautiously worked his way to the foot of the bed and back, giving her a triumphant grin when he made it back without cracking his head. She laughed at his charming antics, wishing that Barrett was there to share the moment, but all too soon he'd tapped on the door to tell her that breakfast was being served.

Daniel now perched on Sister Judith's lap, hungrily stuffing scrambled eggs into his mouth.

"Abigail, if thou art not intending to eat thy ham, we must be on our way."

"Oh. Yes, of course," she murmured, embarrassed that he'd caught her daydreaming.

Mother Superior trailed the couple outside where the horses were saddled and waiting. Abigail hugged Daniel to her tightly, dreading the moment she had to release him to the sisters. She no longer worried about his care; the sisters, though stern, also showed great patience and resilience with the children.

"The cook prepared food for your journey." Mother Superior smiled. "It isn't much."

"It is more than enough, Sister," said Barrett, accepting the packet she offered. "Would that we had something to offer to thee in return."

She waved her hand dismissively. "When you have the means, remember us."

Recalling the coins she'd pilfered as a blind beggar, Abigail removed them from her pocket and handed them over. "I hope this will help."

Mother Superior viewed the windfall, speechless. Then she cried, "Thank you! This blessing is out of the blue and sorely needed."

Kissing Daniel's rosy cheek for the last time, Abigail reluctantly handed him to Sister Judith, her heart wrenching when his small hands clung to her hair possessively.

The sun painted the sky with pinks and yellows as Abigail and Barrett turned the horses down the lane. She swallowed back the lump in her throat and told herself she wasn't going to look back, but by the time they'd reached the end of the lane she couldn't stand it any longer. Twisting in the saddle, she peered through barren branches at the mansion.

Sister Judith stood on the steps, holding Daniel. The austere figure dressed in black blurred when tears blinded Abigail. This was so foolish! It hadn't hurt this bad when she'd been separated from Amelia and Anne-Marie. Tears trickled from the corners of her eyes when she watched Mother Superior try to calm Daniel, who was crying now.

Jerking her head around, Abigail held her body erect in the saddle in an effort to hold back her pain. It wasn't fair. A small boy, both parents gone — it just wasn't fair! Even though Daniel had had precious little time to warm to her or Barrett, they were both all he had in the world. And now they were deserting him.

She choked back a sob, but a hiccup escaped her. Averting her face so Barrett wouldn't see, she stealthily wiped away scalding tears.

"He'll be fine." Barrett's quiet reassurance did little to ease her guilt.

"I know he will." She drew a ragged breath, struggling to control her emotions.

"The sisters raised you well, didn't they?"

"Yes." The sisters had been good, but having a mother and father would have been better.

A meadowlark called as the horses picked their way down the lane. Tears ran unchecked down Abigail's cheeks now as the orphanage gradually faded from sight.

Barrett suddenly reined up and got off his horse. Striding back to her animal he held out his hand to her. "Come here."

Abigail slowly dismounted, uncertain about the delay.

But when he opened his arms to her, she went gratefully into them, her tears flowing again. For the second time in her life she wanted a man to hold her; she wanted a man to make her believe, if only for the moment, that everything would be all right in her life, even though she knew that after leaving Daniel it could never be the same again.

He held her against his chest and she felt his silent message. Daniel had struck a maternal note in Abigail McDougal that wouldn't be easy to assuage. Every passing hour drew her closer to the child.

Her tears dampened his shirt as he rubbed her back consolingly. When the crying spree finally abated, she lifted her head, finding it hard to meet his eyes. "I'm sorry," she said, sniffing.

Blubbering this way in front of him was dreadful, especially after the way she'd made a fool of herself kissing him last night. She was never going to make him see her as a beautiful, sophisticated woman a man couldn't live without. Not when her eyes and nose were as pink as radishes.

Wiping away her tears with the pads of his thumbs, he handed her a square of gray linen. "Courtesy of the Mother Superior. She's an amazingly perceptive woman."

Abigail offered him a feeble smile and brought the linen up to dab her watery eyes. "I'm sorry. I'm such a twit at times."

"For once, I think we're in complete agreement." His impertinent grin made her laugh, but she forgave him for being a man, for there was a sympathetic light shining in his eyes that touched her.

"You're a mess, Abigail McDougal. But a fine one."

"I know." She drew a ragged sigh. "I don't know what's gotten into me."

Drawing her closer, he kissed her. Her eyes drifted shut as his lips brushed against hers — once, then twice — then closed over her mouth.

Very briefly the thought registered that his skin seemed hot, but the thought was so quickly replaced by love that the comprehension never entered her mind again.

"What are we going to do about Daniel?" she whispered when their lips finally parted.

"Abigail, we've settled the question of Daniel. He stays here, where he'll be loved and cared for."

"The matter isn't settled in my mind."

"Then settle it and we'll be on our way." His tone held a subtle warning, but she didn't care. She didn't know why, but she couldn't admit to herself that Daniel was gone from her life forever. She couldn't leave Daniel with strangers. Yes, her convent had been uncommonly good to her and her sisters, and this one looked to be nurturing, but it wouldn't be the best possible life for the little boy — especially when she was willing and able to care for Daniel in every way but means. "I want to take him with us."

Smothering a mild oath, Barrett released her abruptly. "That's crazy! I know what you're thinking, but it's impossible. Time is up, Abigail."

"He didn't slow us down before. And if he did, it was only because he was hungry. With food he'll be no trouble," she argued.

"No."

"Yes."

"No!"

Her eyes locked with his stubbornly. "I'll take care of him. You won't have to do a thing. I promise. I'll find and milk the cows. I'll feed and change his diapers. You won't have to do a thing. Just let me take him with us."

His momentary flicker of hesitation was all the encouragement she needed. Standing on tip-toe, she showered his face with kisses, knowing full well that he was going to give in to her.

"We'll keep him with us until you've finished your business in Shreveport, then we'll bring him back here, if we must. Please, Barrett? Please?"

He shook his head. "This will only make it harder on you. You'll get more attached to the child, and you'll never want to let him go."

"Nonsense. I simply want to make certain that he gets the proper love and care that any child is due. As soon as you've handed Smith the papers and we've started back to Mercy Flats, I'll be more than ready to turn him over to the sisters." She kissed him fully on the lips. "And besides, he'll make it easier for us to travel without arousing suspicion. Who would suspect a Quaker family as being anything other than simple folk?"

Her mouth covered his again, smothering any counter argument he might have been ready to make.

"All right!" He set her back, eyeing her sternly. "But I'm warning you, don't get it in that pretty head to keep him because you can't. No judge would give the child to an unmarried woman."

"Perhaps a judge would never be consulted."

"Abigail . . ."

"Oh, all right. I won't get any *more* attached to him! I promise!"

"Of course you won't. I'm warning you, Abigail —"

But she wasn't listening. She had already reined the horse and started back to the mansion, leaving him standing in a cloud of dust.

"You want the child back?" Judging by Mother Superior's expression, she clearly thought that Abigail had lost her mind.

"Only for a few days. Then we'll most likely need to bring him back."

The nun stood on the porch shaking her head as Abigail galloped off, the child tucked safely in her arms.

Squeezing Daniel victoriously, Abigail gave the horse its head down the long lane.

He's mine for another twenty-four hours, but that's enough.

It had to be enough.

"I've got him," she announced breathlessly when she reined up beside Barrett.

"You don't mean to say we can finally get on our way?"

"We're ready!" Abigail and Daniel grinned at him.

He shook his head and she knew he must still be marveling at how she'd talked him into this one.

They pushed hard the rest of the day, stopping only briefly to allow Daniel to crawl around freely for a few minutes. The child had become so accustomed to the rocking motion of the saddle that he'd slept most of the afternoon. By the time they stopped for the night, the infant was cranky again. Abigail noticed that Barrett was unusually subdued. At noon, he had refused the ham and biscuits the sisters had sent, but Daniel demanded so much of her time that Barrett's behavior slipped her mind.

When he refused the evening meal, she got downright worried. "Are you all right?" She stood before him, her hands on her hips, challenging him to face her.

"I'm fine," he returned shortly.

Remembering how hot he'd felt to her

touch earlier, she knew that he wasn't being honest. "You don't look fine." She reached out to lay her hand on his forehead but he turned his head, overcome by a racking spate of coughing.

"Barrett, you're sick. Your fever's up again. I'm sure of it."

"Don't mother me. I'm fine."

But he wasn't fine. His feverish tossing and turning kept Abigail awake most of the night.

Shortly before dawn, he awoke, coughing violently. She sat up and leaned over to feel his forehead again. His skin was fiery and dry and he was muttering incoherently.

Crawling out of the lean-to, she hurried to the stream and filled both canteens. For over two hours she bathed his face and chest, but almost as soon as she dampened his skin the moisture dried up. Her efforts seemed as useless as throwing cold water on a hot cookstove.

Thrashing about on the pallet, he drifted in and out of reality, at times insisting that Abigail take the papers and ride to Shreveport without him. Each time she steadfastly refused.

"Abigail," he called weakly.

"I'm here, Barrett. Here, you have to drink a little more water. You're burning up

271

with fever." Was there a doctor in the area? She had no idea where to look for one and she couldn't leave him.

Cradling his head against her chest, she trickled water down his throat. He was as hot as Hattie had been — oh, dear Lord. Had he caught whatever killed Hattie? Her heart hammered so hard she thought it would come out of her chest. That must be the cause of the illness. A simple chill would have passed.

His dry hack sounded the same as Hattie's — why hadn't she noticed the similarity earlier?

He managed a few swallows from the canteen and then fell limply back on the pallet.

"You've got to go on by yourself," he whispered.

"No. I won't leave you."

"Abigail," he groaned, clasping his head in pain, "don't argue. Those papers have to reach Smith no later than tonight and I'm too sick to travel."

"No." She forced back her rising hysteria. She wasn't going to leave him here, sick and alone. "I won't leave you."

"Finish this for me, Abigail. Find Smith. He'll send men back for me, but the papers have to reach him. Tell him —" He broke into a coughing seizure and she waited until the spasm passed. "Tell him he'll have to divert troops to attack Banks's advance unit."

"No, Barrett! No!" She wouldn't leave him. She couldn't! Yet she knew how important it was not only to Barrett but to the whole Confederacy that the messages reach Smith in time.

"I don't know where to find him," she said brokenly. "And I can't leave you alone. You're ill, terribly sick."

"There's a small map . . . in my back pocket . . . Get it."

Her hands trembled when she eased him onto his side, following his request, but even that small effort exhausted him. Quickly locating the map, she gently lowered him back onto the pallet.

"Leave now. You should reach Smith's camp before dark."

"Barrett —"

"Don't argue, Abigail. Kirby will send someone back for me."

Daniel's head popped up on the pallet, his blue eyes quizzical when he stared back at them in bewilderment. When he recognized Abigail, he flashed a drooling grin.

Hurriedly changing his diaper, Abigail gave him a biscuit, and then ran back to the stream to fill the canteens. When she returned, she laid one within Barrett's reach along with a folded wet cloth.

"I'm scared," she confessed.

"No need to be. You'll make it. If anyone should stop you, tell them that your baby is ill and that you're trying to reach the child's father in Smith's camp."

Abigail's fingers trembled when she saddled her horse, trying to keep Daniel from crawling underfoot, which wasn't easy with a one-year-old. She'd promised God to stop lying. Would He consider the circumstances and permit her a small slip?

She returned to the fire and pressed her lips to Barrett's feverish forehead.

"I wish I didn't have to leave you."

"I'll be fine. It's just a little cough." He rolled to his side, bending double as another spasm overcame him.

"A little cough?"

"I'm not dead yet, am I?"

She was thankful that he hadn't lost his dry sense of humor. Settling her head on his chest, she choked back tears. "No, but you look like you're close."

"You always could cheer me up," he murmured. A sob caught in her throat as she held him tightly.

You have to pull through this, Barrett Drake.

You have to pull through this!

She rode out shortly after dawn with Daniel tucked in front of her on the saddle, pushing the horse hard, galloping across open fields and down dusty roads.

Daniel, seeming to sense the urgency of their mission, contented himself with chewing on a piece of jerky she had given him. All day she urged the horse headlong toward Shreveport, stopping only briefly to cool and water the animal.

As twilight gathered, she slowed the horse to a walk. He was dripping with heavy lather and she was worried she was pushing him too hard.

Absently poking pieces of biscuit into Daniel's mouth, she studied the map Barrett had given her. The drawing wasn't very clear, but there appeared to be a large square through which he'd drawn the trail. There was an alternate route off to the side with the notation *5 miles.*

Squinting at the disjointed printing, she finally made out the words: *Indian Burial Ground.*

She looked up, her heart sprinting to her throat.

Silhouetted on the horizon were the wooden platforms the map indicated, platforms made of spindly limbs and laced together with rawhide, gaily festooned with feathers and weapons. Surrounding them were pots of food intended to help the deceased on their way to meet the Great Spirit.

An Indian burial ground. Goose bumps rose up on her arms like smallpox blisters. If an Indian warrior died in battle, he was generally left where he fell, but if he died in camp, it was customary to wrap his body in robes with his personal belongings and place him on a scaffold or high tree branch near the camp — her blood suddenly felt like it turned to ice. She turned, peering over her shoulder.

Daniel started to fret and she absently patted his leg, her eyes fixed on the frightening silhouettes of the platforms.

She suddenly became aware of the wind that sprung up with the approaching darkness. It moaned through the platforms, the eerie sound sending a shiver up her spine.

"Oh, Lord," she breathed, "give me courage." In a few minutes it would be pitch dark, and here she sat on the edge of a burial ground. Heaven only knew what — or who — was lurking about . . . waiting for her.

She squinted to study the map again. The five miles Barrett had indicated must be the distance around the sacred ground. If she went around it, she'd lose too much time.

She glanced up, her eyes resting on the long row of scaffolds suspended in the air. She couldn't go through . . . that. Even Barrett wouldn't expect her to go through that!

A burial ground was sacred to the natives. Men had been killed for trespassing.

Maybe there were Indians nearby. Maybe even watching her at this very moment.

Daniel broke into tears, and she hushed him quietly. For a long moment, her eyes fixed on the obstacle that lay in her path as she turned the alternatives over in her mind.

What would Amelia do? She'd turn around and run.

Anne-Marie? The answer came as swiftly as the question. She'd ride right through.

Abigail watched from the corner of her eye, half-expecting to see a tribe of the deceaseds' relatives bearing down on her.

Swallowing dryly, she shifted Daniel to settle his cries.

What would Barrett do?

A picture of him lying so ill prodded her. Kneeing the horse, she knew what she must do. Barrett was counting on her to get the papers to Smith. And the sooner she reached Smith, the sooner Barrett would get help.

A week ago she couldn't have imagined a man on earth that could make her ride through an Indian burial ground with darkness approaching. A week ago she could never have imagined a man who would inspire her to ride *anywhere.* But Barrett Drake could and had, and she loved him enough to do anything.

Loved him enough to do anything.

The revelation was nearly as startling as the thought of what she was about to do.

"Barrett Drake, you owe me for this," she muttered as she nudged the horse forward. Her heart pounded so hard she could hardly breathe. Urging the mare to a faster gait, she gingerly picked her way through the line of platforms.

Oh. This is awful. "Father God, I know I've sinned and I don't have the right to ask You for anything, but —" She broke off in a shriek as the horse shied, his rump bumping a platform support.

Her heart lodged in her throat when she watched the platform sway and then gradually steady.

"I'm sorry," she whispered, and truly meant it.

Her eyes were as round as Daniel's when darkness closed in. An owl called, startling

Daniel. He screamed and she thought she was going to faint.

"Shhhh, it's just an owl," she soothed. "It won't hurt us."

She felt as if a big hand were encircling her throat, shutting off her air supply. Her heart hammered so hard it drowned out the sound of the horse's hooves, but nothing blotted the keen of the ghostly wind.

Squeezing her eyes shut, she prayed that the horse would find his own way. "Father, I'm aware of what I've done to deserve this, but I swear I won't ever do it again."

A strange clicking sound penetrated her terror. Forcing her eyes to open, she saw a grotesque mask staring back at her from the pole of a burial platform. The wind swayed the mask back and forth, then forward and back, banging it against the pole.

"Amazing grace, how sweet the sound," she sang. Fear told her not to look up, but morbid curiosity made her wonder if it was true that the deceased were buried with their knees pulled close to their bodies.

"That saved a wretch like me!"

Tilting her head upward, she squinted, trying to make out the robed figure lying atop the scaffold. Man or woman? Chief or squaw? She couldn't tell; she no longer cared. The object looked like a lump of robe lying up there.

"I once was lost, but now I'm found —"

Fixing her gaze straight ahead, she held her breath as the end of the burial ground came in sight. So far, nothing had come out to snatch her.

It took hours or maybe only minutes to leave the sacred ground. She was never sure.

When the horse passed the last scaffold, she finished in a rush. "Was blind, but now I see."

Kicking the horse's flanks, she was off again at a full gallop.

NINETEEN

A full moon bathed horse and rider when Abigail rode into the outskirts of Shreveport. She spotted a large encampment over the rise and she prayed it was Kirby Smith's battalion. The campfires resembled tiny candles flickering through the treetops. The horse was lathered, and Abigail's dress was soaked with perspiration. She shivered in the chilly air. Daniel had fallen asleep, and her arms cramped from supporting his weight, but she had made it . . . hopefully, in time.

Reining up in the shadows, she studied the camp, trying to make sure that it was Confederate. When she was able to make out the Confederate stripes, she breathed a sigh of relief. Even if it wasn't General Smith's camp, they could tell her where he was.

Prompting the horse forward, she wondered how her arrival would be met.

"Halt! Who goes there?"

"Is this General Smith's camp?"

The young man, who couldn't have been more than sixteen, stepped out of the shadows, carrying a Mississippi rifle. His voice still changing, the tone cracked in the midst of his attempt to sound commanding. "Who wants to know?"

Abigail hesitated. "I have a message for General Smith."

"I'll pass it on."

"It . . . it's a personal message," she called. "I must talk to him in person."

He turned and shouted to someone behind him, "Brown! Tell the general a woman has a message for him."

"Please inform the general that I have word from Hershall Digman."

"Diggon?"

"Digman."

Abigail couldn't see the young man's face for the shadows, but she could hear the doubt in his voice.

"What's your name?"

"Abigail McDougal."

His gaze skimmed her clothing. "Tell the general a young Quaker woman, Abigail McDougal, has word from Hershall Digman."

The seconds dragged by. Abigail's horse

shifted restlessly as she waited. A few minutes later a voice called back.

"Bring her in."

"Follow me." The young man turned and walked toward the fires.

Abigail knew that it was late. The few men lounging around the low camp fires watched her curiously when she rode slowly by them.

When they reached a large tent, the young boy held the horse's bridle while she dismounted. Daniel murmured in protest when her feet touched the ground, but he quickly drifted back to sleep.

A second soldier led her horse away when a guard at the opening of the tent pulled back the flap.

The man sitting behind a makeshift desk looked up, frowning. "You have word from Drake?"

"Yes, sir."

Kirby Smith stood up, eyeing Daniel inquisitively. "Speak."

Abigail glanced at the man standing behind the general.

Smith said quietly, "Alvin Moore, my aide. He can be trusted."

She hesitated. "May I lay the baby down?"

The general motioned toward a small cot. "Excuse my lack of manners. Lay him on my cot. And please, sit down. You look as if you've had a long journey."

"Thank you. I have."

She laid Daniel on the cot, turning his face away from the light. The boy curled bottom up, sighing as he snuggled deeper on the thin blanket.

Pulling a chair from the table, the general offered Abigail a seat. A cup of hot coffee appeared in her hand and she smiled her gratitude at the young corporal. She brought the cup to her mouth and flinched as the bitter liquid burned a path down her throat.

"Drake sent you?"

She nodded. A wave of fatigue washed over her.

"You're carrying a message from him?"

"How do I know you're Kirby Smith?"

Clearly taken aback, the general smiled. "Ah — Drake *would* send a cautious woman." He leaned back in his chair and soberly considered her. "How do I know you're a Quaker?"

She shook her head. "I'm not."

"Then Barrett encountered trouble."

Relief flooded her. He *was* Kirby Smith. "He's very ill. I'm afraid it may be the fever."

"Yellow jack?"

"I'm not sure — I pray not. Through an odd set of circumstances, we came into contact with a woman along the way here who was very ill. She was coughing continually, and she had a high fever." She glanced at the sleeping infant. "The woman and her child died during the birthing, leaving this boy an orphan. I'm not sure if Hattie died from childbirth or from the fever, but a day or two later Barrett developed a cough. He tried to make it here to deliver the papers, but he was so ill this morning he couldn't continue the mission." Reaching under the table, she withdrew the packet containing the message from beneath her skirt and handed it to him. "Barrett said it's imperative that you divert troops to head off Banks."

General Smith opened the papers, his features somber as he read the note in the dim lighting.

"Please, Barrett is so ill . . . You must send someone back for him immediately."

"Sergeant Douglas!" Smith bellowed.

A rough-faced man appeared in the opening of the tent. "Sir!"

General Smith's eyes pinpointed Abigail. "Can you draw a map of where you left him?"

She rose and removed her bonnet. "I'll show the way."

"Nonsense. You're exhausted. You will

remain here in camp. My men will find him." Turning back to the sergeant, he barked, "Take three men and follow the map she draws. A member of my staff needs assistance. I suggest you approach with caution. He's sick with fever and may not be capable of sound judgment, and he's an excellent shot under any circumstance."

"He doesn't have a gun," Abigail said wearily. "We were posing as a Quaker couple and we didn't think it wise to carry one."

The general stared at her for a moment, and then broke into a chuckle. "Excuse me," he said, obviously trying to get himself under control, "but the image of Barrett Drake posing as a Quaker confounds my imagination."

"Have you met Hershall Digman?" He nodded. "Just as confounding." She busied herself drawing a map on the paper that he provided.

The general chuckled again when he handed the map to the sergeant after she'd finished. "Drake will be dressed as a Quaker."

"My drawing isn't very clear," she said. "I want to go with you."

Studying the crude sketch, the sergeant nodded. "We'll find him."

When the soldier left the tent, she sank back onto the chair, closing her eyes in exhaustion.

"Forgive me, Miss McDougal. I'll have one of my men escort you to your quarters."

"I would be ever so grateful," she admitted.

The general called out again, and a tall, blond man stepped inside.

"Sergeant Dobbs, find a place for Miss McDougal and the baby to sleep."

"Yes, sir."

"Thank you, General," Abigail said wearily.

"Thank you, Miss McDougal. When you're rested, we'll talk again."

"Yes," she returned vaguely. "We'll talk." She was numb with weariness, yet her heart grieved for Barrett. Would they be able to find him using the hopelessly inadequate map that she had drawn? She could only pray that they did . . . and soon.

Sergeant Dobbs picked up Daniel and then escorted her out of the tent.

Abigail viewed the exhausted sea of men when she walked across the campground toward a long row of tents. Bloodied faces, weary eyes.

"You'll be sleeping in Lieutenant Bennett's tent. He won't be needin' it for a while," the sergeant said.

"He's not —"

"No, ma'am. He took a bullet in the ribs, but he's going to make it. Doc's got him over in the hospital tent." She traced his gaze to a long, dimly lit tent. The silhouette of a portly man moved about inside between row after row of occupied cots.

"Here ya are," the sergeant drawled softly. "You and the boy should be just fine."

"You're very kind, Sergeant."

"If there's anything I can do for you, you call. I'll be close by." He gently laid the sleeping Daniel in the center of one of the two cots in the tent.

"I'll bring some fresh water. I'm afraid the facilities here aren't the best for a lady —"

"I'll need very little, Sergeant. Thank you again." The young man had the nicest smile she had ever seen. When he smiled she saw a hint of dimples in both cheeks.

When the canvas flap fell into place, she sank onto the edge of the cot and closed her eyes wearily. "Oh, Barrett," she murmured. She missed him so much her heart ached nearly as much as her body.

Pulling the pins from her hair, she released the mass to fall over her shoulders. Massaging her scalp for a moment, she leaned over, lowered the lantern flame, and stretched out on the cot and prayed for Barrett and for the men General Smith had sent to get him.

Let Barrett live, she whispered into the darkness. *I may not deserve a man like him, but some fine woman on this earth does.*

She only wished it was her.

Abigail woke with a sudden start. Sitting up, she tried to orient her thoughts. The sounds of the camp confused her for a moment, until she remembered where she was.

Daniel was awake, entertaining himself with a hat that had been hooked on a tent pole.

"Miss McDougal?"

Sergeant Dobbs's voice drifted from outside the tent.

She hurriedly raked her fingers through the tangles in her hair before starting to braid the long strands. "I'm awake, Sergeant. Come in."

Dobbs pushed back the tent flap and bent to step inside. As he straightened, his gaze met hers, holding it for a moment. "Thought I'd escort you and your son to breakfast."

"Oh," She tried to talk around the pins in her mouth as she twisted her hair into a coil at the nape of her neck. "Daniel isn't my son. Captain Drake and I assumed his care after his parents died."

"Oh." The Sergeant's eyes filled with concern. "Indians?"

"Idiots," Abigail muttered, recalling the father's senseless death.

"Then you and the captain are . . ." He broke off, a flush dotting his fair complexion.

Abigail half-smiled and then his implication sank in. "Oh, no, nothing like that."

"Well," he released a sigh of relief, "that's nice to know." He grinned broadly. "Isn't often we get a woman in camp, and it'd be a shame if you were already taken."

"Oh?" She tilted her head teasingly. "Why, thank you, Sergeant Dobbs." The sergeant seemed so young. Barrett was so much older and more experienced and more handsome and more . . . She stopped her train of thought.

He blushed, his eye moving to Daniel. "Would you join us for breakfast?"

"I'd love to."

"Can't guarantee how good it'll be, but the cook's pretty good at makin' what little we have edible."

She quickly changed Daniel's diaper and when they left the tent, the sergeant insisted on carrying him as they walked to the commissary tent.

The tent, with all four sides rolled up, was slightly larger than the field hospital. Several men sat at crude tables. Others lounged outside. All had respectful but appreciative looks in their eyes when Abigail passed.

She didn't find their glances alarming; it had been some time since they'd seen their wives or sweethearts, and she understood how lonely a person could get when he was separated from his loved one. She left Barrett hours earlier and she ached to see him.

Sergeant Dobbs settled her and Daniel at a table and went to fill their plates.

"Pardon me, ma'am."

Abigail turned to find a young man wearing a gray uniform jacket bearing corporal stripes and a mismatched pair of butternut brown trousers standing beside her.

"I wondered . . . if the boy took to me, could I hold him a bit? My boy was about his age when I left home. I reckon he must be about four now."

Her eyes softened with concern. "You haven't seen your son in three years?"

"Once. But he was asleep and didn't know I was there. We were passing by; I only got to stay a minute."

"Of course you can hold him, Corporal."

The war had barely touched the lives of

the McDougal sisters. Abigail never thought about men who hadn't seen their families in months, sometimes years. The deplorable conditions in camp made her realize for the first time how much these men sacrificed for their cause.

"I think Daniel would let you help him with his breakfast," she offered.

The corporal bent and began getting acquainted with the baby, who, after a moment's shyness, soon basked in the attention of the corporal and others who watched the boy's antics with delight.

"They're lonesome for their sons." Sergeant Dobbs set a full plate of gruel and hardtack in front of her. "Chicory coffee. Sorry."

"Are you a family man, Sergeant?"

"No, ma'am. And I'm grateful. The war's hard enough; I couldn't bear leaving a wife and kiddies behind."

She sipped scalding coffee, watching the men play with Daniel. "Do you know Mr. Drake?"

"The captain? Yes, ma'am. Know of him, least ways."

She felt unsettled when she thought about Barrett. Had the men found him? Was he . . . no, she couldn't think the worst for fear that it might come true. "What's he like?"

"Well, I can't say, ma'am. He keeps to himself most times. But the men highly respect him."

"Has he been in the service long?"

"Quite a spell. They say he's content with military life. Rumor had it his great-grandfather fought in the Revolutionary War and his grandfather in the Mexican War. Born to it, they say, followin' the men of the Drake family in graduatin' from the military academy."

"You and Barrett have the same accent. Are you from Georgia?"

"Yes ma'am. Different ends of the state. How about you?"

"West Texas."

"West Texas? Well, call me a polecat. You're not far from home."

Just how far, though, she wasn't certain. Mercy Flats seemed an insurmountable number of miles away — miles she might never cover.

Daniel had quickly discovered that any antic he tried brought boisterous laughter, and he was busy outdoing himself entertaining the growing group of men gathering around him.

Abigail sprang to her feet when a sentry's

voice suddenly rang out, "Riders comin' in!"

She raced out of the tent to the edge of the camp, her eyes fixed on the three riders approaching. One animal pulled a travois, and her pulse quickened. She raced to meet the group, running beside Barrett's stretcher. Tears of gratitude to God blinded her. He looked so very still. Reaching out to touch his hand, she willed him to open his eyes and respond. His lips were cracked, and his breathing was so shallow that she had to feel for a pulse to make sure that he was still alive.

The camp doctor stepped out of the medical tent and waited. The horses stopped and the men quickly dismounted and carried the stretcher inside the tent, Abigail close on their heels.

Barrett's appearance alarmed her. Even with the two days' growth of beard, she could see that his fever was dangerously high.

"How is he?" she asked anxiously.

The doctor barely glanced at her, focused as he was on cutting away Barrett's shirt. "Fetch me that bucket of water," he directed.

She complied, dampening a cloth and bathing Barrett's face while the doctor listened to his heartbeat. When she had left him twenty-four hours ago, he'd been tossing with fever. Now he seemed ominously still. The doctor felt for a pulse. When he released Barrett's wrist, it fell to the cot limply.

"I think it might be yellow fever," Abigail supplied. "Am I right?"

"Good Lord, that's all we need." The doctor walked to the end of the stretcher, removed Barrett's boots, and tossed them to the end of the cot. While he proceeded to unfasten Barrett's trousers, Abigail busied herself with rinsing out the cloth. When she turned around again, Drake's clothing was piled on top of his boots and he was covered with a light sheet.

"We have to get his fever down," the doctor said more to himself than to her.

"I want to help."

The doctor glanced up and then went on working. "If it's the fever, you're in danger."

"I was around the baby's mother too."

The doctor set to work with Abigail at his side. It was an hour before they stepped back, wiping their hands on a cloth.

"What happens now?" she murmured. The fever was lower but still evident.

"We wait."

"Wait?" Her heart fell. She'd hoped that by now Barrett would have responded. But he lay as still as death, his body racked with fever.

"Try to get some water into him. I'll have the cook make a broth. You can spoon it down his throat as long as he'll swallow it. See that he doesn't choke." The doctor moved on when two more wounded were carried into the tent.

Sergeant Dobbs assumed full care of Daniel, allowing Abigail to remain with Barrett. She spent the morning alternately washing the patient's face, chest, and arms with a soft cloth and then carefully dribbling teaspoons of water and broth into his mouth.

The day wore on and darkness fell, but she refused to leave his bedside.

Burying her face in her hands, she listened to his hacking cough, praying for some small sign that he would live. "Father," she prayed, "I offer everything I have to give. I promise to give up all my evil ways and devote myself to living according to Your Word. Please, Lord . . . just let Barrett live."

"Miss McDougal?"

She glanced up to find Sergeant Dobbs standing in the doorway.

"Sergeant. I'm sorry, if Daniel . . ."

"He's fine. The men are enjoyin' the diversion. Helps them feel like they've got a little bit of home." His brow furrowed with compassion. "You need to rest. I'll sit with Captain."

"No, I want to stay with him — but thank you."

"You're going to make yourself sick. At least let me bring you somethin' to eat."

For the first time that day she noticed that she was hungry. "I'd be very grateful, Sergeant. Thank you."

"No trouble at all, ma'am."

"Please, call me Abigail."

"Yes, ma'am, it would be an honor. I'll be back shortly."

When he returned, he was carrying a plate of stew, a chunk of bread, and two steaming cups. Pulling his chair closer to the cot, he drank coffee while she ate.

With half her attention on Barrett and the other half on their conversation, Abigail found herself telling him about Anne-Marie and Amelia, their mission, and the bizarre way she'd met Captain Drake. "As good as the sisters were, I couldn't leave little Daniel yet," she confided. "At first, I thought I might take him back to Mercy Flats with me, but I'm not sure that's wise. I wonder if there might be a childless couple in Shreveport who would want to adopt him."

"Might be. I'll tell the men to keep an ear

open — but the war's left so many widows . . ."

Abigail studied the young sergeant's face and found it to be handsome in an aristocratic way. Not rugged and breathtaking like Barrett's, but infinitely kind. "What did you do before the war, Sergeant?"

"I taught school."

Abigail smiled. "A teacher? How strange to find you in a sergeant's stripes."

"I find it so too," he admitted. "But every able-bodied man has been called to support the cause."

"The cause. I guess I'm like a lot of people. I thought the war was about the issue of slavery, but Barrett says it's really over the right to govern ourselves."

"Well, not entirely, but I do believe in self-government. As a teacher, I reported to a school board, most of whom didn't read or write and some of whom didn't see the importance of education at all. In their eyes, a teacher is an expendable item.

"When I tried to explain the importance of a boy knowing how to read and work his sums, the importance of knowin' something about the history of his country and of the world, the board plain didn't understand. Gettin' money to buy books turned into a major issue. I guess I was ready to give up

298

teachin' and try somethin' new when war broke out."

"And now? Will you return to your position once the war is over?"

"Ignorance is no excuse for anythin'. I'll go back to teachin', and I'll buy the books and supplies myself if I have to. Children need to be taught not only the basics, but philosophy and literature as well."

She sighed, tucking the blanket closer around Barrett. "My sisters and I were educated by nuns at a mission. We learned to read from the Bible and what few books folks donated."

"Bein' from Texas, I guess the Spanish influence is very strong at that mission."

"Yes, I knew very little about what was happening anywhere but in my world." She smiled. "I know Barrett must think I'm pretty unenlightened."

"Not unenlightened. Unaware," Dobbs corrected. "A pretty woman like you could never be accused of being ignorant. I guess you were raised Quaker so you wouldn't know anything about violence."

"I know enough, and no, I'm not Quaker. This is only a disguise. Barrett thought it necessary for safe travel."

"Well, he's a good man — a man of God. I'm sure he didn't abuse the dress."

"He didn't." Then it hit her. She had transgressed against God. Lowering her head, she silently repented. *Forgive me, Father. I was young and foolish; I now see with shocking clarity what I have become.*

"Beauty and intelligence combined with courage," the sergeant mused. His gaze softened. "Incredible courage. I don't know of many women who'd be doin' what you're doin'."

"Well, seems I've always been long on determination. Stubborn, I believe the sisters at the mission called it."

"I'm sure determined is more like it. Could I bring you fresh water from the creek?"

"That would be very nice of you."

"I'd be happy to do it. Is there anything else you need?"

"You can check on Daniel for me." She felt bad about virtually deserting the child. "When the men get tired of playing with him, you can bring him to me."

"The boy'll be fine. I'll keep an eye on him for you. I imagine he'll be wantin' to go to bed soon. I'll bed him down in your tent."

"Thank you, Sergeant."

"Doyle." He smiled. "And may I call you Abigail?"

"Of course. Thank you, Doyle," she amended.

His name brought a big smile to his face. "No, ma'am. Thank *you.*"

Word immediately circulated throughout camp that the Quaker woman wasn't Quaker after all.

Just one fine-looking single woman.

Toward daylight the second day, Barrett began to toss and moan, rolling around on the cot.

Abigail jerked awake and stood up. "Doctor. Doctor!"

The doc rolled out of his cot, half-asleep. Pushing to his feet, he walked to Barrett's side and began to examine him with his quick but competent hands.

"Looks like he's coming around. His temperature's lower."

"But he's still unconscious."

"And he could be for a while. He's not out of the woods yet."

As the sun broke through the clouds, Barrett's mutterings became more coherent.

"You sure you don't want to go on over to the commissary and have a bite to eat?" the doctor asked Abigail when Barrett called out a woman's name again.

"No, thank you." Leaning over Barrett with a cool, wet cloth, Abigail's lips thinned when she caught the tail end of the name he was calling. Mona.

Ramona. He's actually calling for his late wife.

Tossing the cloth into the half-empty bucket, she parted the canvas and stepped outside the tent to gain control of her temper.

"Ramona! Oh, Ramona!" she mimicked. "My foot he isn't still in love with her!" She paced back and forth in front of the tent. "I'm sick. Ramona. Rub my forehead, rub my back." No wonder the doctor was so insistent that she go eat. Men! She despised them all.

By afternoon, Barrett seemed worse instead of better. It was all Abigail could do to keep the blankets on him. Concern creased her forehead in a perpetual frown, but the doctor seemed to think that it was only a matter of time before the fever broke.

She wondered exactly where his experience lay, with animals or people. Her eyes shifted back to the patient.

"Ramona," Barrett murmured. "Ramona?"

"I'm here, Barrett." It galled her to appease him this way, but if he lived, she'd see to it that he'd pay. She irritably wrung out the cloth and wiped his feverish face.

"Did you feed the dog?"

"Yes."

"Did he eat?"

"Yes," she returned stoically.

"Ramona . . ."

Glancing over her shoulder to locate the doctor, she wadded up the cloth and wedged it between his lips.

"Raoooooaaa . . ."

"Miss McDougal."

She started, jerked the cloth out of Barrett's mouth, and dropped it back into the pan of water. "Yes, Doctor?"

"You should eat something," he called from across the tent. "You're getting cranky."

Doyle entered the tent carrying a tin plate. "I've brought her supper, Doctor."

"Good." The doctor sent her a stern glance. "I'll remind Barrett that he's in your debt."

"Come on, ma'am. Let's go outside," Doyle coaxed.

"I'll eat here." She dropped onto the chair next to Barrett's cot, holding her hand out for the plate. "I don't mind, really."

Shrugging, he handed the meal over. "Never saw a woman so protective," he grumbled.

He sat with her as she ate. Tonight they talked of gentler times, of his home and his family. Abigail was aware of the young sergeant's attraction to her, but she was too tired and too polite to openly discourage his interest.

Dobbs finally left to stand guard duty, and as darkness fell, Abigail continued her bedside vigil.

The lantern's rays bathed Barrett's features in the shadows when she knelt beside his cot. Her eyes filled with love when she noticed how much thinner he'd grown during the past few days. Somehow it made him more handsome, carving his features more finely.

A stubble of beard shadowed his cheeks, and since he was lying still for the first time in hours, she decided to shave him.

It took a bit of finesse. She carefully anticipated any abrupt movement on his part to keep from cutting his throat. It wasn't a perfect job, but she managed.

When she was finished, she washed his face and admired her handiwork, satisfied that he looked better and must surely feel better, whether he realized it or not.

The doctor returned and checked his patients one last time before bedding down at the back of the tent.

Abigail's back ached with fatigue, and she seriously considered going to her own tent for the night. But when Barrett coughed, she knew that she couldn't.

Corporal Bower stopped by to assure her that Daniel was fast asleep, exhausted from the big day he'd had. He promised to keep an eye on the boy for her.

Knowing that she couldn't stay awake another night, Abigail decided that the best thing to do was to make herself a pallet beside Barrett's cot. That way she'd know if he needed anything during the night and the doctor wouldn't be disturbed. She'd seen the shadows of exhaustion beneath his eyes and the weight of his years stooping his shoulders.

"Mona," Barrett murmured.

"Hush up, Barrett," Abigail muttered as she made her pallet.

She lay down, knowing that she would get very little rest, but some was better than none at all.

Barrett called out Ramona's name again and she heaved a sigh and reached out to gently pat his hand. "I'm here, darling," she whispered, "I won't leave you."

He immediately settled down, seeming at ease now.

■ ■ ■ ■

Rays of warm sunlight filtered through the tent when Abigail awoke. Barrett stirred on his pallet.

Sitting up, she felt a pang of guilt for sleeping so soundly. It must be very late, she realized as she heard the commotion in camp.

"Don't concern yourself," the doctor said from the bedside of a cot nearby. "You and he both needed the rest."

"I — I'll get fresh water," she stammered.

"I'll do that for you," Doyle called from the door of the tent.

"Thank you . . ."

"I've brought your breakfast, and Daniel is playing in the commissary."

"Doyle, really. You don't have to keep doing this for me."

"But I want to," the sergeant said.

Throughout the day, he carried her meals and brought Daniel to visit her for brief intervals before sweeping him off to play again. The child was glowing from all the food and attention he was getting, so Abigail didn't feel so bad about leaving him.

That evening Barrett seemed to be resting comfortably. His forehead wasn't nearly as hot, and she was almost tempted to believe the doctor when he said the captain had turned a corner.

When Sergeant Dobbs stopped by with her evening meal, he mentioned that several of the men were playing cards over in the commissary.

"Oh?" She was good at cards. She and Amelia used to sit up all night playing for hours. "Do they play often?"

"It's the only thing to do, unless we're on patrol or standin' guard. Until the next battle, that is."

"I suppose playing cards does pass a lot of time," she mused.

"It sure does — though it wouldn't be something a lady would understand." He grinned. "A Quaker lady," he teased.

She got to her feet and stretched lazily.

"Perhaps you might enjoy watching the game tonight," the sergeant suggested.

Abigail studied the young man's earnest expression, disappointed that he was so gullible. It wouldn't be fair of her to take advantage of the men, especially considering that they'd all been so nice to her, and yet . . .

"I'd love to watch, but I can't leave the captain."

"I could have the men move a table over

here. Why, you might even get to play. Just for fun," he clarified.

"Oh certainly. Just for fun," she agreed. "If you don't think the men would mind."

"They wouldn't mind a bit. I'll ask when I take our plates back."

"Well, don't insist," she told him. "I don't want to be any trouble."

"It won't be a problem."

Thirty minutes later, a table stood in front of the medical tent. Abigail watched four men play poker as Doyle explained the finer points of the game to her — incorrectly.

"Would you like to sit in on a hand?" a corporal invited.

"Oh, no, I couldn't . . ."

"Here," another man offered, springing to his feet, "take my chair. I've got watch in a half hour anyway."

She reluctantly sat down and picked up the cards she was dealt. Guilt assuaged her. She'd promised the Lord that if He'd heal Barrett she'd change her ways — but she had given all the money she'd earned begging to the last mission. But maybe just one hand . . .

The men allotted her a measly amount of matchsticks, but the stakes weren't high so she wasn't concerned. All assumed that she was being cautious because of her inexperience, and they had a grand time teaching her the rules during the first two hands.

Then, when it seemed that she was getting the hang of the game, they settled down to more serious play.

"Why, I can't believe my luck!" she exclaimed, scooping up the handful of coins they were using now that the men were convinced she was an imbecile.

"Beginner's luck," one of the sergeants complained, throwing his cards on the table.

She took the pot the next four hands in a row.

"Why, I do declare, gentlemen. Can you believe such a stroke of luck?" She batted her eyes, clearly aghast at her good fortune.

"Yeah. If I didn't know better, I'd say you'd played this game before," a sergeant grumbled.

"Me?" Abigail smiled, expertly cutting the deck. "Odd, isn't it?"

When she won the next two hands, two of the men gave up but another two were waiting to take their places.

She was careful to let one or the other win a pot now and then, but she saved the big ones for herself.

One surly corporal watched her from the corner of his eye like a hawk, openly complaining that she was dealing from the bottom of the deck. By midnight there were more than a few disgruntled players at the table.

"Don't that beat all you ever seen!" a corporal cried, throwing his hand on the table when Abigail laid down a royal flush.

"Well, it has been delightful, gentlemen, but it's getting late." She delicately yawned, feigning exhaustion.

"Yeah, real delightful," Sergeant Stredevant mocked. She smiled nicely back at the sore loser. "Thank you ever so much for teaching me the finer points of the game. It's been an experience. Don't you agree, gentlemen?"

Doyle shot the men a swift visual reprimand. "Our pleasure ma'am. It isn't often we're whipped by someone so pretty."

"Why, Sergeant Dobbs, how you do turn a phrase," she replied modestly. "Thank you again, sirs, but I must bid you a good evening now."

On her way to the privy, Abigail stopped by the general's tent. He glanced up when she tapped at the entrance. "Yes?"

She appeared in the doorway, framed by lantern light. "I wanted to give you something." She walked to his desk and laid down her complete winnings.

He stared at the pile. "What's that?"

"The men and I got together and decided so many needed new shoes." She smiled. "Please take it all and buy what's needed. And you're welcome."

TWENTY

On the third day in camp, Abigail began to notice increased activity. It was obvious that the men were preparing for a coming battle.

"How's your patient today?" the doctor asked that morning.

"Better, I think."

He stepped to the bed and checked Barrett over, and then drew the sheet back over him. "I don't think its yellow jack."

Abigail sagged with relief. "Are you sure?"

"As sure as I can be. You'll begin to see an improvement any day now."

"I'm still worried that he hasn't regained consciousness."

"Patience. He'll be up and about soon enough," the doctor encouraged. "If he isn't, it won't be for lack of care. Wish I had a dozen like you." He smiled at her before continuing to the next bed.

Sitting down on her stool, she folded her hands and waited. That seemed like all she'd done lately, but she didn't mind. As heat began to build in the tent, she nodded off. An annoying fly buzzed overhead, darting on and off her cheek. Brushing the pesky insect away, she tried to keep her eyes open, but they felt as heavy as weights.

Swiping the fly away again, she was vaguely aware of the moans surrounding her. There was so much pain and suffering inside the tent and so little anyone could do to ease the agony.

She nodded off, waking with a start a moment later. Forcing her eyes open, she glanced down at Barrett, and her heart nearly stopped.

His eyelids were moving. As she stared at him, one eye flickered open, blinking as he tried to adjust to the bright sunlight streaming through the tent opening.

"Barrett?" She jumped to her feet, knocking over her stool. "Can you hear me?" She clasped his face between her hands, leaning closer. "It's me, Abigail. Can you hear me?"

"Abigail?" he asked in more of a croak than a whisper.

She grinned. "Yes! We're in General Smith's camp. He has the messages, Barrett. We got them here in time."

"In time?"

"Yes! Oh, my darling, you've been so

313

sick." She hurriedly reached for the cloth and wrung it dry. Though his eyes closed, he appeared conscious. Abigail's heart filled with joy as she bathed his cool face with the water. He was going to be fine. *Thank You, God!* He was going to be fine!

"Where are we?"

"Kirby Smith's camp. Just outside Shreveport. We've been here three days."

"Three days?"

"Yes — three." He tried to sit up, but Abigail pushed him back. "No. You must rest. Everything's fine. The general came by this morning to tell me that without your efforts, the army would have been unprepared for General Banks's advancing troops."

Barrett seemed to relax after the news and drifted off again. This time his rest was more peaceful.

She sat on the stool watching him for a long time. When she was certain that he was comfortable, she decided that she could take the opportunity to check on Daniel.

Walking through camp, she smiled, exchanging pleasantries with the men. She'd come to know many of them in such a short time. None seemed disturbed by the recent fleecing she'd given them at the card table. She was struck by the bonhomie the Johnnie Rebs shared. They all wore ragged uniforms, half wearing gray, the other half wearing butternut brown, with a goodly number wearing both colors. She had listened to their dry humor that seemed to break out at the least provocation. Though they seemed like soldier boys, they were obviously grown men who knew their responsibilities.

Many were homesick, and the songs they sang around the campfire were of home and sweethearts and wives left behind. They sang lustily and with abandon, and she'd discovered that many of them had very good voices. Tents and camp equipment were threadbare. Spades and axes were a luxury. One of the main jobs assigned to a detail was the task of gathering wood for the fires each morning, especially the cook fire. Another detail was sent to scour the countryside for food, butchering any animals they could scavenge from local farms and bringing in "donations" of flour and staples from others. The war had gone on so long that there wasn't much food left for anyone, even an army supporting a cause that most in the area considered just.

Besides poker, the men played seven-up and vingt-et-un. Others spent their free time polishing their muskets and bayonets with well-moistened wood ashes. What a contrast — bright muskets and tattered uniforms.

Abigail knew now why Barrett had chosen the role of a shoe salesman for his guise. Many of the men had completely worn out the soles of their shoes, and more than a few were entirely barefoot. She smiled, knowing that her ill-gotten gains from the card game would supply a vast need.

"Howdy, ma'am," a redheaded, freckle-faced soldier greeted Abigail warmly.

"Hello. How are you this fine day, Corporal?"

"Fair to middling, I'd say."

She smiled, entering her tent for the first time in days. She found Daniel playing with Doyle, the two having a grand time.

"How's the captain this morning?" Doyle asked as he caught Daniel by the seat of his pants when he tried to shimmy out of the tent.

"He's awake!"

Doyle glanced at her, the smile fading from his lips. "You think a whole lot of the captain, don't you?"

"I try not to think about the captain any more than necessary," she conceded, because she knew how hopeless it was. The kisses had been dalliances; the warm smiles a polite gesture. If he had feelings for her, he'd surely lost them during the illness. Ra-

mona dominated his thoughts even unconscious.

Now that Captain Drake was on his way
to recovery, he'd be taking her to Mercy
Flats before long, and then she'd never see
him again.

"What day is it?" she asked the following
morning.

"Well, I'd say it's April." The doctor
finished examining Barrett, seeming pleased
at his progress. "I would imagine somewhere
about the sixth or seventh."

"April sixth," Abigail mused. So much had
happened in the last week and a half that
even thinking about it made her mind whirl.

The doctor straightened, meeting her eyes.
"He's doing fine. He should be staying
awake for longer spells now."

That evening Abigail stood outside the
medical tent and watched as most of the
men in camp were called to company. They
marched out to the accompaniment of a
muffled drum. Something about the sight
made Abigail uneasy.

"Where are they going?"

"To Mansfield, I hear." The doctor stood
watching the exit with her.

"Where's that?"

"Some eight to ten miles south of here."

Apprehension filled her voice when she whispered, "Will they engage in battle?"

"Yes, ma'am. Rumor says General Banks is movin' troops clean across Louisiana. Could be as many as twenty thousand or more."

"General Smith can't seriously be thinking of trying to fight that large a force with our men —"

"No, General Taylor and General Smith are looking to combine forces in Mansfield."

Abigail's eyes closed with relief. "We'll give those blue bellies a run for their money."

"Well, I think I'll get some rest." The doctor turned away. "We'll have casualties by tomorrow noon."

Abigail tossed and turned that night. Although she was back in her tent with Daniel, her thoughts were on Barrett and on the men who were marching to meet Banks's troops at Mansfield.

The men's faces drifted before her eyes, both young and old. She wondered if young Corporal Howard would ever see his infant daughter, or if Sergeant Miller would come back to marry his Suzanne, or if nice Lieutenant Madison would ever get to hold his new grandbaby.

She didn't believe fighting solved anything, and she didn't know much about the cause, but she knew those men, and she wondered if anything could be worth the loss of even a single one of them.

Barrett's eyes were open when she entered the medical tent the next morning. Though he was weak, she was encouraged to see that he was improving every hour.

"I hear there's a battle."

"Yes, I'm afraid so."

"Well, the men are well trained," he murmured. "And Smith has sound judgment."

By his tone, he was angry because he wasn't marching with them.

She straightened his light blankets. "It saddens me to think that some won't be coming back."

"Sounds like you're worried about someone in particular." She noticed that he deliberately kept his tone casual.

"No," she replied. "All the men in camp have been exceptionally good to Daniel —"

"Miss McDougal."

Abigail turned to see a young corporal standing in the tent opening. "Yes?"

"Lieutenant Moore has sent me to invite you to join the general for supper tonight."

"But . . . but I thought the general left with —"

"General Smith will be joining his men immediately after supper," the corporal stated.

"Oh. I see. Then please tell the general that I'll be happy to dine with him."

"Thank you, ma'am." He automatically saluted, and then flushed with embarrassment when Abigail smiled.

"Seems you've made a few conquests since you arrived," Barrett grumbled.

"Don't be silly." She unconsciously smoothed her hair. Dinner with the General. How nice.

"Suppose I can't blame them. Most of them haven't seen a woman in months. Anything in skirts would look good right now."

Stung by his implication that any woman, no matter how homely, would have sparked the same courtesies, Abigail flung the washcloth at the pan of water and stalked out of the tent. His wicked chuckle followed her.

Oh, he's better all right! And too infuriating for his own good!

That evening she was dressed and waiting when the corporal came to escort her to the general's tent.

The young man's features broke into a smile. "You look real nice, ma'am."

"Good heavens, Corporal." Abigail viewed him chidingly, Barrett's earlier observation still bedeviling her. "This is the same dress I've worn since I got here."

"Yes, ma'am." The boy's face flushed beet red. "But somehow a man don't seem to notice."

Though the food was exactly the same as served in the commissary, the general managed to give the meal an air of class and decency. All in all, it was a pleasant evening and Abigail strolled back to the medical tent later, humming a tune that she'd heard the men singing earlier.

"So you've enchanted the general," Barrett commented from the shadows.

She smiled, elated he was now up and moving around. "Sarcasm? I take that to mean you're feeling better tonight?" She walked past him without a glance.

"I feel like I've been trampled by a herd — hey!"

"Hey what?" She never broke pace.

"Aren't you going to check on me tonight?"

"You appear to be doing fine to me." She continued on, disappearing into her tent a moment later.

That night battles and bodies occupied her dreams. Men — fathers, sons, brothers

— flailing on the fields, blood spread across the fronts of their uniforms. She awoke almost as tired as when she'd gone to bed.

There were few troops at breakfast in the morning. She was surprised when Sergeant Doyle sat down beside her.

"I thought you'd be gone with the others," she exclaimed, immensely relieved to see him.

"Someone has to stay." He passed a piece of hardtack.

His expression gave no indication of how he felt about being left behind, and she didn't ask. Some men would be sensitive about the choice. Others, like Doyle, she suspected, might be just as glad they weren't involved in the killing. Abigail couldn't fault him for that. War, she decided, was an inhumane business, no matter what side a man favored.

Barrett was sitting outside the medical tent when Sergeant Doyle walked Abigail back to her tent.

Daniel, who was obviously enamored of the sergeant, sat atop his broad shoulders and Abigail realized they resembled a family — a very happy family. She felt Barrett's eyes on her back when they sauntered through camp, laughing and talking like they were a typical young couple and child out for a morning stroll.

Late that afternoon, she stuck her head through the opening of the medical tent. Drake was gaining strength rapidly, but his scowl didn't indicate it. "Good afternoon, Captain," she said.

"Doyle's tent is three down."

"I know my direction. I thought you might need fresh water."

"If I need water I'll get it."

Petulance? Understandable but unlike the captain. She let the remark pass. He'd been sick, and the doctor said he'd be cranky for a few days. "Daniel truly enjoys the men's attention."

"Daniel? From what I hear, you've hardly seen the boy since you got here."

Sick or not, he was unreasonable. What he'd said was true, in part. The men had dominated the child, but not for her lack of care. Entering the tent, she picked up his discarded pillow and fluffed it. "The men so enjoy Daniel's company. You wouldn't believe how much he's changed. He's chattering like a magpie now — nothing clear but you can make out a few words."

"Doyle is teaching him to talk?"

"Why, Barrett Drake!" She bit her lower lip, counting to ten. Then, "You need a nap."

"I don't *want* a nap."

Her eyes narrowed on him warningly. "Take one anyway."

"Go spend time with Doyle."

"Thank you. I'll do that."

"Fine."

"Fine."

She pitched his pillow on his cot and left. And stayed away from the medical tent one whole day. Doyle carried Daniel and accompanied her to dinner. There she enjoyed the attention of the few men left in camp, who wound up laughing at Daniel's antics. He was a typical one-year-old now, trying to learn to walk. He'd taken his first unbalanced steps from one soldier to another, and Abigail clapped her hands with praise. Daniel's two front teeth shone as he smiled at the accolades heaped on his accomplishments, and he'd gleefully toddle from one man to the other. Even the few falls he'd taken hadn't wiped the grin from his face.

Abigail kept a close eye on the child, understanding for the first time why women were so proud of their children. Seeing him achieve the smallest accomplishment, watching him change in personality from a sad-faced infant to a smiling little boy, made her beam with pride.

After a long game of seven-up, Sergeant

Doyle walked her back to her tent, carrying a weary Daniel. When Doyle placed the boy on the middle of his cot, he was already fast asleep.

Abigail stepped outside with Doyle, closing the flap behind her. When the sergeant bent down to kiss her, she wasn't surprised; she'd expected his affection and found it mildly pleasant. Not exciting like Barrett's, but gentle — and sweet.

Barrett sat outside the medical tent, watching the nauseating spectacle. His lips firmed, and the muscle in his jaw twitched.

She thought she was bothering him but she wasn't, not in the least. Doyle didn't know her true nature — he hadn't witnessed her gall.

But he'd noticed her finer points.

Barrett made sure he saw little of Abigail these days. It wasn't hard to keep her at a distance, though — she was always in the company of Sergeant Doyle.

Should he tell her that she was making a fool of herself? Warn her that men's feelings in battles didn't necessarily hold in peace?

On her way to her tent the following night, Abigail paused in front of the medical quarters. She'd let Barrett stew in his juices for one whole day; surely that was enough penance for him. She'd wager he hadn't noticed her absence. Taking a deep breath, she called out before lifting the flap. He glanced up from the book he was reading.

"Anything I can get you?"

"Nothing. Oh, I'll be riding out of here in three days."

"Three days? My, you are improving. The doctor didn't mention this miraculous turnabout." The captain was stubborn as a mule and twice as cantankerous. "I'll make preparations to leave."

"You still want me to take you?" he asked without looking up.

She frowned. "Why — yes. Why would I change my mind?"

"Doyle comes to mind. You and he seem pretty friendly lately. Thought he might decide to take you."

"I'm certain that he would, but he has du-ties."

His gaze met hers and she saw hurt — even a hint of betrayal — in their depths. "What's so special about Doyle?"

Her cheeks burned. Why, he was envious! Of a gentle man who'd been nothing but gracious to her. "You're delirious and talk-ing gibberish again. Any minute you'll be calling for your darling Ramona again!"

Whirling, she left the tent, biting back tears.

If she made it through another three days with him, they'd need to name a mission after *her.*

TWENTY-ONE

"All right. If you're looking to rile me, you have."

Abigail glanced up later to find Barrett filling the doorway of her tent. Snatching the pins from her hair, she freed the thick mass to fall to her waist. Obviously he had more to say, but she wasn't in the mood to hear it.

"Now it's your turn to go away," she said.

"What's this fascination with Doyle? Are you aware you're turning this camp upside down by being here? These men are fighting a war, not running a courting service."

"I assume you're rattled because you happened to witness Doyle's innocent kiss the other night." She yanked the brush through her hair. "Well, it was just that — an innocent peck."

"That peck didn't look so innocent to me."

"It's late, Barrett. Obviously we don't see

eye to eye on my choice of company." Satan had a way of turning a comfortable relationship into something tainted and immoral. She turned to meet his eyes. "Were you spying on me?"

"Spying on you? Every man in camp saw the exchange."

"I hardly think *every* man saw it, and even if they did, there's nothing shameful about an innocent kiss. You've kissed me." The comparison between Barrett and Doyle rattled her. Doyle had kissed her; Barrett had *kissed* her.

His tone softened. "I have no call to be your guardian, but you're under my protection until we part."

Circus, traveling show. Spectacle, innocuous kiss. He viewed things differently than she.

The muscle in his jaw twitched. "Are your feelings for this man serious? What about the pact you made with your sisters?"

"The pact," she reminded him, "was childish. You said so yourself."

"Then you have changed your mind about men."

"Not all men, but Doyle is an attractive man, nothing more. My plans haven't changed. As soon as you're able to travel, I'll ride out with you." Sergeant Doyle was a fine man, but he wasn't *her* man. She cleared her throat. "It's late, Barrett, and you need your rest. The doctor says you're still very weak."

His eyes moved to Daniel's empty cot. "Where's the boy?"

She closed her eyes and jerked the brush through her hair. "The boy's name is Daniel."

"Shouldn't he be with you?"

"Not necessarily."

"He's with Doyle?"

Barrett's tone annoyed her. If he truly cared for Daniel and her, why didn't he simply say so? She'd certainly had no trouble making her feelings for him appallingly apparent lately.

"Daniel is with Corporal Maddox tonight."

"Corporal Maddox." She noted the flash of relief in his eyes.

"Corporal Maddox asked permission to keep him overnight."

Abigail had been hesitant at first about the corporal's request, but then she recalled a prior conversation with Doyle. Maddox's wife and two sons had perished in a Yankee raid on their hometown a few months earlier. The corporal had withdrawn into a shell, preferring to keep to himself since the tragedy. But when he'd seen Daniel, he'd smiled and lowered his defenses.

When Abigail recalled the tragedy, she'd readily agreed to share the child. It was comforting to see how such a small boy could bring happiness to so many lonely lives.

The last she'd seen of the two, the corporal had been busy whittling the boy a toy soldier from a stick of birch while Daniel raptly watched from his perch on the corporal's lap.

She pitched the brush onto the cot and rose to her feet. "Was there something you specifically wanted, Barrett?" For the first time in her life she was more interested in the thoughts and feelings of someone other than herself, and he challenged her discretion. He'd forgotten that she wasn't the reckless, headstrong young woman he'd met a scant time ago — or had he even noticed the change? It had taken hard knocks from the Lord to get her attention, but she was awake and aware now. She once was a wretched soul, stealing from men, playing Robin Hood in childlike behavior. Well, her Robin Hood days were over. Daniel had changed her life — Daniel and Barrett. If he wasn't so blinded by jealousy — *jealousy.* That was it. He was envious of her relationship with the other men. The Bible was full of the havoc the ugly sin provoked. If Barrett's state hadn't been so grave she would have laughed. Every man in camp had been a perfect gentleman, but her favor fell with one man, one very stubborn and prideful man who didn't know a good woman when he found her.

It was obvious that after she'd carried his message to General Smith she'd ceased to be of use to him, yet for some reason he found his male ego mortally endangered when other men found her desirable.

And she should be the envious one. As uncaring and spoiled as Ramona had been, in spite of all the hurt she'd caused Barrett, it was still her name that he'd called when he lay delirious with fever.

Her name he called in his darkest hour.

If that didn't prove where his loyalties lay, nothing did.

"It's very late. Goodnight, Captain Drake."

Their gazes refused to yield to each other.

"Are you in love with Doyle?" he asked.

"Goodnight Captain."

"Are you in love with him?" he repeated. His tone demanded an answer that she was not prepared to give. In love with Doyle? She'd never given it a thought. She respected and admired what he stood for, but could she fall in love with him? Was love — true love — possible in such a short span of time?

The second answer was clearer than the first. Hadn't she fallen in love with Barrett in less time? Even when she thought he was Hershall Digman, pitiful, bumbling Hershall Digman, he had struck a responsive chord in her that no other man had ever tapped before.

"I need an answer, Abigail." His voice turned husky now, more uncertain.

"I admire Doyle and I enjoy his company, Barrett, but I am not in love with him. Are you still in love with Ramona?"

"Why bring her into this conversation?"

"You mistook me for her in your delirium. Not once but several times. I must remind you of her." And her betrayal. That was the crux of the problem. She reminded him of everything he resented in his unhappy marriage.

Surprise and then resignation colored his features. "You're nothing like Ramona."

In a calm voice, she said softly. "I'm not the one you need to convince, Barrett."

Something foreign entered his eyes, something dark and forbidden. "You think I'm still in love with my dead wife?"

"Yes."

"You think that one failed attempt to find love has me thinking that I could never love another woman?"

"Yes."

Taking her hand, he carted her out of the tent and propelled her through the center of camp. He'd lost his mind! Where was he taking her and for what purpose?

"Barrett, stop this," she warned. "You're making a scene."

Ignoring the men's calls and friendly jeers, he moved her along, defying her protests.

She pictured his face dotted with anger — no, resentment — no, determination — and it occurred to her that maybe he had decided to take her off and shoot her after all. She thought about screaming for Doyle, and then realized that it would only serve to incite the situation.

The doctor stepped outside the medical tent, surprise registering when Barrett pulled Abigail past.

Smiling lamely, she waved as Barrett hustled her by the tent. "Evening, Doctor."

The doctor slowly removed his pipe from his mouth. "Evenin', Abigail."

Through the camp, by the creek, and up a wooded thicket Barrett strode with Abigail struggling to free herself from his steely grasp, but he held her firmly in hand.

"I'm calling for Doyle!"

"Go right ahead."

"Barrett!" She kept up, trying to retain her composure. She felt so humiliated that she could die! He had dragged her through camp in front of all those men!

Once outside the camp, he drew her into a thick growth of bushes, still refusing to release his hold.

Wrenching free, she glared at him, rubbing her wrists resentfully.

"What is the meaning of this?" she demanded in a tight voice.

"I wanted a little privacy. All right? No Doyle or other doting men."

Shivering, she rubbed her arms. "All right. We have privacy. Is there something you need to say?"

"Something I need to do without having every man's eye in camp on me."

He was starting to scare her. He had been nothing but a gentleman; did he plan to change? Turn into a brute who might . . . She shook the thought away. This was Barrett. She had absolute confidence in his principles. Straightening, she met the challenge "What do you want?" Her breath caught when he pulled her to him and kissed her. Hard.

Her knees went limp as he held her, and he caught her slight weight and supported it. The kiss settled into a sweet, overpowering exchange that sent her head reeling. Her arms drifted around his neck and she rested against his strength. It was many long minutes before he released her . . . and then with reluctance, she sensed. Meeting her stricken gaze, he touched her cheek. "You think about that kiss next time Doyle gives you a 'peck.' "

Think about it? She knew the earth-shattering embrace would never leave her mind.

Not if she lived to be as old as Methuselah.

Abigail awoke before dawn with a song in her heart. Her first thought was to go to Barrett, but she suppressed the urge, knowing that if the moments they'd spent together last night meant anything to him, he would come to her. So now, as in the past, she waited.

She could no longer imagine her life without him, yet he had said nothing about a future together. The word *love* hadn't been spoken, while many others had come so easily to her mind.

Around mid-morning she grew restless. Daniel was napping, so she decided to stroll to the commissary in hopes that she might bump into a certain handsome captain. The memory of his kiss still made her blood race, and she longed for a brief glimpse of him.

She asked a lieutenant who was hanging around outside her tent to peek in on Daniel occasionally. He said that he would, and she set off.

Casually ambling past the medical tent, she glanced inside and felt a letdown when she discovered Barrett's empty cot.

"Mornin', Abigail."

"Good morning, Doctor," she said in a rush, hoping that he wouldn't mention the ruckus in camp the night before.

"Looking for your captain?" There was thinly disguised amusement twinkling in the doctor's eye.

"No — well, sort of. Just getting a breath of fresh air while Daniel's napping." Filled with acute disappointment, she meandered toward the stream. It was a lovely day. The sun's rays nestled warmly upon her shoulders, and for the first time in a long time she wasn't preoccupied with thoughts of Amelia and Anne-Marie. She'd found a new path. Amelia and Anne-Marie would always be a part of her but now she had a new life — one with a man she deeply loved.

Anne-Marie and Amelia would die when they heard that news.

Strolling along the bank of the stream, she idly brushed her fingers across the blooming weeds, sending their frilly tops spiraling into the air. Birds chattered back and forth; a running creek gurgled lazily through the rocks and logs strewn in the water.

"Hello, love."

Turning sharply, Abigail spotted Barrett lazily sunning himself beside the stream.

Suppressing her elation at seeing him, she made her smile as casual as a woman could when she was with the man she loved. "Captain Drake. How nice to see you again." Their gazes met, and the emotional undercurrent made her stomach curl with warmth. "Sunning yourself like a lizard, I see?"

His mouth curved with an unconscious smile as he crossed his arms behind his head and stretched out more fully. Patting the empty spot beside him, he beckoned to her. "Come sit with me."

"Well . . ." She pretended to think about it for propriety's sake only. She owed the good sisters that much. "I suppose I could — for a moment." She sat down beside him, conscious of his closeness.

"You look mighty fetching this morning,"

he observed. "Sleep well last night?"

"Very well. And yourself?"

"Very well, thank you." His grin was decidedly smug.

She closed her eyes, wishing that the moment could last forever. An hour spent together seemed like a moment to her. Barrett's health was improving so readily that they were bound to be leaving any day now. She studied a passing cloud. That prospect was painful, yet she knew she couldn't complain. The extra days she had been granted with Daniel were blessings, ones she hadn't anticipated.

But giving up both Daniel and Barrett — at the same time! — was more than she thought her heart could bear.

She studied Barrett's handsome profile from the corner of her eye. If she'd changed on the inside during the past week, he'd changed on the outside. It was hard to remember him as a persnickety little shoe salesman, more concerned with his spectacles and white spats than her welfare. She smiled when she recalled how she'd considered him to be short and frumpy, an insult to the male gender.

Now, just looking at him made her weak with desire.

He wasn't particularly tall, hardly taller

than she. But he had a commanding presence about him. How had she missed that in the beginning? How any woman could resist him, no matter who he was pretending to be, was beyond her comprehension now.

Leaning back, she kicked off her shoes and skimmed her toes through the water. The creek was cold, but the water felt wonderfully refreshing.

"Out here, like this, it's hard to believe there's a war going on," she observed, thinking about the men who had ridden out of camp. "General Smith will meet the Northern forces today — I heard talk at breakfast this morning."

"He expects to engage Banks's advance unit today."

"How very sad."

She caught him studying her and she turned to meet his gaze. "What?"

"I don't think I've thanked you. You did a good job getting the message through. It couldn't have been easy, with the baby and all."

"No. And you didn't mention the sacred burial ground." The thought brought an involuntary shudder. "It wasn't easy."

He grinned. "You're afraid of the dark, aren't you?"

She blew out a breath. "How did you know?"

He chuckled. "How did I know? Let me see, it might be from the way your eyes grow round as silver dollars once the sun goes down. Those burial platforms couldn't have set you to rest."

She accepted his teasing graciously because she was in an acceptable mood this morning. Sometimes he could look so stern but when he laughed like this, his eyes reminded her of a sunny summer day. He was cranky over the attention she'd shown Doyle, but he was a gentle man. She shouldn't have, but she felt a tingle when she thought of his rather possessive mood. In fact, she rather liked it.

He looked uncommonly handsome this morning. His hair curled over his shirt collar and over his forehead, giving him a roguish appearance.

"You plan on getting married someday?" he asked her as casually as if he were conducting a survey.

Her pulse skittered at the question. It seemed odd, coming from him. They could pretend that nothing unusual had happened last night, but they both knew better. An invisible thread bound them whether he liked it or not.

And they both were aware that he didn't want to marry again.

"I've never planned on it," she admitted softly. Until recently. Lately the subject had dominated her mind.

He studied a bird in flight. "I suppose, like all women, you dream of marrying a tall man."

Now that seemed a peculiar observation. Was the tough Barrett Drake sensitive about his height? "I don't know." She shrugged. "I've never thought about it."

"A tall man who'd give you tall children," he mused.

"And a tall house with a tall tree in front and a nice, tall picket fence around the tall grass that grew in the yard," she bantered. He *was* sensitive about his height!

"I'm serious."

"So am I."

"Be honest with me. Wouldn't you want your husband to be tall?"

Sighing, she leaned forward to catch a leaf floating by. "How tall are you?"

The telltale muscle above his jaw twitched. "Tall enough."

"That's exactly how tall I'd want my husband to be." She looked directly into his eyes. "Tall enough."

They sat for a moment sharing the silence

before she glanced away as a disturbing thought occurred to her. "Would you want a tall wife?" She wasn't exactly a giant. Perhaps he preferred tall women.

"No, I like runts your size."

"I'm not a runt," she scoffed.

"No, but you are quite a lady, Abigail."

She didn't know why that should make her feel so heady, but it did — oh, how it did.

"And you've turned out to be an acceptable man, Captain Drake."

She met his gaze and knew that love shone in her eyes, but Barrett's gaze wasn't quite as readable.

"Acceptable, huh?"

"Acceptable," she confirmed. They lifted their faces to the bright sunshine.

"Abigail, we'll leave soon — maybe not as soon as I'd hoped, but soon. I've neglected my duties as long as I can," he said quietly.

Sadness washed over her. Though she'd expected the announcement, she'd dreaded this moment. "I thought that might be the case."

"I plan to keep my promise to see you safely to Mercy Flats. We'll leave Daniel at the orphanage, and with any luck you'll be back with your sisters in a few days."

"All right." It broke her heart to think of

leaving Daniel at the orphanage, but they'd deal with the matter later. She wanted to care for the child as her own. Plucking a floating leaf from the water, she twirled it between her fingers. "Will we travel as Quakers?"

When the silence stretched, she finally glanced at him. His eyes were closed as if he were in deep thought.

"No," he said finally. "I'll request a troop escort."

"That's wise, since I've promised the Lord I'd change my ways."

He grinned. "About time you did something about your ways."

"You needn't worry. I have every intention of keeping my promise. I've asked for forgiveness, and when I unite with Amelia and Anne-Marie I'll make them see the error of our previous ways."

"Praise God."

Rolling onto his side, he idly trailed a blade of grass down her arm, and she laughed, pushing his hand away.

"We won't be able to pose as Mr. and Mrs. Levi Howard," he teased in an intimate voice that reminded her of the night before.

"I know."

"You don't mind?"

"No."

"You're mighty obliging all of a sudden."

Twirling the flower between her fingers, she gave him one of those mysterious smiles intended to make a man wonder what a woman was up to. "When my sisters and I were young and full of fancy, we used to pick flowers and make necklaces out of them, or we'd pick the petals to decide if a boy we didn't care for liked us."

"A test that I'd stake my life on," he said.

Abigail calculatingly plucked a petal from the flower, her eyes locked with his teasingly. "He loves me." She plucked another. "He loves me not. He loves me . . . He loves me not."

He shook his head. "I marvel at your enthusiasm; always looking for a bluebird, aren't you?"

"And I'll find one someday," she promised.

"Well," his voice grew lazy, "maybe you underestimated yourself, Abigail McDougal." He swept the blade of grass across her cheek.

"Barrett." She paused, mindful of the painful subject, but it was on her mind hourly. "You called for Ramona when you were ill."

"Did I?" He chuckled. "Must have been quite a nightmare."

"You still think about her, don't you?"

"She's dead, Abigail."

"Is she, Barrett?"

The need in her voice bled through and she felt a weakness much like the one that had consumed her the night before.

"You worry too much," he admonished softly. His fingers wrapped around her wrist and pulled her gently toward him.

"I know, but . . ." He silenced her with a long, heady kiss. Not an answer to her inquiry, but good enough for the present.

Twenty-Two

Abigail and Barrett exchanged curious glances when they returned to camp and noted the activity taking place.

Stretchers were arriving and the stench of tar filled the camp, a gruesome reminder that the war was still going on. There would be human limbs piled high in back of the medical tent by morning.

The battle had been fought at Mansfield, and the first reports filtering back to camp were encouraging. Instead of capitalizing fully on the fall of Vicksburg, the North had diverted over twenty-five thousand troops for General Banks to lead across Louisiana with the intent of capturing Shreveport before moving on to invade Texas from the northeast.

When Abigail stepped into the medical tent her nose wrinkled at the stench. Barrett bent over a wounded solider. "They say it was a major battle."

"General Magruder rushed as many men north as he could spare. General Taylor and General Smith took almost nine thousand men to attack Banks's advance unit." He shook his head. "They're calling it a decisive victory, but the South is taking a heavy toll in human suffering."

Abigail pitched in, offering what help she could. Working side-by-side with Barrett, they assisted anyone who needed an extra hand.

She left late in the afternoon to retrieve Daniel. The long evening and the fight to save the wounded wore on. When Abigail entered the commissary late that night, she was near collapse. Her dress was slick with blood, and she had witnessed so many deaths and amputations in the past few hours that she was numb. But Daniel begged for food, and there was no available soldier to feed him.

Moving through the serving line, she was barely aware when Doyle approached and took the boy from her arms. Handing the child to a corporal, he drew Abigail to a table, sat her down, and pressed a cup of coffee between her hands. "Drink this."

Nodding dazedly, she brought the cup to her lips, barely aware of the hot liquid spilling down her throat.

"You shouldn't be seein' this," Doyle said.

"No." She caught his hand, trying to ease his agony. "It's all right. I'll be fine after I've rested a moment."

He brought her a plate and she tried to eat, but the food lodged in her throat. Doyle sat with her, brooding and pensive. Abigail sensed that something besides the battle was troubling him.

"Take a walk with me," he said when she had finished. A young corporal had left with Daniel with a promise to put him to bed.

She glanced at the row upon row of bodies lying on the ground, moaning. "I'm needed —"

"Just walk with me a ways."

She saw the grieved look in his eyes and wondered how life could be so cruel. Doyle was a gentle man, sickened by the ravages of war. It was a war he'd neither started nor wanted, and yet he'd been asked to give up all that he held dear to fight it. "All right, but I need to make it brief."

Barrett glanced up when she walked past the tent with Doyle. Averting his gaze, Barrett continued to wrap a bandage around an injured man's leg.

It was obvious to Abigail that something was bothering Doyle. She wondered if he was being sent to join the battle. He'd been so good to her and had helped her so much that saying goodbye to him was going to be difficult.

Ironically enough, Doyle walked toward the same stand of bushes she and Barrett had visited earlier. He strode beside her, more like a man who was intent on walking instead of talking. When they reached the bushes, he paused and turned to face her.

"I saw you with him at the stream today."

Color crept to her cheeks. She glanced away, wondering exactly what Doyle had seen. A couple enjoying the sunshine? Or a kiss?

"It doesn't matter," he said, as if he could read her thoughts. "I just wanted you to know."

"I'm sorry." Abigail laid her hand on his arm to comfort him.

"Your feelings for Drake show on your face."

"I'm sorry," she offered again simply. She hadn't wanted to hurt him.

"Rumor has it you and the captain plan to leave straight away."

"Barrett feels he has to return to his duties."

"Does he still plan to take you to Mercy Flats?"

"Yes."

His eyes met her evenly. "He hasn't offered his hand in marriage?"

"No. Please, Doyle. This isn't the time or place." Diverting her eyes, she wondered if her feelings were obvious to every man in camp.

"I know it appears that I'm out of place, but I might not have another opportunity," he said quietly.

She glanced up.

"I know you'll be leaving with the captain, and I may have to join the company at any time," he went on.

"Perhaps not —"

"I will, if the battle continues."

Resting her hand on his arm again, she told him quietly, "I'll pray for you."

"Thank you, I'd be much obliged. But that's not what I'm needin' to say. Abigail, I don't know how you feel about me, but I'm in love with you and the boy."

Her jaw dropped, but he stopped her before she could speak.

"Even if you don't love me now, you could grow to care for me."

"Doyle —"

"Just hear me out. Please." He caught her hands in his and studied them for a long moment before going on. "I know how much you care about Daniel. I know you

351

love him, and how you would like to see him have a real mother and father. I'd be a good father to him, Abigail. If you'll marry me, we can be a family."

"Oh, Doyle." She struggled for words — proper words, not ones that would wound him sharp as any sword. He was so good, so kind, but she didn't love him. "You've only known me a short while — you can't know the real me."

"The past doesn't matter; I know you're a good woman and we wouldn't have to marry right away. I know you're worried about your sisters."

"Doyle, I . . . I don't know what to say." Her mind raced. What he was offering had never occurred to her, and oh, how she longed to keep Daniel with her. Marrying Doyle would solve the problem and give the child a future. Under other circumstances she might consider his hand in marriage, but . . .

"All I want is for you to promise you'll consider my proposal."

The indecision in her eyes must have been evident, and it lent him hope. "Rumor has it you're sweet on Drake, but I'm willing to fight for you and the boy."

"Doyle," she said softly. "I don't love you. The captain and I —"

"I know. You're in love with the captain, but that doesn't matter to me. I don't mean any disrespect, but he'll never ask you to marry him. The men say he's still in love with the memory of his first wife, and no other woman will ever take her place."

Her heart knew that he spoke the truth in love. "Captain Drake will never marry me. I'm aware of that."

"Then permit me to earn your love and respect."

"That would be unfair, Doyle. I want to keep Daniel so badly I ache —"

"Then marry me." Grasping her shoulders, he held her solidly between his large hands. "I'm offering you the chance to keep the child and marry a man who loves you, Abigail. I can't do any better than that. I'm not Drake, and I never will be, but I promise you'll never want for anything."

She shook her head, sorely tempted to accept his offer. Though her heart belonged to Barrett, Doyle would permit her to keep Daniel with no questions asked. But he would need to know her true emotions; that she loved Barrett with heart and soul and she would never forget him. "Doyle, my heart . . ."

His eyes captured her gaze. "It doesn't matter, Abigail. If you'll marry me, I'll devote my life to winning that heart of yours."

Pulling her close, he murmured her name and she rested her head on his chest. It was a good, solid chest, worthy of so much more than he was asking or than she could offer him.

"Go to Mercy Flats and see about your sisters, Abigail. Think about what we could have together, and when the time is right, I'll come for you, if that's what you decide," he promised.

Dazed, she closed her eyes wearily. "All right, Doyle. I'll think about it."

Squeezing her tightly, his voice trembled with gratitude. "Good girl. Just you, me, and our babies. As God is my witness, Abigail, I'll make you happy."

TWENTY-THREE

When the battle ended, General Kirby Smith had captured one hundred fifty loaded supply wagons, twenty-two cannons, and twenty-five hundred prisoners before falling back to Pleasant Hill, some thirty miles west of Natchitoches, Louisiana, to regroup.

Twelve thousand Confederates fought savagely to cut off the Union escape route, but they were driven off with a loss of some fifteen hundred.

Although Union losses were not as heavy, Banks's campaign to move into Texas was broken and the scheme abandoned.

General Smith and his troops returned to camp, and Abigail worked by the doctor's side until the last casualty was treated. Collapsing on her cot that night, she stared at the ceiling, too exhausted to move.

"Are you hungry?"

She opened her eyes to find Barrett standing over her, holding a cup of coffee and a plate of stew. "I've never been so tired in all my life." His gaze lit with what she would like to think was admiration, but on closer examination, she decided it was spent appreciation.

"I'm proud of you. You've grown up in the last two weeks."

"Really? Is this what being a grown-up is all about?" She closed her eyes, sick at heart from the sights, smells, and sounds surrounding her.

Setting the plate and cup on the ground, he drew her into his arms and held her close to his chest. Sighing, she let her eyes drift closed and savored the moment of closeness.

"The bluebird is getting more elusive," she admitted when fatigue overcame her.

"We've done all we can do."

"But the doctor —"

"We've done all we can do," Barrett repeated softly. "We leave at first light." When his mouth lowered to hers, she pushed aside all thoughts of tomorrow. If she was going to have to say goodbye to him, she wanted to make sure he would never forget her.

Sunrise found Abigail in the commissary,

coaxing a fussy Daniel through breakfast. A few men sat at the table watching with long faces when Barrett led the horses to the front of the tent. He'd said little to Abigail that morning, except to tell her that the general had assigned a small contingency to escort them to the border. Once there, the contingency would turn south and ride for another camp.

He heaved the saddle onto her horse, tightened the cinch, and then dropped the stirrup back into place. "You about ready?"

"All ready."

Daniel held his arms out to Barrett, and Barrett took him.

"Thanks again for your help, Abigail." The doctor walked beside her when she prepared to mount up.

"I wish I could have done more."

His eyes met hers as he took her hand and graciously lifted it to kiss her fingertips. "It has been an extraordinary pleasure, madam, having you in camp. Drake is a fortunate man."

With a smile, she nodded graciously. "The pleasure — what little there's been — has indeed been mine, kind sir."

"Captain." The two men shook hands. "Take care of her. She's a rare find."

Barrett's gaze turned solemnly affectionate when he bent to check the horse's hoof. "That she is, Doctor."

After mounting up, Abigail reached for Daniel, refusing to look at the soldiers who stood in the doorway of the tent. Some wore bandages around their heads while others supported their weight on crudely fashioned crutches.

Barrett swung into the saddle and then turned to salute the men. The troop straightened and briskly returned the salutation.

The small escort quietly closed ranks. "Forward, ho!" The horses trotted out of camp, and Abigail refused to look back.

The couple rode side by side all morning. She concentrated on keeping Daniel entertained by pointing out the various birds and animals they saw along the way.

Barrett coaxed him to repeat the sounds, and then laughed along with the other men at his fractured pronunciations. The toddler giggled delightedly with them, blissfully unaware that he sounded silly.

During their noontime rest, Barrett fed the child while Abigail ate. She picked at her food, choosing to distance herself from the men. She sat by the stream, staring dispiritedly into the water. Though Barrett appeared taken with the child, Doyle had dominated the baby's every waking hour.

Of the two men, Doyle was nurturing but Barrett's eyes too shone with pride when he focused on the little boy.

Close to noon the following day, the small company halted in front of the lane leading to the orphanage. Abigail's eyes blurred with unexpected tears as she read the weathered sign. Forcing back the painful lump in her throat, she dropped back to ride behind Corporal Nelson. She didn't know why she felt so resentful toward Barrett — yes, she did know why. In her opinion, he was the only one who could have prevented this moment. She didn't intend to hand Daniel to strangers — surely he must know her better than that. But his stiff stance indicated that was exactly what he planned.

"Looks like a peaceful place," the corporal commented encouragingly as they rode along the lane.

Barrett moved up beside her, a concerned look in his eye. "Do you want me to do this?"

"No, I'll do it." She kept her eyes fixed stoically ahead of her. *Bluff, Abigail. Bluff him until the last possible moment. He can't mean to hand Daniel over like a parcel.*

"Are you sure?"

"I'm sure."

Mother Superior stepped out onto the

porch. Her eyes fixed on the riders as they drew closer. Abigail knew she must wonder why Levi Howard wore confederate gray this morning.

The horses halted. Dust settled. Abigail met the sister's quizzical gaze evenly. "Reverend Mother."

The nun nodded. "We were beginning to wonder if you'd changed your mind about leaving the child."

"I'm sorry. We were delayed." Taking a deep breath, she dismounted and handed Daniel to the sister. *Not for long, sweet baby. Just long enough for Drake to come to his senses.* "He's walking everywhere now, and he eats almost anything. And he's learned a few words," she added.

Mother Superior nodded, trying to hold on to the squirming child. "We were about to sit down to the noon meal. Will you join us?"

"Thank you, but we can't stay." She lingered for a moment, and then said stoically, "Captain Drake, is there anything you'd like" — she bit her lip, modifying her choice of words — "is there anything you have to say before we go?"

The men exchanged uncomfortable looks. Clearing his throat, Barrett said softly, "Take good care of him, Reverend Mother."

"We do the best we can, Mr. Howard."

"I'm sorry we had to be dishonest with you, Sister. My name is Drake. Captain Barrett Drake, and this is Abigail McDougal."

The nun's eyes held understanding. "We all do what we must, Captain."

Abigail quickly climbed onto her horse and reined in a circle, refusing to look back as she galloped down the lane. She'd be back — she and Amelia and Anne-Marie — and they would claim Daniel and no one would ever take him from her again.

Barrett handed her a square of gray linen when he rode past her a moment later. She accepted the offering but refused to look at him. She kicked her horse into a faster gait.

The pace quickened during the afternoon. By nightfall, they'd reached the Texas-Louisiana border.

As they made camp she sat by herself, listening to the men discuss plans to head south the next morning. She ignored their chatter as she rolled into her blanket early and tried to sleep. She was numb now; nothing penetrated her mind.

The company rode out early the next morning, and for the first time in days, Abigail and Barrett found themselves alone.

"Ready to leave?"

"I'm ready if you are." Barrett wouldn't meet her eyes as he saddled the horses.

She pitched the remains of her coffee into the fire and then silently placed the cup in her pack before mounting up.

Dawn streaked the sky when they started off again. Abigail knew that she should break the silence that hung between them like a shroud, but she didn't know what to say. Should she beg him to marry her? Should she plead with him to go back for Daniel? Or should she remain silent and keep her promise to free him of any further obligation to her once he returned her to Mercy Flats?

She decided on the latter, since his continuing silence appeared to indicate his preference.

They made camp that night, speaking only when spoken to. After supper, she rolled up in her blanket and turned her back to him. By tomorrow night she'd be in Mercy Flats. One more day and Barrett Drake would be rid of her. Tears stung her eyes.

One more day, and she'd be rid of Barrett Drake.

"Are you warm enough?"

His voice penetrated the darkness. Other than asking her if she wanted more coffee, he hadn't spoken to her that night.

"Fine, thank you."

"Stop being so polite," he snapped. "You either talk my head off or you don't talk at all. You are driving me crazy!" He sat up, throwing back his blanket. "I know what you want — you want me to declare my love. Well, maybe I can't. The only other woman I declared my love for ran off and joined the circus!"

Gritting her teeth, Abigail spat back, "And I wish —" She caught herself before she expressed her desire. She was through wishing for bluebirds; it didn't do an ounce of good. Clamping her eyes shut, she focused on a more pleasant subject: Doyle. She would marry him. Barrett didn't want her; he didn't want Daniel either. If he had, he would have stopped her from giving him to the orphanage that morning.

Oh, it was a bitter pill to swallow. She should never have allowed Barrett Drake to disrupt and invade her life. Her lips trembled, and she was appalled to feel hot tears rolling down both cheeks. He had reduced her to a silly, vapid girl.

If you marry Doyle, you can go back and get Daniel tomorrow morning.

Rolling to her side, she struggled to blot out the tempting thought. It was foolish to wish she could keep Daniel, but she did wish it. On one hand, she told herself that she could raise him with the help of Amelia and Anne-Marie, but on the other hand, logic argued that motherhood would be a staggering task.

Abigail wanted so much more for him. She wanted him to have a real father, and Doyle could be that for him. Yet it wouldn't be fair to marry a man she didn't love for the sake of one small boy. *I don't love Doyle,* her heart cried out. He'd pledged his love to her, but it would be a lie to offer hers in return. A few weeks ago she hadn't minded how many lies she had to tell, but the Lord, through Barrett, had worked on her heart and changed that. She both resented and loved Barrett even more for it.

And what would she do if Amelia and Anne-Marie weren't at the cemetery? What if they never returned? What if they were — dead? The unbidden thought was so painful that she couldn't bear to think it. The two men who had taken them could have been murderous, uncivilized misfits. Hershall E. Digman cared for her — protected and sheltered her. Could she live without knowing what had happened to Amelia and Anne-Marie? And if they were awaiting her return, could she leave them again to marry Doyle, sharing her hopes and her dreams with them only through infrequent visits and letters?

Morning dawned, and they broke camp in strained silence. Abigail wasn't sure why Barrett was so subdued. She prayed because the imminent parting wore on him as well as her, that he was plagued by as many doubts and as few answers as she. His eyes, once so expressive, were unreadable now.

The countryside gradually faded to the familiar for Abigail. She and her sisters had spent their lives riding the hills and valleys they were traveling now.

When they were within a short distance of Mercy Flats, Abigail urged her horse into a full gallop. Giving their horses free rein, the couple rode side by side, racing toward the border town.

As they topped a small rise, they slowed, and a smile broke across Abigail's face when she gazed at the town that had been the only home she'd ever known. Mercy Flats wasn't much to behold, just a few adobe buildings that looked as if they had seen better days, but it was home.

A dust devil provided the only sign of life this afternoon. It was siesta time, and not even the old coon hound that lay in front of the trading post bothered to stir.

"It's not much, is it?" Abigail admitted

softly. "Over there," she said, pointing to a small dwelling on the outskirts of the town. "That's the Mission San Miguel, where I was raised."

They sat on the horses as tears misted her eyes. "Over there is Church Rock, the cemetery where my parents are buried."

Resting against the saddle pommel, Barrett centered his gaze on the small cemetery beside the mission. The graves lay in the shade of tall oaks, and wildflowers bloomed in riotous colors around the headstones.

"It looks real peaceful, Abigail. A man could be happy here."

Flies buzzed the horses. Bridles jingled when the animals shook their manes to rid themselves of the pesky insects.

"My parents are buried beneath that tree just to the left — see it?"

His gaze located the two graves, and he nodded.

Side by side, they sat, gazing down on the tranquil scene. The cemetery appeared deserted, but that didn't mean that Amelia and Anne-Marie weren't there. It didn't mean that at all. They were probably at the mission this minute, having tea with the sisters.

"Well, I guess this is where we say good-bye," she acknowledged, trying to speak above the mass crowding her throat.

"Yeah, guess it is." He was silent for a moment, then spoke again. "Abigail. I've been doing some serious thinking. This whole trip has made me realize that I'm weak and I need to work on my faith a little harder."

"Yes." She sighed heavily. "Me too. I hear that God has a way of getting your attention when He has something to say."

"You think He threw us together to try and tell us something?"

"Well — we're together. At least for the moment. And we've both been rather poor examples of Christlike living, duty or not."

"True."

"So what do you think God's been trying to tell us?" Barrett asked.

"Better get serious about your life and faith. Life's a short journey."

He nodded. "I was thinking the same. Of course, we're not responsible to anyone but ourselves. We're not raising kids or anything."

"We're responsible to God," Abigail said quietly. "Folks might not know about our indiscretions, but He knows."

"You're right. He knows."

The horses rippled their hides. "You think Amelia and Anne-Marie are waiting for you?"

"Oh, yes. They're there." She hadn't had a lot of security in her life, but her sisters could always be counted on to show up when they were needed.

"Yeah, I expect they are."

The moment stretched. They'd shared a lot the past couple of weeks. "Barrett?"

"Yes?"

She sighed. "Nothing, I guess."

The horses grew restless and stamped as the flies buzzed around their fetlocks.

"What do you think you'll do when the war's over?" she asked, unaware until that moment that she would ask that question. The second the words were out, she wished that she'd kept silent. He could not be goaded into love — or common sense.

Gazing at the valley below, he said softly, "I've got a hundred acres of prime farmland in Georgia. Once the war's over, I'm going home."

"That sounds real nice."

Their heads turned and their eyes met.

"What about you?" he asked.

She looked away. "Doyle asked me to marry him."

Pain flickered briefly in his eyes. "I know. We talked briefly before I left. Are you going to accept his proposal?"

"He's a good man, Barrett. He wants to

adopt Daniel."

"He is a good man, and he'll make Daniel a fine father." They sat in silence another moment. "Are you in love with him?"

Abigail hesitated. "I could grow to love him."

He straightened, almost with resentment. "I thought you weren't in the market for a husband."

Love shone so clearly in her eyes that she didn't see how he could fail to notice it. "Well, I didn't think I was either," she said crossly. "But then you came along and . . ."

"And what?"

"What? You know what." She shouldn't have to tell him first. It was a man's duty to tell a woman first that he loved her.

They sat for another moment. Apparently neither one knew their duty. Barrett broke first.

"Well, I've been thinking. Once the war's over, I might settle down. Take a wife. Have some children."

Abigail's heart leaped to her throat. "I thought you weren't in the market for a wife."

His eyes met hers. "I didn't think I was either."

She waited, praying that he could get the simple words past his lips. *I love you.* Easy as pie. Shouldn't cause a man or woman any undue worry. Moments ticked by.

"You haven't said if you're going to marry Doyle."

"No. I don't plan to marry Doyle." She thought too much of the man; he deserved a woman who cared for him deeply. It would seem that she was back to plan one: raise Daniel with her sisters. If they could be convinced.

When he didn't comment, she thumped her heels against her horse's sides, sending him down the hill.

"Hey!" he called. "Where are you going?"

"To find me a bluebird!"

Surprise followed by a grin crossed his face. Spurring his horse into a gallop he yelled, "Hey! Wait up! I was about to tell you that I love you!"

Grinning, she rode harder. *Thank You, God! Thank You!* "I *love* you? That the best you got, Captain?"

"Okay! I *adore* you and Daniel — come back here so we can settle this!"

Oh, it's settled, dear. You just don't know it. Thank You, dear Lord! It seemed Captain Drake was looking for a wife and baby boy after all.

ABOUT THE AUTHOR

Lori Copeland is the author of more than 90 titles, both historical and contemporary fiction. With more than 3 million copies of her books in print, she has developed a loyal following among her rapidly growing fans in the inspirational market. She has been honored with the Romantic Times Reviewer's Choice Award, The Holt Medallion, and Walden Books' Best Seller award. In 2000, Lori was inducted into the Missouri Writers Hall of Fame.

She lives in the beautiful Ozarks with her husband, Lance, and their three children and five grandchildren.

The employees of Thorndike Press hope you have enjoyed this Large Print book. All our Thorndike, Wheeler, and Kennebec Large Print titles are designed for easy reading, and all our books are made to last. Other Thorndike Press Large Print books are available at your library, through selected bookstores, or directly from us.

For information about titles, please call:
(800) 223-1244

or visit our Web site at:
http://gale.cengage.com/thorndike

To share your comments, please write:
Publisher
Thorndike Press
10 Water St., Suite 310
Waterville, ME 04901